Fran Cooper

The Two Houses

For Jules,
Hope you enjoy!
Fran x

H
HODDER &
STOUGHTON

First published in Great Britain in 2018 by Hodder & Stoughton
An Hachette UK company

1

Copyright © Fran Cooper, 2018

A CIP catalogue record for this title is available from the British Library

Hardback ISBN 978 1 473 64157 0
Trade Paperback ISBN 978 1 473 64158 7
eBook ISBN 978 1 473 64160 0

Typeset in Sabon MT by Palimpsest Book Production Limited,
Falkirk, Stirlingshire
Printed and bound by Clays Ltd, St Ives plc

Hodder & Stoughton policy is to use papers that are natural, renewable and
recyclable products and made from wood grown in sustainable forests. The logging
and manufacturing processes are expected to conform to the environmental
regulations of the country of origin.

Hodder & Stoughton Ltd
Carmelite House
50 Victoria Embankment
London EC4Y 0DZ

www.hodder.co.uk

The Two Houses

Also by Fran Cooper

These Dividing Walls

For my parents, who taught me to love wild places.

Crack

I

The Two Houses sit grey and brooding beneath a pale sky. They cling to the hillside, cowering from the wind, because always, before everything up here, there is the wind. In the not-quite-light of a November afternoon, this whole strange world is beaten by it; the spindly trees, the long sedge grasses, even the houses themselves seem to bend under its assault.

The Two Houses were not always two. But if it is human to build – even up here, in this blasted northern hinterland – it is human to break, too.

And he could not have known – the man whose hand carved *1712* in deep, angular strokes above the doorway – that his work would both last and not last. For it is more than three hundred years that this wind and these stones have been battering each other, more than three hundred journeys around the sun, and still his stones stand. But the middle of his great house is missing. Its central rooms have been cut out, removed, sliced clean away as if a stinking wound or canker. His one great house rent and rendered into two.

Jay walks out into the space between, into the gap between the two houses that, in *1712*, were built as one. A house so haunted, the locals say, that its last owner simply took out the middle. Took out the rooms where objects hurled them-selves across the carpet and dogs whimpered and even in the heat of summer – what summer there is, up on these hills – the air could on a sudden turn to clouded ice in front of you. One house made two; void and vacuum in between. Bad things happened here, they murmur; this is bad land.

Jay walks out into the space between, because it is in this

space that the builders have been digging. Because wouldn't it be perfect, they said, to have her studio here; to connect the two houses, to bring them together again? And Simon, with his architect's brain, with his love of stone and glass and building, had eagerly put pen to paper.

Up here, high above the world, the rain is as relentless as the wind. In the silence of the fading year, Jay has been making a taxonomy of it. Thin rain, fat rain, rain that doesn't fall but hangs around you like a shroud; rain that drives itself horizontal, pricking dull needles into the skin. Today it drips, ticklingly slow, down the back of her neck, catches dew-like in her hair and eyelashes.

You see everything and nothing from Two Houses. Everything, because they sit above the valley's road, looking out over the sweep of empty hillside, the curved fells with their wind-whipped green and ochre grasses. Nothing, because the village is further up the dale, hidden from view, and it's ten miles down to town the other way. They are the only souls for miles, Jay and Simon, the builder and his lad.

There are spades lying on the earth between the houses. A digger, abandoned, its claw limp against the ground. Beyond the damp, Jay can smell the wetness of newly churned soil, its rich secrets meeting air for the first time. Her knees crack as she bends down to the place on which all eyes are fixed.

'Jay—'

It is Simon, hovering behind her somewhere. He is always so sensible, her Simon.

'—maybe you shouldn't . . .'

But it is too late. Her fingers have touched it, this strange, unearthly protrusion from the land at which they are all looking. And as they do, everything swims into crystalline focus. Every sharp intake of breath when the Two Houses are mentioned; each darkly guarded reference to the things that happened here. Suddenly, she understands.

Behind her, the builder's lad retches. The smell of his soured breakfast carries on the bitter air, and a new silence descends as they wait, held in uneasy tableau around the unburied earth. For there is no doubting it now: this thing beneath her fingers has the irrefutable hardness of bone.

Break

2

This is how it starts, on a Thursday afternoon in high spring with the frantic choking of birdsong outside the window. A crack in the firing. A line, filigree-fine. And as she turns the vessel with her hands, suddenly it is as if she herself is on the potter's wheel, her feet unrooted from the scuffed and dusty floor, and she is turning. Turning, turning, and she is falling now into this crack, this infinitesimal maw that has opened up in front of her. Crack break rupture ruin, and in their frenzy of mating and making the birds don't care, louder than ever in their feathered song. Jay spins faster than the world on its axis as the great cracked vessel slips and falls, its porcelain shattering in long seconds across the ground.

It happens, she tells herself that afternoon. That evening. Through the suffocating hours of that sleep-starved night. It happens it happens it happens. But when Simon finds her pacing the kitchen in the cold dawn of the third day, in those half-light hours where everything is silvered and white, her hands shaking uncontrollably, her heart a leaping dance inside her chest, she is forced to admit that the break is in her. That, somehow, it is she who has broken.

She cannot work. No difference, the calendar on the studio wall with *13 May* circled in ominous loops of red marker. No difference, the telephone calls from gallery assistants, then gallery directors, asking in increasingly panicked tones about the appearance of her work. No difference, the friends who come and who she refuses to see. The telephone rings. The meals that Simon makes grow cold and congealed on her plate. Her head and heart have fallen into that porcelain void, and there is nothing – no words, no thoughts – only white and aching emptiness.

It is absolutely *not* about not being able to have children.

'Is it about not being able to have children?' Podge asks delicately, his hand on her forearm, his voice overly prepared and sickeningly sympathetic.

No it's bloody not, she wants to scream. I am more than the sum of my parts, the fruit of my womb, the torpor of my ovaries.

'No, Podge.' Podge, with his shaved head and his big silver earrings, her best friend these twenty years, and yet somehow he could ask that question. 'It's about the work. You know me.'

Podge nods solemnly. 'I know you. It's always about the work.'

And yet and yet and yet, slamming her forehead into the bathroom wall just for the cold, reverberating crunch of it. This agony of not being able. She, who sailed through school, sailed through Chelsea. First to get a dealer, first to get a sale, a show, a four-figure advance. The only one of the cohort to be having a retrospective – a retrospective at forty-two, for crying out loud, that's something to talk about. She who walked into a room, locked eyes with Simon, picked him, married him. She who has done everything she ever wanted without even having to think about it. To her, this inability is corrosive. It gnaws at her unproductive innards.

And no matter, really, the question of whether she wanted them. Whether she wanted to swell up, to be leached off, thick and blubbery as a whale. She thinks of Sally Armstrong, the weakest of the Chelsea set, fat and happy in the suburbs last she heard, oozing with milk and maternity like some great dairy cow. Jay never could stand Sally; the frilly lips of her vases, their twee glazes.

And yet, and yet (the *clonk* of her forehead, bruised now,

against the tiles). It is novel, this not being able within her skin. She wants to rip it off, to cleanse herself of it.

She spends the summer in her bed. Friends whispering anxiously at the bedroom door, on the threshold, the cusp. As if breakdown might be contagious, as if despair might be caught.

White sheets, white walls, the black and white collie dog fluff of Bella lying in the bed next to her. Bella, growing fat now that her walks have petered out. Jay diminishing, folding in on herself while the dog fills out, tongue and tail lolling in the summer heat.

The broken vessel haunts her dreams, flits across her retinas in this strange, timeless place between wake and sleep. Things have broken before; *obviously* things have broken before. The magic of the kiln is quicksilver, inscrutable. But this had been so long in the planning. A vessel – not vase, not urn – half as tall as she is. Wide curved sides tapering to a small, delicate mouth. Months of experiments, trials, tests, and finally she'd worked out how to get the clay so fine it would feel like paper. So pale that coming into the workshop at dusk, it seemed for a moment as if you'd stumbled upon some smooth, fallen moon. A planet brought down to earth.

A summer in bed squeezing her eyes shut, and yet still she feels the clay's coolness against her palms, the strong vital curve of it, waxing rich and plentiful beneath her hands. How she'd coaxed it; the hours, the weeks. For what? A crack in the firing. A hollow shell. Worthless, unfulfilled, unfilled.

She cannot explain to Simon, who sits by her side, that her mind is a dance of all these forms unformed. That the date of the retrospective approaching – being – passing – does not make her feel sad, for she does not feel anything at all.

3

'I don't want to be here any more,' she whispers. Her words cut through the stale heat of the bedroom, the thick summer air through which Simon, in turn, is delicately folding a page of newspaper. It dangles, black and white and ever so slightly trembling, from his hand.

I don't want to be here any more.

Outside, there is a team of men drilling in the street. In a garden, someone's child is crying; next-door's builders have their radio blasting. A bus tears along the main road and planes circle lazily overhead. It is London in August, its noise and chaos hurtling in through the open windows.

And Simon, gently replacing his page of newsprint, chooses to take 'here' as London. Chooses the specificity of time and place, the airless bedroom and the particularly noisy coordinates of Southwark. It is warm, his skin is sticky, and anyone would be forgiven for finding the city's smog and rattle overwhelming. Greased by the beads of sweat that have been forming on his brow since long before dawn, Simon's glasses insist on sliding down his nose. Pushing them back up for the umpteenth time, he refuses to entertain the possibility that 'here' might mean something larger.

'I think we should get out,' he says.

Her turquoise eyes stare up at him from the pillow into which she has sunk these last few weeks, skin and bone.

'What?'

'I think we should get out. Find a place outside London. Somewhere to do up. For holidays, weekends. We always said we would.'

His wife looks at him, pale and listless, her long red hair fanned out behind her. A Pre-Raphaelite portrait; Millais's Ophelia, drowning in her bed. She is so pale now, her skin faded to milk, networks of blue veins criss-crossing her like a map. Even her hair has dimmed, as if the pigment has been leached out of her.

The woman Simon married was full of colour, bright and vivacious, a russet mane and dazzling jewel-like eyes. She was the life of the party. Always making, creating. If she wasn't at her wheel or tending her kiln, he'd come home to find her up a ladder stringing garlands around the living room, or in the kitchen cooking an impromptu supper for fifteen of her nearest and dearest. These are not things that Simon would have done himself, but he has always enjoyed them, in his own quiet way; has always looked on admiringly from the sidelines, waiting patiently, contentedly, for the moment when the front door closes and he has her to himself again.

Simon has, on occasion, worried that he's too sensible for Jay. He suspects that her artist friends find him rather square. Podge, the painter, whose shaved head and bulging belly share the same round form; Gavin, the stick-thin poet; Hélène, who doesn't ever seem to do anything except travel to Nepal and Bhutan in search of *inspiration*. To them, architecture is about lines and measurements. They deal in the business of creativity – in the uncorking of bottles, the staying up into the small hours – while he goes to an office for early-morning meetings, wearing a tie to boot. (Not that he says it to Podge and co, but Simon actually thinks his knitted ties are pretty avant-garde.)

But Jay has never said any of this, never begrudged his early-to-bed, early-to-rise nature. She has always pored over his plans, talked through his trickiest installations, offered ideas and solutions while he stared mesmerised by the light playing over her auburn hair. When a pair of outrageously coloured jays took to pottering around their tiny London garden, pale pink and turquoise, he started calling her his Jay-bird. She laughed, strutting like a crow and feathering their nest. His Jay. His Jay-bird.

'Space, Jay-bird,' he says gently, over the whine of the drill and the hum of the traffic. 'Peace and quiet.'

She pulls herself up in the bed, wrapping her arms around her knees. With her shoulders arcing forward, he can see each veterbra jutting out from her skin, the dark, newly cavernous recesses beneath her collarbones.

'You sound like Podge,' she murmurs. 'I don't want to join the rest of the circus down in bloody—'

Margate. Simon knows that's where she's going. Margate and Rye and, lately, Whitstable, and all the other once-abandoned seaside towns, newly taken over by the trendy London crowd, the same faces there at the weekend as you'd find in Soho or Clerkenwell during the week.

'No, Jay-bird, not Kent. Really out somewhere. Somewhere wild and remote, where we can just be us.'

Where we can just be us and you can just be you again, he adds silently, somewhere between hope and prayer.

'Weekends?' she asks thoughtfully, twiddling the ends of her long hair.

Simon nods. 'Weekends. The odd week here and there, even.'

Jay sighs.

'I don't know. How far could you get in a weekend anyway?'

She turns from him, back to her pillow, her horizontal world. But Simon remains undeterred. He saw the faint glimmer of interest. And he is an architect. He knows that things are only built stone by stone, brick by brick.

Later that night she comes downstairs to find him at the kitchen table, maps and train timetables spread across its surface.

'I mean it, Jay. Let's go.'

*

14

'It'll only be for weekends,' he overhears her telling Podge the following week as she packs a bag for their northern expedition. Podge, his fellow nursemaid and gatekeeper during this – Simon doesn't know what to call it. The doctor said 'breakdown', but he was sat behind a shiny mahogany desk in the padded comfort of his private practice, and Simon found his terminology trite, his consultation scant for the fees demanded.

Podge's nasal voice rings out, high and incredulous. 'Weekends?'

For all the uneasy truce of their relationship – Podge's perpetual need to assert that he was Jay's best friend long before Simon came along – Simon has to admit that he has been a brick these last few months, staunch and stalwart.

'Long weekends,' Jay counters. 'Simon can work from home, sometimes.'

'And what about you? What are *you* going to do in the *country*?'

There is something vulgar about the way he says it, as if the dirt and manure it conjures have somehow landed on Podge's tongue.

'I'll work. It'll be peace, quiet—'

Podge mutters something that Simon cannot hear. Packing up his work for the night, he wonders what Podge makes of Jay's newfound lack of work. Jay, who has always been working, always busy with her fingers – until now. To Simon, it seems somehow just as improbable that she would start again as that she had stopped in the first place. The low utterances continue in the bedroom until Podge exclaims dramatically: 'I don't know why you don't just come to Margate with the rest of us!'

And Simon, victorious, smiles.

4

'Shit!'

The Volvo swerves violently up onto a verge, its hulking great nose stopping just centimetres from the drystone wall in front of them. Simon sees his wife thrown against the passenger side window, hears the soft *clunk* of her head against the glass as they grind to a halt.

'Are you alright?' he asks.

Jay rubs her temple. 'What was that?'

'No idea.' Simon readjusts his glasses, hands trembling.

'A pothole?'

'The wheel?'

They clamber out into a rough-edged afternoon, the air chill and damp. No matter that London talks of an Indian summer. They have come north, climbing high above the sunlit cities and picture-postcard valleys. No one sweats in deckchairs here, or pulls out the sundresses they had thought to retire for the year. September has barely started its rotation, but already the light is dribbling limply through the clouds; a few hours yet off dipping, but with that autumnal laziness that knows a long night is coming.

In the city, people will be stepping out into baked streets, braving a Tube journey in tropical humidity. They will be rushing past each other, unlooking, unheeding, spun off course by the *thump* of colliding into someone else's shoulder. Simon and Jay are a long way from that on this empty stretch of road. The brown grass whispers, flattening itself under the air's command, and in the distance, a bird – or perhaps it is the wind? – sings a mournful note.

Simon joins her on the passenger side and together they stare down at the front wheel, or what's left of it, all sag and warp around the hubcap.

'Can you drive on it?'

Simon crouches down, touching his fingers to the rapidly cooling rubber as if to coax it back to life. 'We can limp on, I think.'

Jay kneels next to him, but it is not the wheel that meets her hand. He watches her fingers stretch out towards the ochre mud. She pushes it between thumb and forefinger, and somewhere inside him a memory stirs.

'Are you sure you want to be touching that?' He gets up and leans on the Volvo's bonnet, rolling his shoulders, cracking his neck. This is their fifth hour in the car today, the fourth property, and it's impossibly far from anything to be the one they're looking for.

She does not move. Turning in on herself again, he thinks, as she buries her nose in the clod she's pulled from the earth. Yet another thing that closes her off from him.

'Come on.' He calls her back, a sharpness he can't account for in his voice. A gust of wind whips along the deserted road, and if he could he would call back his words. But the wind carries them off, and she is standing up, letting the earth fall, slipping wordlessly back into the car. Simon remains on the roadside, wishing for all the world that he had not extinguished that brief, familiar spark.

They do limp on, wonkily, the moan of the wheel like an injured dog, as if the car itself is hurting. The sides of the valley rise steeply above them, grey-green and foreboding. There are few trees here, just bare land criss-crossed with stone walls and tumbledown barns. The outside hush creeps into the car. The radio has long since stopped spluttering, and Jay and Simon peer out cautiously, silently, at the barren landscape.

It was arbitrary, in the end, the choosing of place. Simon's maps crept across the kitchen, unfolding themselves across every surface, and ultimately it came down to the blind stabbing of fingers against the crinkled paper. Not Kent, they'd decided that. Not the Cotswolds (too conservative). Not the Peak District (too touristy). Wales was, in Simon's words, too . . . *Welsh*. Finally Jay had searched for the land that was the least veined, the least laced with roads and arteries. Oxygen bubbles in clay cause explosions in the kiln, and if the summer in her bed had been a self-starving of air, a compression not unlike the way she wedged and pounded clay to push those bubbles out, she wanted that here, too. Looking down at the illustrated land as if it were a body, she did not want the embroidery of roads, veins, lifeblood.

She did not like the first houses they saw. A twee cottage with falsely jolly window boxes. A sixties bungalow replete with gun turret windows and metallic floor tiles. The third appealed to Simon, an old vicarage looking over a postcard-perfect village green, but Jay stood stony-faced and shook her head. Already there were old ladies peering through the lacy curtains to get a look at them, stopping Simon on the garden path to make pointedly casual conversation.

'I want to be left alone,' she told him.

'Is there anywhere else?' Simon asked the estate agent, his mouth downturned.

'Afraid not, not down here.'

Simon was just turning back to her, wheeling around ready to admit defeat, when the man said: 'Well, hold hard. There is somewhere. Much further up dale. A bit of a wreck, to be frank. Council finally getting around to selling it off. Let me ring Herbert, see if he can take you round. You'd have to drive up on your own, mind. Out of my way, is that. A dead end, to boot – top of the dale just stops, like.'

So now with their busted wheel they are crawling slowly up the single road at the bottom of this deserted valley, this dead-end dale. 'Nel-der-dale,' Simon announces cautiously, one eye on the road, one on the map. They pass through a tattered town, grey and run down, half its shops out of business, their blanched facades barricaded against some unknown threat.

'You sure you want to look up here?' Simon asks.

Jay does not answer, because she is looking, leaning forward to drink in this strange world. For it is strange to her, with its great treeless hillsides rising above them, rounded over like so many hunched backs, so many cold shoulders. As if, like her, the land wants to keep itself to itself. From here the hills look velveteen, vast and unpeopled. They climb, the road looping serpentine along the valley floor, and their ears pop as they pass first one abandoned house – windows boarded, roof collapsed – and then another. By the side of the road an ancient telephone box comes into view, its once-red walls faded now to pink and rust.

'Can you stop?'

Simon's head snaps around to look at her, eyes wide behind his glasses. 'Stop?'

'Yes, stop, stop.'

He does, and she scrambles out of the car, turning back to the telephone box, strange relic of a bygone time. The wind is fierce, metallic cold, but she doesn't know if it's that or the thrill of pulling back the old glass door that pricks gooseflesh along her skin. Inside, it is quiet, musty. Cocooned from world and weather, it is a tiny space from another time, with its rotary telephone and politely printed notices, faded now and age-stained. *Little's Sheep Dip – the most trusted. Arkwright Cough Syrups – best for man and beast.* The wires have long been cut, but for a moment Jay peers out through grimy glass at the empty landscape, not a building in sight, and wonders who could have made a telephone call here. How lonely it must have sounded if anyone ever tried to call back, its peals ringing and ringing across the desolate valley.

'Jay—' Simon is pulling open the door and with him comes a roar of chill air.

Her fingers alight on the cold buttons. 'Isn't it magical?'

He nods, pulling the collar of his jumper up around his neck. 'Amazing. But we should go, the man is waiting for us.'

Buffeted by the wind, they stagger back to the car like drunks, the force of air plunging them in zigzags across the road, Jay's hair lashing itself into wild tangles before her eyes.

'Simon?'

But this wind, this wind, it snatches the words from her, whisks away the sound of her voice before it reaches him.

'Simon!'

Halfway into the driver's seat, his head pops up comically above the roof of the car.

'Yes?'

'Why is it called "The Two Houses"?'

He pauses. The wind drops, leaving a silence that is sudden and soft. 'I don't know, Jay-bird. I think the agent said something about there being a bit missing.'

'Like me, then.' She flashes a hard smile and sinks into her seat.

Simon frowns, concentrating on the road. Her words echo between them, reverberating in the cool air until they are almost nothing. Words for which there are no easy answers, no pat responses. Words it is easiest to ignore, to leave until the silence grows loud enough that it is as if she had hardly said them.

'Oh, hello,' Simon murmurs. In the distance, Jay can make out the tubby figure of a man, arms waving, pointing them up off the road onto the hillside. 'I think we're here.'

Somewhere in the pit of Jay's stomach, it feels like homecoming, and the fingers that have been clutched around her heart release.

5

Folk say that time does not make a noise. That time is dull and silent. But folk say stupid, unfounded things, because a house – or two houses – left to their abandonment would tell you about time's noises. As would we, abandoned, who listened to them.

You stand still enough, long enough, you'll hear it. The creep of ivy growing through a window, its tendrils sucking, clasping, against a bedroom's walls. The flake and fall of paint, each loss fluttering, clattering to the ground. The shriek of water frozen in a pipe. The bullet crack of glass in the dead of winter. Oh yes, there is a cacophony to decay. A favourite word of my mother's, cacophony.

It is loud, time, and it is cruel, for no matter how hard you tug at the weeds, how hard you try to remember what things once were, it marches on, deafening.

Wood splinters. Windows break. Leaves find their way in under doors, rattling against the floorboards until they are paper skeletons, until they are mere dust. And even the dust hisses, moved by the wind that breathes inside the walls, trampled by the footfall of children who've no right to play here or the rodents that come by night, and if they could have seen it thus, oh . . .

Mouldering curtains sigh. Ragged wallpaper chatters in the breeze. The hooks of a heavy light fixture creak and groan as gravity does its worst until one day the whole glass orb falls, shattering clean away, and it does not matter, then, how much it was loved.

A world is not silent just because there is no one left to hear it. I was left to hear it.

*

Jay's eyes take a moment to adjust to the gloom, her ears to learn the loud noiselessness of this place, as if they are hearing quiet for the first time. In front of her, a wide hallway appears; a dark wooden staircase, complete with two turns. It is grand, elegant in its decay; the kind of staircase in hotels or stately homes that makes her feel she's lady of the manor. Even in the half-dark, though, she can see that most of the bannisters are missing, that the handrail is caked with years of bird shit. Its pale, lunar excrescences are strangely familiar to her; she smiles, thinking of the clay splattered on the studio floor.

She feels her way into the first room. Its wide bay windows are cloaked by dark curtains, arm-achingly heavy. Hauling them back, she frees decades of dust whose motes dance and sparkle in the new shafts of light. Herbert, the tubby estate agent, walks into the cloud of it.

'Of course,' he splutters, trying to clear his throat, 'forty year empty's left a fair bit of muck.'

And yes, the windows are silvered with grime, argentine, but with what light there is Jay can make out an ornate fireplace, frothy Victorian cornicing, a vast room littered with years of neglect. Old newspapers lie forgotten on the floor beneath chunks of fallen plaster; a leather-bound book, its pages bloated with rain; odd forgotten bits of wood and metal. Heavy floral wallpaper sags away from the walls, and the air reeks of acrid smoke, the black stains of long-ago fires streaking up the walls.

Jay does not see what Simon and Herbert see, does not hear the sensible things they discuss ('empty a long while . . . going for a song'; 'good bones . . . a decent floor beneath this muck' . . .). Instead, she is moving out of this room into a second hallway, peeling away the stiff, flocked wallpaper like wrapping paper and running her hands over the plaster beneath. Cool, clay-like, mottled beautiful with age.

Beyond this corridor is a kitchen, its tiled walls still keeping the air frigid. There is a sour smell in here, something half-decayed and maggot-moving in the corner. But Jay finds that if she presses her cheek to the tile, runs her fingers along the great black cooking range, she can imagine warmth, as if some heat is held residual, locked away in the very walls. She can close her eyes and smell bread in the oven, something rich and meaty on the stove. Surely that is the sound of water boiling, its steam rising up over the tips of her fingers. Opening her eyes, it flies from her, but she is not sad to be left alone in this dark, mouldering corner.

Sidestepping guano and broken planks, she climbs the stairs. In one bedroom she finds a thimble – silver, dented – that fits perfectly on her finger. She turns to tell Simon who has come into the room behind her – 'Si, look' – but he is not there, and those cannot have been footsteps she was so sure she heard approaching. She pauses, waits to see if the steps will start again. But they do not so she creeps on, into another empty room whose bedframe has left a trace of itself against the paint, ancient bedposts in perfect silhouette; into another whose child's wallpaper has faded almost into nothingness, so that pink-jacketed riders and ghost horses jump along its walls. Here, there is fade, but in other rooms, colour: rich russet stains in the bathtub, a lace curtain turned crisp and ochre, a vibrant green flourishing of mould next to the grand staircase, where the beginnings of a corridor suddenly stop.

'Simon?'

Again, she thought him closer than this, could have sworn he was just in the next room, just a few steps behind her. He is not, and for a time she is alone with the pounding of her heart, the faint clouds of her breath peppering the dark air, the creak and groan of long untrodden floors. *There's no such thing as ghosts*, she tells herself.

'Yes, love?'

Here he is, picking his way gingerly up the staircase, the small, somewhat queasy-looking estate agent in tow.

'What's this bit here?' She points to the indentation in the wall, where the skirting board and cornicing turn, as if around a corner, before coming to an abrupt halt.

'I don't know, Jay-bird.' Simon runs his hands along the wall, steps back for a moment to take it in. 'It looks like it was meant to be a doorway of some sort.'

'But why does it just stop?'

The agent speaks, licking his lips nervously before and after. 'That's where they cut it out.'

'Cut what out?'

'Middle of the house.'

'What?'

'Middle of the house. It were symmetrical before. Hestle Hall they called it, same name as the village up yonder. Look.' The agent shuffles through the printouts he's holding. They quake and flutter in his hand, but sure enough she sees it now. He's pointing at a photograph of the house they are standing in: a large bay window on the left, a front door that was once the centre of the building, and then a gap, a space, before another slender building on the right.

She points at the other building. 'Is that part of it too?'

'Yes, ma'am.' It sounds like he's saying *mam*.

'But you have to go outside to get to it?'

'Yes. Across the grass. They put a door in at the back. Two Houses. Been called that since they took the middle out.'

'When was that?'

'Oh, long time ago. Must be seventy year at least.'

'But why?'

'Jay . . .' Simon's voice has the slightest edge of warning, as it does sometimes when she asks too many questions, asks too much of people. Both of them are mildly surprised by it: her last few months have been so quiet that there have been no probing questions asked, no interrogations to stop.

'Well . . .' The agent swallows hard, blinking furiously behind his glasses. 'They said it were haunted, like. Dogs barking and that. Things that moved. Odd noises. He'd lost his wife, the last one of them, the owner that is, that was. Lost his wife and then it started – only in the middle rooms, mind. So he cut it out. Cut out the rooms that she were haunting, her rooms. Long time ago now, as I said. Sure there's nothing to it, like.'

But Jay can sense the sweat on his palms, can see it beading on his upper lip. She catches Simon's eye. He has that look he gets sometimes when he is thinking about work or trying to solve a difficult crossword clue. He is her wise owl, he is a grandfather clock, for though his pale face is calm and inscrutable, if she holds her breath she can hear the whir of gear and mechanism beneath.

'Can we see the other house?' she asks.

'See it from here. Look.'

Herbert the agent marches over to the window, wrestles with the long-rusted catch. It swings open with a gasp, a shock, as if the whole house recoils at this sudden violation, this sudden inrush of other air. Obedient, Jay and Simon hang their heads out of the window.

They look out over the unhallowed land, over the space between in which all these ghostly things have happened. Evening is rolling in, a chill mist with it that cloaks them all in an extravagant whiteness. The rain spatters the backs of their necks as they crane out at the other house. It is exactly that: the other part of the house they stand in. It looks, from this sideways window perch, of the same stone, same scale, as if it had just drifted free one night in a flood. Bobbed its way across the garden to a place where it could breathe, a place where it could be.

'Fascinating,' Simon murmurs, his cogs turning. 'I wonder, which way do the beams run? You might almost think of putting them back . . .'

Jay thinks back to the clutter of their London street; new builds and old flats and tiny terraced houses all crushed together. The endless honking of angry drivers unable to pass, unable to park. The tree roots bringing the pavements up into sharp volcanic mountains, as if they, too, were yearning to break free. How claustrophobic it had become, suddenly, to hear someone else's television through the wall; to be privy to the sounds of love and anger. To look up through the fume-haze to a sky latticed by aeroplane trails, and to have always, *always*, the builders, the roadworks, the lorries, the buses, the foxes, the wailing babies, the shrieking mothers on their mobiles – to have that as the soundtrack to everything.

The estate agent's hands jitter, fumbling with his dossier. The clatter of paper, the fall of rain. And beyond that, there is silence. A dark, desolate world in which they can cocoon themselves. In which they can find peace. Jay remembers standing barefoot in their scrubby square metre of London grass, trying desperately to ground, to connect. There is so much space here. So much earth.

'Simon, it's perfect.'

Her breath makes clouds in the quickening night, and just like that, it starts.

6

The rumour of it flies up Nelderdale. Past the desolate tumble-
downs, the abandoned farmhouses, the forgotten phone box
faded to pink and rust. It swoops along the ribbon of road,
high up along the hillsides, up above the empty schoolhouse
and the deserted mine workings where old scars rend the
land, spilling ancient rock waste onto the hilltops. Finally it
circles down through the village streets, arriving at those few
still lived-in houses Hestle has to offer, slipping in on the air
under doorways, down chimneys, through the cracks in the
windows.

It is not clear how the news arrives. It never is, in a place
like this. But it settles as snow on those who are left, dropping
uneasily onto their shoulders, onto the very tips of their noses.

Someone drives the twelve miles down to town and asks
Little Herbert the estate agent about it. He's not little any
more, squat and sweaty behind his thick varifocals, but
nothing changes here, least of all a nickname.

'Aye,' he says, swallowing loudly. 'Buyers for Two Houses.
London folk.'

But he refuses to divulge any further information, and so
the rumour takes to wing again, hovering above the village,
fluttering its feathers until the air is nothing but wing-beat,
loud and panicky above them.

Even Tom Outhwaite can't help looking as he drives past.
Tall and greying, with a chiselled jaw and no-nonsense eyes,
he's not the sort to succumb to idle chatter. To drive out to
look at the houses as if they'll offer up some kind of secret.

Only one road in the valley, he tells himself defensively, but he can't deny the long glance as he passes, the letting up of the accelerator. As he looks, the car stalls. Furious, he starts it up again, ramming it full throttle along the darkening lane.

Tom draws up into the village and parks in front of the pub. His pub, or the pub he runs, at least. The pub that got passed on to him when Norman Neal left the village, and Tom . . . well, Tom needed something to do.

The pub is a square, slate-coloured building. Two benches with broken slats flank its doorway, alongside a faded sun umbrella. He turns off the engine and sits for a moment; he can't remember a time of proper sun. What he does remember, against his will, at all hours of the day and night, are the swirling patterns of the ancient rugs that line the pub's floor. The noisy, glinting labels of the bottles. The burn of the electric light behind the bar deep into his retinas, so that, in bed at nights, it is this harsh, bright world that swims endlessly before his tired eyes. He was not made, Tom, to work indoors.

And now this to-do at Two Houses, a to-do he could have done without. It's been a long time coming. They all knew it might, knew the council might one day, finally, get round to selling the old wreck off. And yet . . .

Ridiculous, he chides himself, unloading the cash and carry bags from the boot. Daft. To get so het up over a load of London folk who aren't even here yet and who'll likely take one look at it in the cold light of day before pushing off back where they came from. Probably won't last two months up here. Why would they? Probably nothing to worry about.

But as he walks into the pub it is abuzz with worry, as abuzz as a pub with a half dozen customers can be.

'You heard about them new folk?'

The question is out of Angela's mouth before the door closes behind him. Angela, her peroxide hair piled on top of her head, cigarette dancing nervously between her lips. Tom heads over behind his bar.

'You're not meant to be smoking them in here.'

'Oh give over, Tom.'

'I mean it, Ange. My name above door. Me who's in trouble if the authorities come knocking.'

'Like anyone comes knocking round here.' She stubs it out nonetheless, her long, painted fingernails clacking against the ashtray. Out of habit, Tom glances at it. Three cigarettes, all lipstick-stained. He can always tell Angela's at the end of the night.

'You heard, then?'

Tom pulls out a tea towel and begins methodically drying the glasses on the tray. They're not really wet, but he'd rather this than look at her. 'Heard what?'

'About the new folk at Two Houses.'

'Well?'

'Well what?'

'What do you want me to do about it?'

'I don't want you to do anything, Tom!' Angela's voice is shrill and sharp, and Tom is glad he doesn't have to hear it too often.

There was a time he thought Angela Metcalfe the best thing in the world. When his awkward teenage self would have done anything to walk next to her in the haze of cigarettes and cheap perfume and run his fingers through her blonde hair. It was only years later that he realised how thick with hairspray it was, sharp and straw-like. She'd picked another bloke by then, anyway. Tony Hanley, two years older, with a motorbike and muscles, a liking for the drink and fists that flew too easily in her direction. By the time she came back to the village in her late twenties, she was smaller, paler, shriller, bruised. Besides, Tom was married then, and glad of it. But there are moments now – not when she's working, helping out in the pub, but in the lonely minutes of his sleepless nights. Then, sometimes, unused to the cold vastness of an empty bed, Tom wonders . . . But then he sees her, and the cloud of perfume, as strong as ever, has lost its allure. Tom wants something real. Something to hold on to.

'John says it's true, Tom.' She starts again. 'That they're really buying.'

John has stains on his shirt. When he shifts in his seat, his potbelly drags against the edge of the bar. He is a man old before his time. Years of too much drink, too little work have turned him fat and grey; grey eyes, grey skin, grey teeth.

'Is that so?'

'Yes.' John rolls his jaw around, clicking it loudly. 'And soon at that.'

'Right.' Tom turns back to his glasses.

'Well?' Angela's voice is even higher now.

'Well *what*?'

'It's not good, is it?'

'Not good, not good,' comes a quiet murmur from the corner of the bar. It is Jacob, Tom's kid brother.

Special, they called him at school. *Sensitive*. Jacob, with his clenched fists and turned-in knee and the shoulders that slope diagonally from left to right. Jacob, who came out of the womb with the cord around his neck, who's spent his whole life scrunched and strangled. Jacob, in his late-thirties now and still helpless, mooning over his half pint as if the suds of froth might give him a message, might tell him something as he rocks back and forth, back and forth on his bar stool. Tom claps a forceful hand on his brother's arm, bringing the rocking to a stop.

'Nothing to worry about, pal. They're just city folk playing country. They'll be out in a month or two. What the hell would anyone want up here?'

The pub is temporarily silenced. John toddles, unbalanced by the heft of his stomach, towards the ancient jukebox. Simon and Garfunkel start up, their voices thin and reedy on the old machine. It's the last thing Tom wants to listen to, but he is glad of the distraction. He avoids Angela's eyes, caked in mascara and steely above her pint glass. Three songs later, as the music peters out, the door opens.

The woman in the doorway is old. Small and skinny, she has a puff of white hair that makes her look like a dandelion. Her leggings gape around her ankles and age has hollowed two perfect o's in the centre of her cheeks. She hovers uneasily on the threshold, left hand clamped firmly over right.

'Evening, Heather.'

'Evening Tom, Jacob.' She keeps her eyes firmly averted from Angela. Old battles. Tom can't even remember what that one was about.

'What can I do you for?'

'A sherry please Tom.' Heather pulls her cardigan more tightly around herself as she approaches the bar. She has the coins ready in her hand.

'Here you are.'

'Thanks.'

She takes a slow sip from the glass. There is a pause.

'What of Two Houses, then, Tom?'

'Nothing to it.'

'No?'

'They'll be out before we know it, Heather. Mark my words.'

Slowly, she finishes her sherry. Tom can hear the faint tapping of her rings against the glass.

'Night then, all.'

7

Tom is glad for the solitude of closing time. He stands alone in the darkened pub, with its tatty rugs and mismatched chairs, the sweet but souring smell of beer spills. He watches John and Jacob meander unsteadily towards John's car. Traces Angela's journey in the glow of her cigarette, round the curve of the road and up the alley. A few more village folk had wandered in over the course of the night, dribs and drabs of them, and he is glad to see them go too. Glad to no longer keep up the pretence.

Every night, the same routine. Wetting a cloth and sloshing it unevenly along the bar, across the sticky, scratched-up tables. He doesn't bother too much about the tougher stains or the crisps underfoot. Angela will be in tomorrow anyway, and she needs the money, eking out her pennies to look after her boys. He has to remember to stop doing her work.

Tom prefers this place in the dark, with its strange shapes and the peculiar glint of glass and metal. Every night as he makes his final round – locking the door, drawing the curtains – he comes face to face with the case displaying 1934's prize trout, with the brass horse buckles and old fishing nets and stuffed birds that have hung on the wall for as long as Tom can remember. Nailed up in a time where somebody cared.

'Beggar off,' he says, by way of greeting, to the glass-eyed trout.

For the last two years, Tom has lived above the pub. Has walked sideways up the tiny, awkward staircase to a handful of tiny, awkward rooms. Guest rooms, some of them, for when the walkers come. Not that they come often. Nelderdale's not got much to offer them, the village of Hestle even less, and the ones that come are quickly off again. Tom recognises now that uncomfortable way they have of looking around, as if to say, *is this it? Is this what we walked all day for?* And they stay, because there's nowhere else to stay. Eat the dinner that Angela lobs at them, the breakfast he inexpertly fries. And then they're off. Walking on, walking through, walking off. With every step, the village behind them gets a little smaller, and with every departure, Tom feels the weight of it more heavily on his shoulders. The weight of going nowhere.

Every night, the same routine, the same sideways shuffle up the staircase which his feet are too big to walk up properly. The same moment's pause outside Zoe's bedroom, the same subtle recalibration of his cells as he remembers that his daughter's not here. That he can't go in to ask how school was, or say goodnight, or joke about that thing on telly, because she's twelve miles down the dale in the crumbiest part of town, with her mother and a man vying to be her new father. The posters on her door are peeling off, and Tom dutifully pushes each corner back into its blu-tack by way of goodnight.

He continues on to the cramped parallelogram of a bathroom, none of whose walls fit together properly. Splashing his face in the pastel-pink sink, Tom catches himself in the speckled mirror. Roman nose, ruddy cheeks; eyes the colour of moorgrass, his mother told him as a boy. Bare-bulb reflections aren't too flattering when you reach his age, and he rubs the towel viciously across his face, wanting to rub away the evening's fretted conversations. Because there's truth in the worry, he knows that well enough.

He wonders again what these people at Two Houses could possibly want from them. They're no national park, no tourist trap. Not anything enough to be of interest any more.

Over the last fifty years almost everyone has upped and gone. Off to the town, the city, the rigs, anywhere that might stand a better chance than this. The great trickling exodus of too many hard years that has left them a ghost village, half the houses empty. A dale that died. Or that didn't quite die, with the few of them still here, still hanging grimly on. Would have been better off, Tom thinks, in his darker moments, if they'd all just left. Made an end of it. Better dead than half, better nothing than something. It couldn't have been worse than this limbo in between.

Limbo. They used to get a smack saying that word as kiddies. A wallop. *None of your bloody Irish business here.* No confession, no redemption in this valley. Just a life of toil and grind, then a wooden box that came calling for you at forty when the despair or the back-break of it finally carried you off. Tom's gone forty now. Waiting for his box, then, he figures, switching off the bathroom light.

But it's not a box coming up the valley towards him, trailing its way up the corpse road where once bodies were carried down off the distant farms, down valley to the churches. It's these new people, these offcomers, and whatever strange business they're bringing to Two Houses.

'This dale has enough ghosts,' he murmurs to the darkness of his empty bed.

Tom has more than enough to worry about without these offcomers – father, brother, daughter, self – yet it is their spectre that stands in the corner of his bedroom tonight, their as yet unknown faces that people his dreams.

8

Simon delights in how quickly the deal concludes. The council seem only too happy to get rid of the place, and well below the asking price. Relishing this victory, he does not expect the difficulty he encounters in getting someone up there to clean the houses, the impossibility of finding anyone to carry out even the most preliminary work. Herbert evades, mumbles, seems to imply it'd take a lot to get builders up that end of the dale.

In the end, Simon asks Jimbo, a strapping redhead of Irish extraction who'd been the saving grace of several London projects in the early days when the firm was starting out; who'd done all the work over the years in their London house. Jimbo, with his peculiar commute between a girl-friend in Willesden and a mam in Newcastle that Simon's never quite got to the bottom of, but which comes in handy for their northern escape. It is Jimbo who picks up the keys, who takes a first gander at the Two Houses, who strips the wallpaper in the rooms of the main house, gives them a fresh coat of plaster, has the unenviable job of redoing the ancient wiring.

'So,' Simon asks one night on the Gray's Inn Road, waiting for Jimbo to hand the keys to him. 'What do you think?'

Jimbo chuckles, a deep throaty laugh that reverberates throughout his vast torso. 'That's a haunted house all right. What a place!'

And Simon – who has been daydreaming of nothing but the Two Houses, sketching out plans in meetings and on the back of napkins, hunched beneath his desk lamp late into the night making the first excited scribbles of what they might do, how they might build there – pauses. Jimbo claps him on the shoulder.

'I'm kidding, man!' That laugh again. 'Was just a big job, wasn't it? Dirt and muck and all on me own, like?'

He is politic, Jimbo. Sees the crestfallen look on Simon's face and decides not to dwell on the years of shit and animal bones he found up there. The mould, the rot, the mysterious noises. The rattling windows and slamming doors that had him – a six and a half foot tall bruiser – hopping outside in his sleeping bag at two in the morning to sleep in the van rather than take his chances in the house.

Simon looks nervously down at the fat envelope in his hand. 'Was it – I mean, are you sure this is enough?'

Jimbo takes the envelope, laughing. 'Too much of a worrier, you are. It's grand, man, thank you. Hope you'll be very happy up there.'

'Well,' Simon blusters, 'it's just for weekends.'

'Aye, right.' Jimbo touches his hand to an imaginary cap by way of goodbye. 'My best to your missus, like.'

At home, the missus is knee-deep in packing boxes, her turquoise eyes fever-bright.

'Blimey, Jay-bird, are we taking the kitchen sink too?'

She kisses his cheek. 'No, but my studio.' Passing him a pile of as yet unassembled boxes. 'I'd like my studio.'

In the end, it is too much for the Volvo, its wheel mended though just as creaky under the weight of their life in boxes. Simon hires movers. Jay decides that it's better to take their London furniture up north – sofa, bed, table – and he can't argue with her logic when she points out how much harder it'll be to get things delivered up there.

On the final day, as they bid their half-empty house adieu, Jay murmurs something about renting it out.

'But we're not going forever, Jay-bird. A few weeks now to get set up, then weekends, no?'

'Of course,' she smiles vaguely, her mind already wandering somewhere else. 'Silly me.'

Even when the people are gone – the people who should have been in this great house, the people who should not – there is the roar of it. The slow roar of decay as things fall apart.

Quieter, there is also the reverberation of what was. Of things caught in the atmosphere. Words suspended in the air like dust, for echoes last a long time in an empty room.

It is a long while that pain reverberates.

They arrive as September is drawing to a close and the scant leaves on the ragged trees are turning. Paler, the valley grass already looks sun-starved, and the air is taking on a new, crisper chill, as if the whole landscape has tilted itself towards the darkening north. The light is ebbing, slipping between their fingers, the last of the year beginning to turn in on itself.

'It's just for a few weeks, Podge,' Jay had said during their goodbyes. 'A few weeks at first to get everything sorted.' Though Podge, his great silver earrings quivering in his earlobes, seemed to know that she was grateful to get going.

Now they are here, London and all that is familiar hundreds of miles away, the Two Houses silhouetted against an electric-blue twilight. Simon switches off the car and looks at her, Bella the collie dog bundled in her lap.

'So,' he asks, 'where do we start?'

They walk towards the larger of the two houses, towards the great doorway with 1712 etched in its stone, where Jimbo has concentrated his work. 'Can't be doing both, man,' he'd joked, 'I'll never leave.' The other house is smaller anyway, with a door hacked into its side like an afterthought. Simon declares it'll be great for storage, but Jay does not hear him. She is already on the threshold, stepping into a new house, a new life that is already curiously familiar.

Inside, the same earthy smell, the same still air. But Jimbo has stripped the heavy wallpaper, coated the walls in plaster so that the grand front room gives off an air of ethereal gloom. Hardly knowing why, Jay walks to the mantelpiece, her fingers reaching out for the small, dented thimble she had last seen upstairs, had left in the upstairs room in which she found it.

'Simon, my thimble.'

'Your what?'

'My thimble. I found it upstairs, I left it in one of the bedrooms.'

'Jimbo must have moved it. God, he's done a great job.'

And with that, Simon is off, inspecting the work, unloading the car, carting their temporary kit into the grand living room where, he declares, they'll set up base camp. It'll be a few squeaky nights on the camp bed before the moving lorry comes, and Simon attacks it all with relish. Bella barks, rushing from room to room, sniffing everything, sneezing excitedly at the dust. And Jay leaves them to it. Thimble on finger, she drifts silently back into the main hallway and presses her palms against the end wall – the wall that went up to make this one house into two. It is cold and claylike to her hands.

Pottery first appeared after her mother's death. Jay was twelve, and awkward, and it was too difficult for her father to say all the things that needed to be said. A Tuesday in May, and with the crumpling of metal and screech of hot tyres, the world fell away beneath her feet. She remembers the hazy summer afternoons of early childhood spent spinning, arms outstretched beneath the suburban apple tree; or twisting the ropes of the swing as tight as they would go before the delicious release, kaleidoscopic to her child eyes. Then suddenly she was on the search for a way to stop the world from turning; to make sense of this new, wildly uncoordinated movement. It came, unexpectedly, in the art room at school.

38

Miss Bird, the art teacher, letting her turn a lump of clay in her hands.

The wheel was a way to control things. In her hands, cold wet clay took shape, turned thin and hard. Crouched low and stiff over the wheel, there was no room to think of anything else. Just her and the work, one shape, one form and the *effort* needed for its transformation. Years, it had taken, to build a confident throw, to learn the sheer bloody-mindedness needed to just hurl the material onto the wheel. The lob, the satisfying smack, the whirr, the muscle ache, the intensity of time devoted to this one thing alone. The time, the pure *time* of it.

Her memories come through the prism of this process. School, art school, her practice afterwards – everything seen and felt through the ache at day's end, the taut exhaustion of it. Even the day she met Simon, at a friend's wedding, when she walked up to him and against all expectation let him into her life: she knew that he was special because he'd taken her mind off her work for several full minutes. That was her way. The way she was never quite easy knowing her works were yet to be fired, yet to be put into or pulled from the kiln. The way the clay dried around her fingernails and she would chip away at it, as if being outside the studio she still needed some connection to that maker's force. And then the release, the terrified opening of the kiln door, the sheer egotistical thrill that she alone had made this work. Made beauty from sludge. Magic.

But the magic had left. Just like that. Poured itself into that crack in the vessel she'd been working on for months, the centrepiece, the *pièce de résistance* that hadn't resisted at all. Cracked, broken, worthless, and gone the magic, gone the joy, replaced with freezing inescapable . . . was it fear? Despair? It wasn't anything, really, and yet it was enough to anchor her to her bed, to her pillow, as if even lifting her head would be to risk the world collapsing in around her.

*

'Jay?' It is Simon, excited as a schoolboy. 'Can I show you something?'

Nodding, she pulls her hands away from the wall, watches her ten white fingernails turn pink again.

'Close your eyes.'

She does and he guides her, gently, between boxes, the occasional clunk of cardboard against her legs and Bella weaving excitedly around them both. 'Here, just here . . .' Jay cannot help but giggle and Simon's heart soars. Outside, the wind is circling, its howl dampened by the walls and the door until it sounds like a breath taken over her shoulder. 'OK.' Simon pauses. 'Open your eyes.'

Plans. Architect's plans, laid out on the floor in front of the ornate fireplace. Jay kneels down, her fingers tracing the lines as if they might help her eyes to see it better. Working through the elevations, she sees two houses; one house cut in half where a room is missing. But where outside, in the gathering dark, there is a gap, on the paper in her hand it is healed. The two parts connected again.

'You said you wanted a studio up here,' Simon crouches next to her. 'I thought we could put it in the middle. Put the two houses back together again.'

9

Heather keeps a watch at the kitchen window. Her hands dance an unhappy judder along the countertops. Already she can tell that the tremors are increasing.

Could be one year, could be five, the doctor said. *Ten at a push*. As if she were a bus journey, or delay, or some other quantifiable but ultimately irrelevant thing. The man at the meat and cheese counter slicing blindly: might be one ounce, might be ten. As if years were ounces. As if the measure didn't matter.

Five weeks since the appointment, and already she can see it more. These minute somersaults in her cells. It is exhausting, to spend the day watching the involuntary movement of it, then to lie in bed and wish for sleep, unable to stop herself from jolting.

Today, however, there is a different tremor. A trembling at the base of Heather's lungs that has nothing to do with her years of smoking. No. Word has reached Heather of the offcomers at Two Houses. John telephoned this morning – a rare occasion, his words muffled and phlegmy – to say that they are here.

'They're arrived.'

'At Two Houses?'

'Aye.'

'Not just the builder this time?'

'No, it's them.'

As if on cue, the wind set to moaning, and the whole cottage – all four rooms of it – seemed to shake and tremble with her.

So Heather keeps her watch, though there is little to look at. This run of cottages faces the river. Further down the village street there is the pub, the bridge, the road that leads to town – to everything, really, because beyond the village in the other direction real roads stop and it's dirt track, the hillsides rising high on all sides. Today, the village is especially quiet. No signs of life. At Heather's feet, her greying Yorkshire terrier whines.

'Come on then, Joss.'

In spite of the darkening sky, Heather reaches for the lead.

Tramping out of the village, past the pub and across the bridge and out along the empty road, Heather remembers what this life used to be. Wild men coming down off the farms, unwashed and ragged, heady with animal scent. The one-fire-winters, where it was all anyone could do to keep one fire going, and that endless gnawing worry etching itself into every face that there was not going to be enough. Enough lambs, enough work, enough coal, enough food. Bread and margarine dinners. Coal dust on the air. Clouds of breath as you clambered into bed at night, and the never-ending years of frozen knees as your legs grew longer and your skirt grew shorter and you could never pull your socks high enough.

Beyond the bridge, at the very edge of the village, she passes the house in which she grew up. No different, really, to the house in which she's spent her adult life. Two up, two down. It's empty now, poky windows smeared with dirt, the scrap of garden wild and overgrown. She hears the sound of her mother scrubbing the stone step as she passes, the fresh *crack* of laundry day as the wind whipped their washing up and down the clothesline. She remembers one winter when, the pot empty, her father appeared with a favourite hen limp between his rough hands. Crying out, the children earned a smack about the ears. 'I'm trying to feed this family!' her father roared, spit gathering like the habitual beer foam in the corners of his lips. He forced her mother to pluck it, cook it, but they sat in silence as it was served. Heather saw a single tear fall onto her mother's apron and the bird was turned out, uneaten.

Heather lives in this world of memory now. This half-life, where everything around her is flat and empty yet thick with the resonance of days gone by. A hum below the surface. *Palimpsest.* A word she heard on the radio once and had to look up in the library dictionary (*noun, writing material on which later writing has been superimposed*), which was difficult because she couldn't spell it.

'Not surprising,' she mutters to herself, looking at the world now and seeing the world then. 'Not like anything new happens.'

There was a time when Heather thought she would leave the village. It was the sixties, and it seemed like people could leave home and discover themselves. But Heather made the mistake of so many girls before and since. Quickly, quietly, she was married off to Harold Ellis – solid, dependable Harry Ellis – and before she'd even begun she found herself in a cottage exactly like that of her parents, keeping house, tending to baby, cooking the tea. That brief moment of life being something more burned bright and extinguished itself within a matter of months. It came and went almost without her realising it.

Joss, fat and wheezing, pauses for her at the stile. Without stopping to consider their direction, Heather pulls herself up and through and they set off up across the hill. It's steep, but it'll take them over the tops to Two Houses.

It was a successful marriage, if you count success in terms of length. Forty years, she and Harry were together. Forty quiet, unobtrusive years. Forty years of bums on the sofa, of bodies next to but not quite touching each other in bed. Forty years of baked beans for tea and a quick half down the pub and so many cigarettes ground into the glass ashtray she cannot begin to count. So much for travelling the world – the furthest they ever got was Anglesey. Heather had wanted to visit Blackpool, to see the bright lights and the rides and the circus performers. But Harry had found a sensible caravan park on the northern tip of Wales, and they spent a week sitting in the rain, in a van that smelled of gas while they warmed the usual beans and sausages on the stove.

Their daughter, Jackie, lives down the valley. Down in the town. In her years of teenage rebellion, Jackie was so sure she was going to get out. *I hate this dump!* she'd screamed, slamming her bedroom door. Well, she'd managed twelve miles.

'More than I ever did,' Heather says to the wind.

Jackie calls up regularly now, though Heather has not told her about the diagnosis.

'Why don't you come and live down here? At least there's people here. Shops. Life.'

How funny, Heather thinks, that young folk think the old want life. Heather isn't sure she wants anything any more.

And yet . . . She pauses, holding out her trembling hands. This diagnosis. It's stirred up feelings she's spent forty years trying to forget. These thoughts that go whirring through her head at night have her all at odds. She doesn't want company, but she doesn't want to be alone. She doesn't want anything, she tells herself, and yet there is a longing in her that wants more than she has ever had. She cannot understand it, cannot unpick this complex web of desire that has fired up inside her, red and hot like blacksmith's coals, that is hurtling the past and the present towards each other.

She stoops to pick up Joss, bones creaking, and places her on the stile in front of them. They look out, woman and dog, on the valley spreading out below them. The silver ribbon of river, the flat curl of road. And just beneath this hill, Two Houses, with their two roofs, their two chimneys, and – Heather strains her eyes to make them out – two people wandering in front of them. They've a car unloading in front of the house. Boxes. Stuff.

A chill runs across Heather's skin. It certainly looks as if they're here to stay.

'Come on, Joss.'

They turn, the wind howls, and she can tell the rain is coming.

10

The rain comes and the rain stays, and Tom resigns himself to the fact that the season is over. There won't be more walkers now. Not that he enjoys hosting them, but the cash is handy and there is something sombre in the turning of another year.

The pub is quiet. The rain rattles against the windows, the windows against their frames. At the bar, Zoe rustles a crisp packet, munching idly as she does her homework. Tom can hear Angela humming as she cleans the rooms overhead. In the corner, Jacob is in his own world, trying to mend a bit of ancient fishing tackle.

'What you working on, Zo?'

'Victorians.'

'Fun?'

She groans. Upstairs, Angela's hum is replaced by the whirr of the hoover.

'The old mine buildings probably date from then. Victorians and that. We should walk up there, sometime. It's been ages.'

It's been forever, he wants to add, because you and I have only ever been there with your mother.

'Yeah,' Zoe nods, frowning at something in her notebook. 'Maybe. If the rain ever stops.'

'Right.'

'Dad?'

'Yeah?'

She asks it nonchalantly, looking down at her schoolwork. 'Those mines on Two Houses land now? Like, do they belong to them?'

Tom pauses. 'Yeah, I suppose they do.'

Zoe slams her notebook shut, digs in her bag for a chemistry textbook. 'Bet they don't even know they've got them.'

Zoe is right: Jay and Simon don't know about the mine workings. Don't know that they have half-collapsed buildings and old lead chimneys high up on the land above them, where the seams were richest and the chimneys could carry at least some of the deadly smoke away from the village. They have their hands full with their houses.

Thanks to Jimbo there is electricity now, and running water, though the pipes spit and rattle in protest, and what these amenities have shown them is *dirt*. It is everywhere, legion and deep. No matter how hard they scrub, the floors find more filth to give up. Windowpanes lurk beneath inches of grime, doorframes beneath cosmic splatters of cobweb and muck. The stains of age are stubborn and do not want to be lifted.

In the kitchen, Jay tries to pull up a bunch of unruly nettles that have somehow grown up through a crack in the window frame. They jostle angrily over the edges of her rubber gloves, lacing her forearms with angry welts.

'Ouch!'

A final tug and they at last come free, sending her reeling back across the empty kitchen. She stuffs them absent-mindedly into the great black range that Simon is hell-bent on figuring out, thinking that all fuel is useful. As she does so, she hears footsteps on the bare floorboards above her. The kitchen light – a single bulb hanging down on a long, grubby cord – starts to swing and circle.

'Simon?'

There is no answer. She is sharply aware of her heart inside her ribcage. 'Simon?'

She passes through the kitchen door, crosses the back hallway, into the grand living room, their temporary base camp. They have delayed the moving van until they can get the house vaguely in order, so evenings find them here, tucked up in a squeaky

46

camp bed, Bella at their feet as they watch the embers of the fire die out. There are boxes here, suitcases, objects adrift in a general sea of stuff, but no Simon. Jay strains her ears to follow the sound of steps overhead, tracing their progress until she is in the main entryway, blood pooling at the base of her throat.

By the front door she collides into Simon, a rush of cold air and rain as he re-enters the house.

'Left my pocketknife in the car,' he grins, brandishing the small metal bundle. Then seeing her face: 'What is it, Jay-bird?'

'Nothing, nothing.' She tries to return her breath to normal, tries not to look over her shoulder at the upstairs landing. 'Just creaks in the pipes.'

Filthy weather, this winter. Filthy weather for a filthy house, with the snow blowing in through the missing roof slates, the damp running down the walls. It was never like this, this wet, this muck.

Cold, yes. The winter of '47 the clothes froze on our backs. The sheets cracked as I got into bed. The maid's room was so frigid that she and cook slept in the kitchen. The groundsmen couldn't keep the road clear, so deep was the snow, so hard it froze. Bitter, biting, that cold, and always the wind howling. Oh yes, this place has known bad weather.

But never filth.

Simon sets about lighting the range, delighted and perplexed in equal measure by the number and variety of doors and compartments, the seeming impossibility of regulating temperature. Outside, the afternoon begins its mercurial slip into evening, and Jay keeps only a faint watch on the light fitting overhead.

Soon the range is working, intermittent warm belches escaping from its doors. In spite of the heat, Jay's feet turn cold when Bella deserts them in order to eat her dinner.

'Just going to grab another pair of socks, Si,' she says to

the back of Simon's head, as he comes perilously close to singeing his eyebrows.

The living room is noticeably cooler. They have not lit its fire yet, and already the smells of cold and mildew have returned; a dank metallic twist to the air that reminds her of railway waiting rooms and wintry platforms. Jay half expects to see new mould blossoming across the walls, so perpetual is the battle against the elements.

She is one sock in when the lights go. All of them on a sudden out, and the room is a deep, velvet black.

'Shit!'

'Must be a fuse, love!' Simon calls. She hears him groping his way down the back hallway towards the cupboard under the stairs. Bella barks. Her arms outstretched in front of her like an ungainly ghoul, Jay feels a rush of chill air across her face.

'Jay, shut the bloody door!' Simon calls from the cupboard under the stairs. And she is reaching the front door now, sure enough it is open, but it was not her who opened it.

'I didn't—' she begins. But Simon has his torch now, she can see the yellow glow spilling out from the cupboard, and by the time she has pulled the great door shut the lights are flickering back to brightness again.

Simon emerges victorious from the cupboard. 'Nothing to worry about, love. Jimbo said they were a bit tricksy.'

Jay thinks back over the last few days, the cleaning and the discoveries, the ways in which they have tried to learn the rhythms of the houses: the *whir* and *whoosh* and *roar* of the boiler ('Just the boiler'); the thousand different songs of the wind ('Just the wind'). It is an adventure, clambering into the camp bed at night, being so cut off from friends and emails and the roar of life. And they are happy, she reminds herself, returning to the kitchen with only a moment of a backward glance. They are happy.

I I

Days pass, and Simon too finds himself thinking of their adventures. He and Jay dive into their tasks together, rolling their jumpers up to the elbow as they plunge their forearms into buckets of frigid, peaty water. Together they scrub and together they jump, hearts in their mouths, as the house creaks and groans around them.

'Coming back to life,' Jay jokes, as the wood warms and the pipes expand, though there is something unsettlingly human about this particular symphony.

She shows little interest in leaving the houses, so it is Simon who has been driving the lonely ten miles down to town every few days, for milk and bread and the endless *stuff* of cleaning. He receives short shrift from those who ask where he's living.

'Bad land up there.'

'Haunted, is that.'

Simon does his best to ignore these comments. They are nesting, home-making, and he is working. Drawing up plans and elevations, sourcing materials for the studio that would bring the two houses back together again. Traditional at the front, he's thinking; grey stone, locally sourced – he's seen enough fallen-down barns and roofless houses on his travels to think that this is feasible. Wood and slate, and there must be architectural salvage somewhere up north? Then, at the back, looking out on to the fell, a great wall of glass. A double-height room, so that Jay can have the very best of light; a space high and elegant and (dare he say it) cathedral-like in its magnificence. He falls asleep thinking of floors and finishes. He is excited.

Yet gradually Simon turns and does not find Jay by his side.

She drifts from him, her tread so light he cannot distinguish it from the clatter of rain or the wind's ache or the lonely crow in the tree outside who complains about the weather. They will start a job together and she will wander off, silently, as if one of the spirits the locals talk of. And each time he comes back to the houses – to Jay, who does not want to leave them – her communion with their bricks and mortar is somehow more total.

'Jay?' Simon's voice echoes in the hallway, in the great living room. Bella, curled in front of the fire, raises her eyebrows. He moves towards the staircase, his hand on the bannisters. 'Jay?'

Nothing.

This place was meant to bring them closer. His great plan to reconnect the houses was perhaps not so subtle as he thought; it was meant to reconnect them, too. For a moment, his foot hovering above the first stair, Simon is transported. He hears music and laughter, and in his mind, they are dancing.

He first set eyes on Jay at his cousin's wedding: he, a last-minute invite intended to make up numbers; she, dazzling in a pale silk dress only slightly pinker than her skin. In an uncharacteristic fit of boldness he spoke to her; when the music started he asked her to dance.

He remembers the agonising uncertainty of it; of two strangers drawn close, intimate, trying not to step on each other's toes. He was, as ever, tentative; unsure of himself. All he could think of were the fingertips of his right hand and the way her back felt to them through silk. He was afraid to move, to breathe, even; as if a breath taken too sharply might break the fragile, lilting equilibrium between them.

These last months have felt to him as if they are dancing again. Tentative, unsure. So many things unsaid between them that they cannot be in that first, intimate proximity.

The lilting waltz dies away, and Simon is in the hallway again, the dark creeping in at its corners, the single bare bulb not enough to keep the shadows at bay. Dusk again, already, and he feels the tightening of winter like a grip in his chest, the feather-light tickling of fear along his back. He creeps tentatively up the stairs. It is so quiet, so still, that he can hear the fizz and flicker of the electric light as he passes.

A sudden rush – something flashes past the upstairs window. A blur, a smudge, something made momentarily visible before his eyes. *A bird, it must have been a bird*, he tells himself, but now a faint tune has started in the distance, something high and creaking. He can hardly hear it above the hammering of his heart, dry fear pulsing in his mouth.

'Jay?'

His feet gather pace until he is half running down the hallway.

'Jay?'

He finds her in one of the bedrooms, a bucket and scrubbing brush abandoned on the floor. She is standing by the window, looking out at the rain, and for a brief moment in the blue half-light he does not recognise her, sees only a woman silhouetted against the gloom, hears only the estate agent's words in his ears: *Lost his wife – and then it started.*

'Are you alright, Jay-bird?'

'Hmm?' She looks almost surprised to see him.

'Everything OK?' He goes to touch her hands. They're freezing, but she pulls them away from him, turning some small, secret object over and over.

'Yes, I was just listening.'

A shiver dances across Simon's skin. 'To what?'

'To the rain, silly.'

'Oh.' Relief. 'Do you want me to bring your boxes over, from the studio?'

Her moods are like the clouds that scud overhead, changing the fellside from grey to green and back again. Her face darkens.

'Not tonight, Simon.' She pushes past him. 'It's late, there are jobs to finish.'

Later, adding more wood to the fire, he will find the object she was playing with lined up on the mantelpiece next to her thimble. A tiny music box, rusted and out of tune, and he will wonder whose it is, and where on earth she found it.

This was a house made for dark wood. For heavy furniture, things venerated and handed down. When these stones were placed, things that were heavy meant things that cost. They were here to stay, not least because they were too big to move again. Objects of age and inheritance. This house was built for permanence, for generations. It was a stand against death, knowing that it and its kin would always stand here.

But what of those who do not inherit? What of those who do not beget? Where do we go, who have no kin to look to? Family trees take no account of dead ends.

Jay clatters down the grand staircase, now scrubbed of the years of bird muck, though still missing a tread on one of the stairs, several of its bannisters still absent. In the living room, she crouches in front of the grate, balling up newspaper and arranging thin strips of kindling with which to get the fire started.

Inside her pocket, the music box presses sharp against her leg.

It is almost a year now since the diagnosis was made final. That children were not a possibility for them. It was a piece of news that came slowly, inching towards them over months of appointments, through endless *further tests* and *second chances*. In the end, even the final, decisive verdict was creeping. There was no blunt, brutal reason for it. She would have preferred that. *A constellation of factors*, the doctor said, trying to be kind. But it was her. An inhospitable climate. The inability to support. She who had always prided herself on making, creating. She who had then thrown herself back into work, into making vessels that were, of course, empty. Waiting to be filled.

But that had only helped for so long. Even the work – her ever-faithful work – had deserted her in the end.

Early summer, and they were once again at a doctor's office. She did not like the word *breakdown* any more than Simon did. It was inexplicable to her, inadequate. The doctor – a psychiatrist, this one – spoke to Simon about the pressures of work, marital problems. A temporary – he stressed *temporary* – inability to cope. He'd asked pointedly about children, as if not having them was itself a symptom. Which, in a way, it was.

The music box glinted at her from the back of a cupboard. Cobwebs and bare shelves, and a flash of metal. It called to her, fitted perfectly in the palm of her hand. The cold handle turned, plucking the dissonant metal forks, and she wondered about the woman who died here, the child whose walls had the red-jacketed riders, the ears that must have heard this song.

The flames slowly lick and crackle, and there is something about this barren house, the bare hillsides and leaden skies, that feels comforting to her. As if there might be a rapport between her and this empty, inhospitable place. She remembers the ends of long days in the studio, the way she would scrub her hands and still, later, feel the settling of clay dust on her fingertips. Dust that, no matter how hard she tried, would still make a faint trace across her trousers, a cosmos of it that would settle as she brushed her hair off her forehead. A residue, a trace. And there is a trace of something in this house, too; something left behind. A familiar film of sadness across its surfaces, no matter how hard she scrubs.

Jay stands, rubbing dusty hands along her trousers. She pulls the music box from her pocket and places it on the mantelpiece. Simon is in the kitchen, cooking, and though she does not remember telling the doctor that she wanted quiet and space, she knows that here she has found it.

12

Tom's car pushes grudgingly up the fellside, spluttering, wheezing, as if after all the years climbing this incline, today might be the final insurmountable hurdle. The road is rough and rocky, so that the brief bone-juddering rattle of the cattle grids actually comes as a relief.

There are three gates to pass through on this lonely track up to the farmhouse, and Tom is irked to see the last one hanging open like a loose jaw.

'Bloody—'

The word is out of his mouth – an instinct, a reflex – before he remembers that it doesn't matter. The familiar pang of realisation, a smack in the gut as visceral now as it was two years ago when the last of the herd was finally sold off. It doesn't matter if the gate is left open; there's nothing left to wander through it. The grate he drives over is just a grid; no cattle here. And when the house finally looms into view – long and low against the hillside, an empty barn tacked on to each end – it is just a house. No farm now.

As always, the door is unlocked and the kitchen hits Tom with a wave of stench. Damp walls, old food, cat's piss. A palpable sense of decline. God, he thinks; that it has come to this.

'Oh.' His father shuffles into the room, pipe clenched between his teeth. ''Syou.'

'Hello, Dad.'

A grunt as his father drops heavily into the chair by the cooker. Gas, this one; a seventies addition, from a time where there was still a future here, still money with which to make improvements. The chair has stood in that spot Tom's whole life. He remembers as a little one the big black range, polished up to a high shine by his grandmother's worn hands. It made sense to sit here then, when the range was hearth and home, cooker and heater, and he remembers being gathered into her lap, the scratch of wool beneath his cheek and the fierce smell of Brasso polish.

'Brought your shopping.'

'Aye.' His father nods, leaning forward to relight his pipe. *Put-put-put.* 'Leave it out.'

But Tom can see what happened to the last groceries that he left out. A bottle of yellow milk sitting by the sink. A loaf of white bread blooming into blue and green.

'I'll put it in the fridge. Where's Jacob, Da?'

'Out.'

'Out where?'

'Out there.'

The old man nods towards the window, which frames a blank expanse of hillside. Tom grits his teeth. It's not worth getting angry with him.

'He shouldn't be out on his own, Dad.'

His father turns and looks above him. As long as anyone can remember, Ned Outhwaite has fixed his gaze three inches above a person's head. Tom's whole life, every conversation addressed not to his face but to the air above him. He wonders when those milky eyes last met someone else's. Angering in spite of himself, he shoves bread, milk and cheese into the fridge.

Straightening out, so tall now that he is not far off the low rafters, he says it again. 'I said, he shouldn't be out on his own.'

Ned Outhwaite, with his ruddy face and thin, yellow-white hair, concentrates on his pipe. 'Can't stop a grown man doing what he wants to do.'

Oh but you can, Tom thinks. Oh but you can.

Tom is, these days, profoundly out of his element. Torn from the land on which he was raised, which it had always been intended he would raise in turn. Generations of Outhwaites have worked this earth. His father, grandfather, great-grandfather before that, all out before dawn on the fellside, trudging back in long after dark, ache in their bones and mud on their boots. It is blindingly obvious to Tom that this earth is in him. That he is in this land and of this land. That, more than mere ancestry, his birth was mapped out in stone and sedge. That those first, imperceptible multiplications of cells already yearned for the damp bog air, the squelch of moss beneath foot and finger, the way the wind soars up the sheer face of this valley end like a bird in flight. To have that inheritance taken from him, to be cut off – he is adrift. A man loosed from his own landlocked sails.

The bank manager did everything he could. Tom has to believe that because he and Alan were at school together and Alan seemed to dread their meetings as much as he did, a thin smile failing to cover his deep unease. That last time, when it finally happened, Alan had clapped his hand on Tom's shoulder and Tom would have done anything to escape that heavy, lingering hand, thick with finality. He knew then that it was done. That there was no fighting it.

Tom leaves his father in front of the stained and splattered cooker, his cloudy eyes wandering off towards a past less painful than the present to bear. Ned hadn't said much when the final decision was made. When the last of the ewes were rounded up and driven down to market. He simply turned on his heel, laid down his crook, and walked away, up and over the barren hillsides upon which he had made what little life he had. He has said very little since. There is no anger in him that Tom can see, just sagging resignation, as limp and lifeless as the flesh that falls from him in his old age. Tom rages alone.

He thunders back down towards the village, egged on by

the skid and slip of tyres, the spray of dusty gravel that rises in clouds behind him. Halfway down, just as the cluster of slate roofs appears, his mobile rings. He pulls the car to an abrupt halt. There's rarely signal up the top of the valley. There's rarely anyone to be calling, either.

'Tom.'

His stomach plummets to hear his ex-wife, her voice clipped, pointed. He can imagine her standing by the phone with her arms wrapped tight around herself. Furious before he's even opened his mouth.

'Lisa.'

'Where's Zoe?'

'At the house.' Still, he cannot call the pub his home. 'Why?'

'The farmhouse?'

The word grates against his heart. 'It's not a farm any more, Lisa. Can't be a farmhouse without a farm.'

'Whatever, Tom. I don't need to rehash your sad story. I don't like her being up there.'

'She's not, she's at my . . . She's at the pub.'

'Well she's not answering her phone.'

'She's probably busy.'

'She's always on her phone.'

'Maybe she doesn't want to talk.' He stops himself from adding *to you* but Lisa sucks in her breath regardless.

'Just get back and check on her, will you?'

'I'm going.'

'Fine. The line's breaking up, anyway.'

How true is that, Tom thinks, as he eases the car down the final stretch of track into the village. Lines breaking. He thinks of the big storms of his childhood, when the phone lines crashed and tangled on the earth. The storms that roll in now, breaking the signal. The line between him and Lisa. The family line. Landline. Everything broken, all splinter and shatter.

13

'I'm going to paint the bedroom,' Jay announces one morning.

'Really?' Simon tries not to sound sceptical.

'Why not? Jimbo left us the paint.'

If Simon has reservations about drips and concentration he bites his tongue, and slowly, dreamily, she sets about it. By the end of two days, the walls are white: pure white, the white of fired porcelain, and the paint is smeared across her hands and face.

'Fresh white, fresh start,' she tells him, though in fact Jay has a new appreciation for colour up here. At first she thought the stones of the houses grey, when in fact they are a kaleidoscope – brown bread, oatmeal, gristle, rust – not unlike her many different shades of clay. The hills are not just green; they are bottle, emerald, mustard together. For a while she sits alone in the empty bedroom, looking out at the changing patchwork of fells. Her mind runs through all the things she has made, might make again, and it is almost like being back in her studio, almost like being her old self, thumbs instinctively rubbing against forefingers as if squeezing clay to its desired shape.

I thought it was the wind, when the howling started. The wind circling the chimneys, or myself, perhaps. My grief given voice for once. But it was not me. It was the dogs. The dogs, stood in her drawing room, hackles up, howling at the air.

The delivery van startles her, the tramp of workmen's boots, the loud voices they use to shout to each other. Jay finds it raucous, air-shattering, but Simon is delighted, rushing this way and that with a clipboard against which he checks each item, noting in his neat little hand its ultimate location. Everything, at first, is brought into the hallway: sofa, table, chairs, bed, until, against the pale plastered walls, it looks like a fashionable London shop.

'Do we have to move the bed upstairs?' Jay asks. She is perched on the end of the squeaky camp bed, Bella sat between her knees.

'Oh come on, Jay-bird, aren't you tired of that pile of rust?'

She relents, though secretly she has loved sleeping down here by the embers of their fires, the chimney's whispers. And loved the purity of that empty bedroom, too; a bare stage, a blank canvas that she has not wanted to splatter. But the truck drivers get the go-ahead, heaving and hauling the bedframe up the turning staircase and down the narrow corridor. It is a Scandinavian sleigh bed, smooth pale wood, an outrageous, expensive honeymoon whim – and it is many minutes of muscle and puffing before it stands in the centre of the empty bedroom.

The men don't fancy much more of that, make noises about having to get back, a long journey, a bloody difficult road to manoeuvre a truck down. Simon ushers them out, a grateful wad of notes passing from his hands to theirs. Jay plants herself on the bed, facing the windows, looking out onto the darkening fellside until Simon returns.

'I'll get the bedside tables, shall I?' he pants. She can already see him running through his mental inventory to find them.

'No.' She touches his arm. 'Let's leave it bare a little while. Sit with me.'

So he does, and they do, and at night, without curtains, under the glimmer of a dwindling moon, Jay opens her eyes to find the whole room glowing.

Shut the dogs out then, that's what he said. And we did. But he could not stop things flying through the air. Could not

belt every object down, though I had the belt on me at first
for throwing them.
I never touched a thing.

She feels her connection to the house most strongly at night. A pull that is magnetic, as if from the stones and earth themselves. A rapport on the still air, in the bare boards beneath her wandering feet, as if those who have come before her also flee from sleep.

When Simon's breath drops to that gentle, wispy hush Jay's feet drop to the floor and she is wandering the hallways, putting her hands to wall and window. For what is a ceramicist if not tactile? Who is to tell her that she will not learn the past through touch?

She is fascinated by the ghost story, by the idea of someone who wanted to come back that much. At school, after her mother died, her friends tried to comfort her by saying that her mum might reappear as a ghost. And during their frustrated, imaginative, teenage years, they tried to call her: séances, sat in circles on bedroom floors; once, a Ouija board, though it didn't spell out anything they could decipher. Her mother never did seem to get in touch, but this place, this had a real ghost, so real they had to cut whole rooms away. Someone who did want to come back, who didn't want to go quietly. And Jay is convinced that a ghost wouldn't be tricked by something so simple as taking a few walls down.

Alone, looking out at nights as black as the crow's feathers she has discovered in the grass, she waits. Waits for her eyes to adjust. Waits for the smudge of dawn to appear. Waits for something – someone – to happen. This night world is kind and silvered, and she is not afraid. Not even when she is sure she feels someone standing behind her, or hears the rasp of a skirt against the doorframe, or when she comes down in the morning light to find things not where she left them. Simon, for his part, blames this on her, on a half-hearted unpacking that moves things temporarily: no final resting places here, he jokes, everything transitory, in flux. And yes, she picks things up, places them down, but from day to day she is astonished by the creep of objects from one room to another, no rhyme or reason to their shifting, skulking by themselves in these witching hours.

And maybe it is in the nature of some of these things to move, the little talismans she has been collecting. The dented thimble, the music box, a thin slice of pearl button. A rabbit's skull whipped white and bare by time and weather; a dried seed pod, blonde and spindly. Her latest treasure is a speckled egg, round and perfect on one side, cracked and gaping on the other. *Silly fool*, she mutters each time she catches herself hoping that it was the little feathered prisoner who broke his way out, not the hungry beak of nature breaking in. She places it gently back on the mantelpiece as if it is an altar; as if all these found, forgotten things are another incantation to this earthy, unearthly world.

The eye does not see what the mind does not want it to.

It took him a long time to see it. Finally, he could no longer avoid it. Not when I was sat on my hands at the dining table, the cook and the maid in the room with us. He could not avoid it, then, when things flew in her rooms. When the air turned frosty. When all of us together heard things shatter.

Jay, like Simon, replays the estate agent's words, spins spider's silk yarns in her mind about love and grief and ghosts as she meditates on those people, this place.

'I want to know,' she breathes onto a windowpane one night, tracing patterns in the mouthmist with an idle finger. All the windows rattle here, an endless percussion of chattering teeth, as if the house itself is cold. 'I want to know the story,' she murmurs over the familiar knocking of wood on wood.

Later, she will say these words again, and she cannot know, now, what secrets they will unfurl, what old scars they will reopen. But in this moment, in the nocturne hush, perhaps it is enough to simply state the desire, for in the morning, she will have her answer.

It took him a long time to see it. Only when he could no longer turn a blind eye, no longer turn the blame on me, only then did the builders come.

14

Jay is not the only one who does not sleep. October now, and the nights are an inky darkness, thick as blood. The stars glint knowingly like so many pieces of mica at the bottom of a riverbed, and the village holds its breath. Waiting. Waiting.

Heather dozes lightly, fitfully, her radio on one side, her dictionary on the other. Well, it is not *her* dictionary. Dev let her borrow one from the library, even though the spine says NOT FOR LOAN in faded red lettering. She blushes now to think how wary she was of him at first, his chocolate skin, his bright white smile. He is a good lad, Dev.

The radio splutters beside her, a programme about memory, and tonight it is Two Houses seared on hers, Two Houses that she cannot escape. She is with her mother, visiting the families that took to sheltering there once the old man had died and their farms had folded. Two dozen people living in those ground-floor rooms. Laundry strung up on old rope to divide them into separate quarters. The chimney is smoking, a hen grubs around in the dirt, and a child smaller than Heather goes to the lavvy in a bucket right in front of them.

'Why are they there, Mam?' she'd asked on the way home.

'Because they've got nowhere else to go, duck.'

Eventually, of course, they did leave. Hard to imagine those folk going anywhere better; hard to imagine them going anywhere worse. Then mice scuttled across the battered floor and birds made nests from anything that hadn't been burned for firewood. Heather was a teenager then, and she can't remember now if she believed in the ghost, in old Lady Brathwane who wasn't old and died young of a broken heart, but there was something eerie to the feel of the place. Two Houses was for a different kind of exploring; the way your hands touched someone else's, the feel of someone else's skin on yours.

Out of time and out of place, Heather's memories scud through like clouds blown by an autumn wind and with a jolt she is a child again, her father is locking her in the coal-hole. It is dark and she is screaming, pounding her little fists against the wooden door. It is blacker than the darkest night and she can hear the scurrying of rats among the coals. *Please, please*, she wails, spluttering on the dark and dusty air. It is an eternity of scrabbling against the wooden door before she is finally freed and she tumbles out into the light; soot-stained, gasping, her fingernails bloodied.

With a jolt, Heather wakes, her heart hammering as fiercely as her child hands against that door. Her cry was enough to wake old Joss, who'd been slumbering at the bed's end. The old girl stretches her tired bones and pads up towards her mistress.

'It's alright Jossy, it's alright,' Heather murmurs, more to herself than to the dog. She looks down at her hands, so different from those little sooty fists. No blood now, just age and wear. And, of course, the tremors. With a surge of sadness Heather realises that this is what this disease feels like. That diagnosis threatens to put her back in the coal-hole, claustrophobic, terrified, unable to get out.

'I can't do that again Jossy,' she whispers. 'I just can't.'

The dog looks up at her and cocks her greying head.

And for the first time, Heather wonders if there might be another way out.

Over at the pub it is long past closing. Tom is relieved to have another day lived through, another evening taut with anticipation done with. Angela and John were there as usual, a few quiet others, Jacob in the corner nursing his single half pint. They didn't speak of Two Houses, but it hung over them like the autumn mist, damp and unmistakable. When the door opened they all jumped, but it was only the Oliver lads from the top end of the village.

Tom's hardly seen his daughter, though it is his week to have her. He hates the partitioning of time, the knowledge that, if he doesn't make the most of her now, he won't see her for another unbearable stretch of days. A week seems an eternity up beneath these hills, with nothing to mark the time and nothing to do, and nothing to say to her even when she does come back because her moods are quicker, sharper than the wind and already that talk of walking up to the mines seems a different, kinder century.

She's a teenager. He hears that from everyone. *It's a teenage thing, it's just her age*. But Tom doesn't remember slamming this many doors. He doesn't remember staring his father down with the anger he sees in Zoe's eyes. His daughter. His baby. That impossible, scrawny bundle of blood and brawn that emerged into the world one day, and Tom remembers those early weeks, Lisa weeping and exhausted, sleeping or angry, fierce like the sheepdog that bit his eight-year-old hand when he went into the corner of the barn to stroke a newborn puppy. And he remembers the quiet hours he and Zoe spent alone. Some of his happiest hours.

Switching off the lights, he climbs the stairs. He hovers outside her door.

'Zo?'

'What?'

'School tomorrow. You should go to sleep.'

'Whatever.'

'Can I come in?'

The bedroom is small, papered in the same kind of ancient flowers that adorn all the rooms above the pub. Faded pink carpet and the faint smell of damp, but stronger than that, the sickly sweet smell of Bacardi – Tom recognises it as soon as he enters. Zoe hardly even bothers to hide it, half kicking the bottle under the bed so that only its neck is showing. He lifts it up.

'What's this?'

She is on the floor, her back against the radiator. He takes in her black jeans, her black T-shirt with a rip in it, remembering with a pang her sweetly patterned child's pyjamas. She doesn't look up, fiddling instead with the scraggly bracelets that line her wrists. 'What do you think?'

'Don't get smart with me.' Tom feels his blood rising. 'What the hell are you doing?'

She shrugs, her mousey hair falling limp around her skinny shoulders.

'You're fourteen. You know what happens if anyone sees this? I lose my licence. We lose all this. Is that what you want?'

Another shrug.

'Is it?'

'I don't care.' She looks at him now, and it is always with a mixture of awe and discomfort that he sees so much of himself in her – the freckles, the green eyes – and yet her mother's steely reserve. '*All this.*' She raises her hands, mimicking his gesture. 'It's all shit.'

A tiny collapse. A miniature landslide around his heart. Rain drums against the window and Zoe is on her feet, screwing up her fists, readying for a fight.

Tom does not give her one. Instead, he turns, closing the door behind him. He stands for a moment on the tiny landing, with its dim light and eighties wallpaper and the carpet worn with age and stains. He remembers, as he cradled her all those years ago, the terrifying realisation that parents have no clue what they're doing. That they know little more than those they care for. He falters for a moment, before sinking into his cold bed.

*

66

Overnight, a new wave of rain comes and the weathermen on Heather's tinny radio begin to talk of saturation. Of groundwater and the water table (which always sounds to Heather like one of those inflatable lilos that she's never lain on, in one of those sunlit swimming pools she's never swum in). The water table, they mumble through her dreams, is rising.

15

Above the Hall the hillsides rise like steep roofs, like earthen cathedrals.

A lung-aching, leg-numbing scramble to climb them, these vertical slopes, slick from rain, thick with hidden rocks and crevasses. But you do and the valley falls away beneath you, twisting loops of river and road, the rough-and-tumble spill of rock and earth. Sedge, stone, slate beneath a rushing sky.

Land. Our land. Land that was ours by right. They talk of rights now: rights of way, human rights, public land, but what of the rights of those left behind? The rights of those of us here, beneath the darkening sky?

High above the houses Jay watches the clouds race across the grey-green earth. She stretches out on a flat rock, an exhausted Bella at her feet. Cold, and yet the stone seems to have held some summer heat. The lichen – mustard yellow, olive green – spools out in front of her, cosmic patterns embroidered in the rockface. She loves the feel of it beneath her hand, her face, that soft smooth abrasive graze.

She has been reticent on the phone, to the ever-loyal Podge, to her agent Jenny. *Oh it's beautiful, yes. There'll be lots of time to work, I'm sure. Mmm, mmm, yes. And how are you?* All the while her eyes raised to the hillsides, her mind already wandering, clambering away.

Bella looks up at her, a soft moan and pleading eyes. She's still a city dog at heart, not used to these gradients, to the lash of the wind. It's the fireside she likes, the warm murmur of flames before her belly.

'OK, Bell. Down we go.'

High on air and altitude, they descend. With the wind at her back, it is all Jay can do not to turn on her ankles, not to slip and slide all the way down the damp and muddy fell-side. Bella falls, rolls, her pretty piebald sides covered in thick mud, tail smacking against the moorgrass. The rain is coming, and although they are new they have already learned to taste it.

The wind snatching at her breath, Jay wants to shriek, to laugh and dance beneath the wild sky in this wild world with not a person in sight. Not a person in sight until she reaches a stone wall, almost slams into it with the force of her descent, and comes face to face with a man.

A little cry escapes her mouth, hand flying up to stifle it. Colour floods her cheeks, and she feels like a naughty school-child, caught trespassing where she should not be. *But this is our land*, she reminds herself as she meets the man's gaze, defiant. *I am allowed to be here.*

He seems young, this man. His grey-green cagoule is drawn tight around him, its hood hiding his face from hers. She feels a spike (is it fear?) in her stomach at the sight of his tightly clenched fists, hanging from his sleeves, one arm longer than the other.

'Hello?'

As his face emerges from its waterproof lair, she realises he is not so young as he looks, this man, though he tilts himself away from her awkwardly, as a teenage boy might do, embarrassed by the contact.

''Llo.'

His greeting comes out as one syllable, mumble-growled. And there is something simultaneously grounded and far away in him, as if he is not of this land at all, this plane, this earth. He tilts his head like a bird, eyes bright, his thin nose beaky, as if at any moment he might set to flight. But it is hands that Jay looks at: hands made for holding earth, as scuffed and calloused as her own. They are so worn, these hands, that it takes her a moment to see the rock that he is holding in one of them, his fingers tightly furled around it as if he and the stone were one.

Jay breaks the silence first.

'Are you from round here?'

'What?'

She asks again. 'Are you from round here?'

'What's round here?'

'This.' She gestures, turning her hand against the fear beating in her throat. 'The dale, the valley.'

'We're all from round here. No one comes to this place.'

'I have.'

'Yes you, you're an offcomer.'

'A newcomer?'

'Offcomer. You come from out there.'

'Oh.'

There is a pause, but not a silence. The wind sings and the sedge grasses hiss, the bare branches of the scraggly trees knock noisily together. No crow today, he has other plans. Jay does not want to break this man's stare. Out of the corner of her eye she can see the Two Houses; they are not far off. The man looks away first.

'I wall.'

'What?'

'I wall. Drystone walls.'

'You make these?' Jay places a hand on the rough-hewn stone in front of her.

'Aye.' He nods, blinking at her fiercely, and for the first time she realises his eyes are different colours; one blue, one green. Sky and grass.

'That's remarkable.'

He shrugs.

'I make things too,' she says.

'Aye?'

'Yes.'

'What?'

'Ceramics.'

'A what?'

She feels foolish. 'Pots and things.'

'With your hands?'

'Yes.'

And suddenly his hand snatches forward, grabs hers by the wrist. She tries not to jump, because actually the gesture is gentle, strangely tender as he looks over the old callouses, the bitten fingernails.

'Yes. You make things.'

Slowly he drops her hand.

'I'm Jay.'

'What?' He cocks his head again, eyes screwed up, his torso twisting away from her.

'I'm Jay. My name's Jay.'

'Jacob.'

'Oh. Similar.'

'Yes.' The two-coloured eyes open again, fixing hers.

Later, when she runs this meeting over in her mind, she will not be able to tell herself why, but for some reason she feels a confidence in this man. If not the urge to confide, then the feeling that he might confide in her.

'We live in the Two Houses,' she says. 'Do you know about the Two Houses?'

A cloud passing over a hillside; a quick shadow over his face.

'Everyone knows about Two Houses.'

'You know the story?'

'Yes.'

She waits. Jacob squirms uncomfortably in front of her.

'We had it in a book . . .' he begins eventually.

Still, she is silent. A trick learnt long ago. To hold everything – limbs, breath – in perfect stillness, until the information you are seeking trickles towards you. When Jacob speaks, it is as a recitation, as if these words were learned long ago by rote, a muscle memory rippling uncomfortable, alien words over his tongue.

'Having lost, in quick succession, a child and wife, Sir Edwin Brathwane declared his house haunted. The lights flickered, animals would hiss, and to avoid meeting daily with the sp—, the sp—'

'The spirit?' Jay supplies, but Jacob only screws his eyes more tightly shut, bangs his fists three times against his side.

'To avoid meeting daily with the spectre of his loss, he ordered the rooms haunted by his wife to be cut out. Whether this banished the spirit of the late Isobel Brathwane, a local beauty, we cannot say.'

Jacob's eyes flare suddenly open.

'He died just after, just after the rooms were cut. There, those were the rooms.'

He points towards the gap between the houses.

'Yes,' Jay nods quietly, the ghosts of his story seeming to flutter over her skin like the wind. For a moment, they stand together, looking over the house, each head filled with its story, its spirits crowding round them.

'I'll go now,' Jacob says, his words an afterthought to his feet which have already started away from her. He turns back over a sloped shoulder. 'You have a nice dog. Mine was shot but I had a nice dog once.'

And with that he is off, long legs carrying him quickly over the marshy ground.

'Jay?'

She looks back towards the houses and sees Simon's fair head above the garden wall.

'Who was that?'

She shakes her head as she walks towards him, Bella running excitedly ahead of her.

'I don't know. He said he does the drystone walling.'

She reaches his side and they turn to walk back to the houses together, Simon's clipboard tapping gently against his side.

'I didn't know anyone did drystone walling any more,' Simon muses.

'I suppose someone has to.'

Instinctively, they go to walk back between the two houses, across the space that has been cut out. Bella emits a low whimper. Jay's heart pounds, hot and fluttering, in her chest. Jacob's words ring loud as the wind in her ears. *Whether this banished the spirit, we cannot say.* Quickly, she links her arm through Simon's.

'Come on, let's go the other way.'

16

Let's walk the dog, Jay said. *It won't rain*, Jay said. It was the first time in days that the rain stopped long enough to draw breath, and maybe it was that man she met who put the idea in her head, this idea that they had to go up to the village. Now Simon finds himself running helter-skelter along a dark country lane, slipping and sliding on the gravelled road as the water pelts hard and cold against his face. It is a deluge, a sudden eruption, so that the world went in seconds from silence to the full cacophony of storm.

Simon's hands move instinctively to his side, where a stitch sears somewhere inside his flesh. He is not in as good a shape as he once was. Jay is ahead of him, her jacket pulled over her head, running with Bella towards the village. He can just make them out through the murk. Bella's white patches flash against the dark and he can see but not hear her barking at the fun of it.

Simon does not think it is particularly fun.

After an eternity of wet minutes they reach the pub. Doubled over, dripping, Jay pushes on the door.

The room falls quiet as they enter. This hush is not, surely, just in contrast to the thundering rain outside. Simon is convinced that the place falls quiet as they enter. A smattering of faces look up at them, wide-eyed, slack-mouthed, and it is as if he is in one of those excruciating dreams where you turn up at school naked. He actually sneaks a quick look at himself to confirm that he is, though sodden, clothed.

'Evening.' Jay speaks first, taking the first tentative step away from the threshold. 'Sorry for . . .' She gestures to the pool of wet they are leaving on the ancient carpet. 'We got caught in the rain.'

Silence. Thick and palpable.

She tries again.

'We've just moved in down the way, at the Two Houses.'

The clunk of a glass being set down on the bar. A stifled cough. Simon watches one man actually turn away from them, staring off into the corner. He's heard about locals versus townies, but this is teetering on hostile.

'Aye, Two Houses, of course you have.'

Simon hasn't really noticed the man behind the bar. He's tall and angular, sort of ruggedly handsome, with greying stubble and strong-looking hands. Simon, with his round tortoiseshell glasses and wet city shoes, feels rather effete.

'Come in. You'll catch your death like that. We'll get a fire going.' Slinging a tea towel over his shoulder, the barman gestures them in. He calls to one of the men at the bar. 'Jacob, set that fire.'

'Oh, hello again.' Jay smiles at the figure who turns awkwardly and hurriedly towards the empty grate. And it is him, Simon notes, that strange man.

'You two met?' the barman asks.

'Yes. Jacob was telling me he does the drystone walling.'

Jay takes off her jacket, shakes out her long red hair with her hands. Simon feels strangely mute. He is an outsider to this encounter. He watches the barman watching his wife, and he knows exactly what the other man is thinking, how bewitching she is with her pale skin and fiery eyes and the impossible sheen of her hair. She is more radiant up here than she has ever been, more luminous than at any time Simon can remember, a pearl lustrously at home within a gritty oyster.

'Oh aye.' The barman's eyes flick over to the other man setting the newspaper and kindling for a moment, before holding out a hand in introduction. 'I'm Tom, Jacob's brother.'

'Jay.'

Tom drops his voice as he leans in. 'And it's just Two Houses round here, by the way, not *the* Two Houses.'

Simon watches their hands meet, and he is frozen, unable to move forward into this peculiar space. He looks at them looking at each other, as if something unspoken is passing on the musty air between them, and it is only moments later – he cannot tell how many – that he realises he is being introduced.

'Simon, hi.' Their hands meet. Simon goes for the business handshake, the familiar flash of a smile he's used in so many meetings, wide and empty. 'It's alright, is it, having the dog in here?'

Poor bedraggled Bella has inched her way towards the nascent fire, her legs shaking with cold. Tom looks down at her, momentarily wordless.

'Sheepdog,' he murmurs, in surprise.

'She doesn't get many sheep in London,' Simon jokes, immediately wishing he hadn't. The other man's eyes are almost misty.

'I'll get you a towel for her.' Tom disappears behind the bar again, then proffers an ancient towel in Simon's direction. 'What'll you be having?'

Jay settles herself by the fire with the dog. Simon walks tentatively to the bar, aware that he is watched by a row of unblinking eyes.

'I'll have a pint of that,' he points at one of the taps, his voice unnaturally bright and forced. 'And, err, what wine have you got?'

The reply is flat and unironic. 'Red, white.'

'A glass of red for my wife, then, please.'

Simon can't quite explain why *my wife* comes out with such emphasis. Tom sets to pouring the drinks, and Simon senses that he, too, is performing somehow. That this very polite, slightly too loud conversation between them is meant to signify something to their silent companions. The longer Simon stands at the bar the more of them he sees, their faces looming out of the pub's dark corners. Almost without realising it, he runs his finger along the rim of the glass, checking it for dirt.

'So what brings you to this part of the world, Simon?'

'Oh, we were sick of London, Tom.' Why does he partake in this forced chumminess, this faux-friendly use of first names as if they've known each other for years? 'We wanted to get away somewhere quiet. Somewhere you can hear yourself think.'

'Right.'

'I bet we all say that.'

'All who?'

'I meant, anyone new moving in around here.'

Tom laughs, a short sharp burst that reverberates against the wooden beams. 'There's not many of you around, Simon. You're the only new folk we've had in years.'

'Oh, I see.'

Tom passes the drinks to him and takes the crisp ten-pound note from his hand. 'And you're . . .' He digs in the till with what Simon takes to be studied indifference. '. . . You're happy at Two Houses, are ye? Just for weekends, is it?'

Simon could swear he hears a sharp intake of breath somewhere behind him.

'Oh yes, we're loving it,' he somewhat lies through a firm smile. 'Weekends, the odd week here and there. We'll be here more than we planned, I think.' Simon thinks of his wife and acknowledges that this will almost certainly be the case. 'We've got the builders coming in next week. We're thinking we'll reconnect the houses.'

A pint glass falls and shatters.

'Shit, sorry Tom.' A woman with an extraordinary blonde perm tries to stop a sea of spilt foam from dripping off the bar.

''Salright, Ange.'

'Pass me the dustpan.'

Simon, sensing his chance to escape, carries their drinks carefully towards the fire. Its flames are tall now, licking and crackling, and Bella has stretched herself out to her fullest length, eyes glazed with the pleasure of heat against her belly. Over at the bar, low voices mutter.

'Everything alright?' Jay asks him.

'Mmm.'

Jay gets up and begins inspecting the various things that decorate the walls. Horseshoes hung upside down for good luck; faded prints on yellowed paper; old miners' lamps and brass fittings and a prize trout, caught in a nearby beck in 1934, or so its label proudly states. Simon finds its bulbous glass eyes marginally less alarming than the real eyes around them.

'Jay,' he half-whispers, almost under his breath. 'Come and sit down.'

She spins round, her voice as loud and clear as always. 'Why?'

'I just . . .' No one is looking at them any more, but it is a pointed not looking, and does nothing to lessen the feeling Simon has about the place. He can't put it into words, but there is something in the air, the studied hush of it. 'I just think we're new and we shouldn't be poking about the place too much,' he murmurs.

Jay arches an eyebrow at him, but settles at his side. They sip their drinks in silence, clothes gently steaming, listening to the pounding rain outside and the sputtering of the fire at their feet.

17

Four weeks at Two Houses, and that was the first time they had made it to the village. It was, to Jay, a revelation, even in the dark and the wet, even not being able to see beyond the end of her nose. She liked the pub, with its dark wood and roaring fire. She liked the publican, with his kindly, guarded eyes. She liked the shadowy, secretive tat of it all, and the smell of coal burning and the way the whole place seemed to hold its breath.

Morning comes with a quiet, steady fall of rain. The rain is infinite up here, she is learning. Perpetual. Loud, soft, smooth, erratic, it is one more constant in this largely unchanging world. She stares out from the living-room window, turning her rabbit skull in her hands.

'I'm going to walk into the village.'

'Really?' Simon looks up from the box of kitchen things he is unpacking; knives, forks, spoons, each in their proper, orderly place. 'In this weather?'

'It'll be fine, it's nothing like last night.'

'Suit yourself,' Simon replies, looking mournfully around at all the things that still need unpacking.

The road that runs beneath Two Houses curves up and along this last part of the valley. This is, after all, the dale's end, a dead end; and when she arrives in the village, Jay will not be able to find any roads running out of it.

But first she must walk, a good mile and a half of empty landscape, glazed with the greyish hues of a rainy day. She thinks of the glazes in her studio, the way you dip and swirl a piece through them. The tidemarks, the overlaps, some coarse, some fine, some studded with gritty stars of pigment – and yes, she sees that here, too, in the dozen different shades of slate and marble, the hundred tones of green that fall away before her.

It is different in the daylight, with her boots echoing on the tarmac and the occasional call of a mournful bird. She can see, now, the tumbledown barns up on the hills, the farmhouses abandoned to rack and ruin. Old bits of black plastic still hang on the unused water troughs, the rusted bits of plough and truck that linger on in the empty fields. Her breath and her heart are deafening in the silence, and she walks with Jacob's account of Two Houses rattling around her brain. *To avoid meeting daily with the spectre of his loss . . . Whether this banished the spirit, we cannot say . . .* On she walks, the faceless figure of Isobel Brathwane so close she could almost reach out and touch her. Who was she, this woman? Jay knows her only through loss, a woman who lost a child. But was she young or old? Happy, or not? A good mother? A desperate one? The road twists and turns and, in the dew-wet silence of the morning, with water soaking up the ends of her trousers, the mournful cry of a distant bird and the steady patter of her feet, it is as if the two of them were walking side by side, and once or twice Jay stops, just to see if the spectre's footfall will continue.

At the edge of the village is a bridge. Next to the bridge the pub, somehow bleached by daylight, washed out, with its faded sun umbrellas and broken benches. Beyond the pub, the village street curves along the edge of the river, lined with tiny cottages, half-abandoned, forlorn-looking, and beyond the cluster of tiny dwellings, a larger building perched on higher ground. Jay passes the pub – quiet, shut up at this time of day – and pauses by the river wall.

'Library, is that.'

It is Tom, pointing at the tall, grey building and its peaked roof. He is wearing a woollen jumper in whose stitches the misty rain gathers.

'Does it still open?'

'Oh yes. Council said we had to have a library.'

Tom narrows his eyes, and Jay tastes the sarcasm in his voice.

'What else do you have, then, besides your library?'

'Old chapel. Village shop.'

This last he points out just along from them at the end of the row of cottages, its sign so faded that Jay had failed to notice it. She sees it now, though; sees the woman with the peroxide perm lowering at them from its doorway.

'Don't mind Angela,' Tom murmurs, turning around to stare at the peaty water swirling beneath them.

Jay turns too and leans on the wall beside him.

'Thank you for your hospitality last night. The fire, the dog . . .'

'Nowt to it.'

His eyes are the colour of the fells, she realises; intense as the craggy rockfaces that hang above them, towering over the village and its clustered roofs.

'I feel stupid that we haven't made it down here before. We – well, Simon's been driving down to town for most things.'

'Oh aye.'

'There's been so much to do at the—' she pauses to correct herself. 'At Two Houses.'

And standing this close, it is unmistakable, the way the breath moves in him as she says it. The light that flickers across his face before he turns from her.

'Do you know the story about Two Houses?' she asks innocently. He does not reply. 'You must do, it was your brother who told me.'

Tom whips around, quick as the wind. 'Jacob?' he asks, his voice just for a fraction of a second unsteady.

'Yes.' *How I wish I could read you*, Jay thinks, as he stands before her, open-mouthed. 'The story of the Brathwanes,' she continues, 'the ghost, the haunting . . .'

Tom turns from her again, takes a pebble from the wall and skims it down into the water. 'Oh yes. We all know that one.' He stands, as if to take his leave from her. 'Ancient history.'

His words hang between threat and warning on the cool, rain-drenched air.

'You want to register.' The woman behind the library desk is shrunken, wrinkled, like an apple past its time. The hollows in her cheeks are parodies of dimples, for she does not smile.

'Yes.'

'Proof of address?'

'Oh, I . . .'

That wave again as she pulls out a form. 'No matter. I know where you're from.'

'Yes?'

'Oh yes. You're from Two Houses. Everyone knows everything round here, lovey.'

Lovey. A word Jay's grandmother used to use, but here it is steely, a knife cutting the air between them.

'Well, it's Two Houses I wanted to talk to you about.'

The woman pushes a form and a pen across the desk. It is very low and Jay has to fold herself over in order to fill the paperwork out. She steals a glance at her faded plastic name badge. *Heather.* It conjures purple air, hardy flowers. Jay pushes the form back across the desk, but Heather just sits and stares, her hands folded on the desk, one clamped unnaturally over the other.

When she speaks, it is almost in whisper.

'Now why would you want to go raking all that up?'

Jay's skin pricks. The echo of her heart grows louder.

'I want to know about the ghost story. Why he did it, why he cut the houses up.'

'Ancient history.'

That same phrase.

'Our history, now. Our house, our walls.'

'I wouldn't be so sure about that. Just for weekends, isn't it?'

Before Jay can reply, a young Asian man appears, round and bounding, his face pouched like a chipmunk's, as if he might be hiding snacks in his cheeks. His circular glasses give him a look of perpetual surprise, and there is a twinkle in his eye, even behind the rain-smeared frames.

'Hello!'

'I want to find out about Two Houses.'

'Ah.'

And maybe Simon wasn't imagining it in the pub; maybe there is something to it, this aura around the houses as if no one wants to go near them.

'It seems that everyone's afraid of ghosts,' she says, half joke, half challenge.

The man wiggles his nose, raises an eyebrow. Waddling out towards the shelves, he tugs his knitted waistcoat down over the bulge of belly and bottom. It is quite the concoction, Jay thinks as she follows him; bright red and yellow, pink and green, knitted together with more determination than artistic vision.

'I like knitting,' he says over his shoulder, as if he can hear her.

'It's . . . lovely.' Jay is not good at niceties; they don't come naturally.

His wide smile grows wider. 'I just like knitting.'

They wind their way through the shelves to the very back corner of the library. A battered, water-damaged sign reads OCAL INTEREST.

'Keep meaning to replace that sign,' he announces, and with the missing ceiling tiles, the old leaks raining down the wall in paint, the broken chair with DO NOT SIT taped to it, Jay imagines there's a lot he probably keeps meaning to replace.

'So.' Stopping abruptly in front of the final shelf, he wheels round to face her. 'If we have anything, it'd be here.'

18

They have been working their way – slowly, methodically, as is Simon's wont – through the upstairs rooms. Scrubbing, scraping, abrading away the decades that have accrued, fossil-like, on every surface. Pulling up carpet that has sunk and rotted into the floor. Washing free the grime that has hidden the grain of the floorboards underneath. Taking a knife to long-jammed window frames so that they can open again.

The last room is the nursery, the nursery that was, with its faint riders and ghost horses cantering across the walls. Jimbo stripped them back, plastered away that pale memory of a childhood, but already damp is clouding across the corner of the ceiling, a milky patchwork, and looking out through the gauzy curtains that Jimbo left behind, Jay sees the world cloudy, silvered, as Isobel might once have seen it (for Jay imagines the past in monochrome, like an old photograph).

This is where Jay brings the library books. She waits for Simon to go out, and in the quiet hush of this abandoned corner, runs her finger along the velvety spines. Old books, smelling of age and ink. Pages crumbling away to nothing as she turns them like moths' wings. And somewhere, in all of this, Two Houses, secreted away with their strange story.

'You should work,' she murmurs to herself, thinking of the many boxes of her studio sat, waiting, in the other house. 'You should work.'

But how much easier to hunt for other people's ghosts than to face up to your own. To scan these pages trying to catch a glimpse of the mysterious Brathwanes. In fading light, Jay traces their names and dates in a notebook, the graphite glinting on the page.

Edwin Brathwane, 1885–1950.
Isobel Brathwane, née Pugh, 1916–1946.

It is amazing, the traces left behind. Lines in a book on the history of the county that talk of a once-great family; a word in an almanac about the sale of Brathwane heifers. The Hestle fêtes where Lady Brathwane always presented prizes; the largest marrow, the best homemade jam. Cases heard by Sir Edwin at the local assizes. Carols in the Hall at Christmas. Paper chases whose course ran up over the land above Hestle Hall, and Jay imagines the scraps of paper fluttering down on them here, in the house, pure as snow, and she scribbles furiously across her own paper, trying to make sense of these scraps from the past.

Would Isobel have cared about vegetables and jam, she wonders? Not the Isobel taking shape in her head, the woman built from all these wisps of references. Beautiful Lady Isobel, beloved by locals, who had the benevolence and grace to take an interest. Beautiful Isobel, so mourned in her passing.

But then she finds the story. The story Jacob recited to her by rote, the story he knew almost word for word. *An Account of Nelderdale, in the North Counties*, its pages well-thumbed, thick black print smeared by unnumbered fingers.

Following Nelderdale to its uppermost reach, one finds the village of Hestle. Hamlet is perhaps the more appropriate description for this small grouping of workers' cottages. As in the rest of the dale, lead mining interests above Hestle date back to medieval times, though these seams gave their final fulfilment at the end of the last century. The land, of limited resource and interest, is predominantly agricultural, its people as hard as is the life in these remote reaches.

There is little to see or do, although the keen sportsman will find Hestle Beck rich with trout in the summer months. The living of Hestle and upper Nelderdale lies with the Brathwane family, whose lands stretch as far as the Scotch borders. Reduced in circumstance of later years, the living is had at Hestle Hall, two miles below the village that bears its name. The house is known to attract the curious, following the late Sir Edwin Brathwane's removal of its central wing.

Having lost, in quick succession, a child and wife, the late Sir Edwin declared the house haunted; the lights spluttered in certain rooms, animals would hiss to be brought in there, &c. To avoid meeting daily with the spectre of his loss, he ordered the rooms haunted by his late wife to be cut out. Whether this banished the spirit of the late Isobel Brathwane, a local beauty, rumoured to have met demise by her own hand, we cannot say, Sir Edwin himself passing not long after the excising was complete. Empty these twenty years, the house, or houses, can be glimpsed in passing from the Nelder road.

A lone branch rattles against the window and Jay's breath catches in her throat. *Rumoured to have met demise by her own hand.* This is not the Isobel she had imagined, drawn back to this place by love and longing, some pale Victorian lady taken too soon and yearning hopelessly for her husband again. She gazes out onto the darkening fells and thinks of Isobel, *rumoured to have met demise by her own hand;* wonders what she saw when she looked out at this same hillside.

A pall. A sudden terrible sadness over it all. She looks back through her notes. Married off at twenty. Jay imagines her – pale, nervous, thin-limbed. And he, Sir Edwin, already fifty-one by then. Old enough to be her father. Corpulent, port-drinking, leering at this young, frail, beautiful wife, bought in only for the getting of heirs – that is evident, Jay decides – much as he might eye up a prize bull or seasoned tup.

Having lost, in quick succession, a child and wife . . .

Rumoured to have met demise by her own hand . . .

Outside, the sky takes on a darkling turn; the slivers of pewter light between the clouds gain a harsh metallic edge, their rays scalpel-sharp. Looking down, Jay is surprised to find her hands shaking, her breath rattled. Nothing has changed in these moments since reading; the world, the houses, the very room she's sitting in – none are recalibrated by the knowledge that a child and wife were lost in quick succession, that it was Isobel's own pale hand that was her undoing.

And yet suddenly this place is cavernous with loss. Jay shuts up her books, shuts up this room, walks back along the hallway, back into the bits of the house that have become – for the time being at least – their home. And when Simon returns from a trip to town, Jay is glad to join him. She tells him nothing of this, as if that story told to her on the wild fellside was meant for her and her alone. As if she and this woman, these houses, have their own private kinship. This night, she will keep to their bed, to their present, though it will not stop Isobel from gracing her dreams.

19

Angela does not have much, but she has her dressing table. It has a three-winged mirror, a stool of pale-pink tufted velvet. When first she bought it, it was her pride and joy. She had a bigger bedroom then, with her ex, so the stool didn't jam against the bottom of the bed as it does now, but still, she finds great pleasure in it. It is here she sits in the mornings, and here at night that she whiles away her hours.

The dressing table heaves with pots and potions. Perfumes and hairspray; boxes that unfold into fifty different shades of eye shadow; lipstick and gloss and plumper and liner, and every other product that's caught her eye. This is Angela's ritual, her becoming. No one has seen her without her 'face' on in over twenty years.

Angela is proud of her looks. Blue eyes, small nose, blonde hair that she backcombs to make it look as full as it once was. She does her best to ignore the lines around her eyes, the creases that run from nose to lips. She is thinner now than she has ever been, and wonders sometimes if this thinness suits her. *Brittle.* A word her mother used at her in anger. She worries about that now. *You're just so brittle, Angela.* And she was brittle. Four fractures before she left her ex; though if you compared that to the number of times she had been slammed into a wall, she was less brittle than her mother thought.

Filing her nails, Angela has been worrying over the pub and the folk from Two Houses. What they said, and how she broke the glass. And then Tom talking to the woman, and the way she leaned into him with all that mess of red hair . . .

Angela rises from the dressing table and wriggles into her heels.

'Come on, boys,' she shouts as she totters down the stairs. Declan and Steven, her two teenage sons, slump in gloomy silence over the breakfast table.

'Boys, come on; the bus.'

They shift slowly. Angela is perpetually amazed by their bulk; by the sheer physical mass of them. Not surprising, perhaps, given their father's stock, but even in their mid-teens they tower over her, as if there is nothing of her in them at all. As with so many women, she would have preferred girls. She would have known what to do with girls.

'Boys, get your bloody shoes on!'

She leaves them on the doorstep, blinking like dazed beasts up into the watery light. It is relentless, parenting. She feels like a farmer herding cattle, prodding them endlessly along. *If they were girls*, she thinks again, *if you weren't alone*, but she is alone, so there's a limit to the use in thinking that.

'Bye, then!' she shouts at their hunched backs, trotting off down the village street.

As grey as the fells at whose feet it sits, Hestle village has seen better days. Half the cottages are empty now, colourless. When Angela was a girl, there were children playing in the streets still, herds being walked to market, carts piled with golden hay going up to the barns, flashes of laundry drying in the breeze, housewives nattering in colourful housecoats. It's been years since they had any of that.

A final primp and preen of her hair and Angela is off to work, her heels click-clacking along the wet pavement. She raps at the door of the village shop and Sharon, the manager, lets her in.

'Morning, Shazza.'

'Morning, Ange,' her boss wheezes.

Sharon is gargantuan. Elephantine. Her face a pink bowling ball pricked with sweat, atop an even rounder base. Every morning as Angela watches her waddle heavily back towards the office she wonders how Sharon's bones can bear her weight. She enjoys tottering along lightly in her heels; she is sure that if she turns she'll catch Sharon's red and puckered face staring at her in envy.

Angela leaves her bag in the office, digging for a cigarette to while away the final minutes until her shift starts.

'Just having a ciggie, Shaz!'

'Make sure you clock in!' comes the wheezy return shout.

Clock in, clock off, watch the clock, count the minutes, down to what? The same journey in reverse, the same moody, pock-marked teenage faces, the same evening with the telly or down the pub working. Angela lights up, inhales, presses herself further into the doorway to keep out of the steady fall of rain. Just as she's tapping her ash onto the pavement, Tom appears and Angela's heart leaps.

'Tom!'

She beckons him over. He has his hands dug deep in his pockets, a look of grim determination on his face.

'Ange.'

Angela leans towards him. 'I'm sorry about that glass.'

He shrugs. 'It happens.'

Conspiratorially, she looks up and down the empty, rain-drizzled street.

'Tom, them folk at Two Houses—'

'Don't—'

'But what he said, the builders—'

'Ange, stop it.'

And for the first time, she notices the strain around his eyes. The tension in his jaw. His voice drops and there is almost a hum in his throat as he says, 'What can I do? What can I do? I've got Dad, and Jacob, and Zoe to worry about; maintenance payments to make, the pub to run, and God knows how I can get that place to turn a profit round here. What can I do?'

A sharp wind whips across their faces, and he turns away before she can work out whether the wet in his eyes comes from rain or tears. He presses his palm against his head and, just briefly, the thought flits across her mind how different he was yesterday, with that London woman.

'Alright.' Angela sucks hard on her cigarette. 'What do we do?'

'We just . . .' He shrugs. 'We have to wait it out.'

And for a moment, as the cigarette burns itself down between her yellowed fingers, Angela wonders what life might have been like if she'd picked him. If instead of brawn and flash, she'd picked this man, with his kind heart and sad eyes and the slump of his shoulders; less than his brother's, of course, but still that slight slump that's enough to tell you when Tom Outhwaite's feeling hurt. She watches all the wedding shows on telly, loves the gowns, the veils, the horses and carriages. And not for the first time, on this cold, mizzled morning, Angela notes the difference between the images of love she sees in magazines and on TV and her own little experience of it.

As she mulls this over and her cigarette dwindles between her fingers, Dev from the library rounds the corner on to the village street.

Angela knows all about Dev. He moved to Hestle a few years back. Runs the library, the so-called archive – like the shop, another dictate from the council, that those are services that need to be maintained. Angela's certain the council have never actually come up here as she doesn't know anyone who sets foot in the library. Jobs, not books, that'd be bloody nice for a change.

'Besides,' she'd asked in the pub, 'what's *he* know about *our* library?' He'd done some library school or something, some posh qualification that no one round their way had heard of. 'Alright for some,' she'd said. 'Why doesn't he go back to where he came from?'

But he came from Bradford, so that wasn't much of an argument, though it hasn't stopped Angela's private campaign. He comes into the shop all the time, and she's sure that he smells different; of tea leaves and spice, and she doesn't trust the whiteness of his smile, not in that dark face. So she scowls, and he's stopped smiling, and she mutters when she can to other folk around the village, and they listen, sometimes.

As he passes, she lets slip the phrase 'Bloody Paki.'

Tom and Dev both close their eyes as she does it, and for a moment it seems to Angela she's the only one who sees things clearly.

20

Bloody Paki gets really boring when you're not even from Pakistan. Maybe it's really boring if you *are* from Pakistan too. Dev doesn't know. He shakes it off, shrugs it off, but despite his smile there is an accretion in these things, like so many grains of sand building up over time, settling silently on top of one another until suddenly, one day it turns to rock, heavy and hard. Immutable burden.

Reshelving the latest set of returns – two kiddies' books and a VHS detective box set – Dev's mind wanders. He remembers the first day of his training course. A square, red-brick building in Huddersfield. Stepping tentatively into the echoing room. Knowing instinctively, on the one hand, that he would, finally, fit in here. Irrationally terrified, on the other, that he would not, and that all those dreams of a different life, all the hours spent seeking it, slogging away for it, might crumble in front of him.

What had actually crumbled was his digestive biscuit, as he dunked it too recklessly into a polystyrene cup of tea, burning his fingers on the scalding liquid before he finally gave up trying to fish it out. Sweat pricking along the back of his neck, electric embarrassment pulsing across his skin. But no one seemed to notice. And he remembers vividly that first day of training, the dreamy way the course leader spoke about her *halcyon days*, when libraries were at the heart of communities, when books took people from cradle to grave.

Not so, now. Not when he's the only paid member of staff, with just Heather to help him. When the acquisition budget has dwindled to what feels like mere pennies in his pocket.

When just paying the electricity and the heating is a challenge, and all the dreams and ambitions he'd had in moving to this abandoned corner of the world – a book bus driving round isolated villages, reading groups, creative writing for troubled teenagers – have evaporated into the damp air. Rain, endless rain in these parts, and just as the cement between the bricks is eaten away by it, coursing grain by grain into the gutters, so Dev's plans have been eroded, bit by imperceptible bit. Six years, and he has settled into it, grown wide and plump on the sedateness of it. Settled. Sedentary. Sediment. No time for dreams when the roof is leaking. The council don't answer his calls as often as they used to, and the whole thing clings together as if to a precipice.

Still, he loves it; in the way you love a lame dog or an old jumper run to holes and darnings. The mustiness, the dust. Stepping out of the street and into this quiet, insulated space. The sagging chairs in which people still like to rest their bones. The old map of the world above the doorway, its subtle hint at all the riches inside, though in fact it's hung too high for anyone to read the names of countries – and many of those names aren't right any more. One of the last vestiges of Empire, this map, with its proud calligraphy. Next time he's called a *bloody Paki*, he should point at this map. Point out that Pakistan was a recent – and British – invention.

He hears the door swing open behind him, the familiar rustle of Heather wrestling with her raincoat.

'Good morning, Heather!'

'Is it?'

Dev turns around. That's not her usual reply. They have their repertoire, he and Heather; their routine. 'Good morning', 'good morning', 'shall I make the coffee today?', 'Oh no, let me.' This is how the day starts – how *every* day starts – with these pleasantries bandied back and forth. Dev puts down his books, tugs at the knitted waistcoat that keeps riding up above his belly (one thing that has prospered since he came here).

'Everything alright, Heather?'

She is finally free of her raincoat; untangled, too, from the dog lead that has a habit of winding around her legs. She looks at him from beneath her shock of dandelion hair.

'Yes. Yes, everything's fine.' She runs her hands through her rain-wet hair so that it stands on end again. 'Just didn't sleep that well, is all.'

Dev's wondered about this, these last few weeks. Heather has seemed different. Tired, maybe, but distracted too, as if her mind has wandered somewhere else. Not that he would blame her – volunteering all week to stamp books, watch the kids after school, change the date on the old-fashioned calendar, it's not exactly high-speed stuff. But he values this friendship, if you could call it that; their comfortable way of speaking to each other, dancing around anything too contro-versial (they mostly leave politics and families well out of it).

'I'm sorry to hear that, Heather. Why don't you let me make the coffee this morning?'

'No, no,' she waves him away, 'I'll make the coffee. Got your biscuits too.'

Brandishing a pack of ginger nuts, she and her aged dog make their way towards the kitchen.

Later, over their second cup of extremely milky decaf coffee, Heather asks him about the newcomers.

'What do you make of those folk from Two Houses, then?'

'The Londoners?'

'Mmm.'

Dev dunks another biscuit (his fourth). 'I thought she seemed nice enough.'

He's hedging his bets, here. He knows how suspicious this village is of newcomers. *Offcomers*, they'd say. He's dealt with that first-hand – the wary looks, the withering glances. He'd never admit it to Heather, but he thought the woman from Two Houses was glorious. She had an aura to her. A magnetic pull, a shift in the air. It was almost tangible. He was shy of it, embarrassed by it, and yet he could have basked all day in her presence.

'I'll take these,' she'd smiled, carrying a pile of books over to him at the checkout desk. And it was, in this dark, grey, sodden landscape, as if an actual ray of sun had beamed towards his face. He'd stuck out a hand in eager formality.

'I'm Dev.'

'Jay.'

'I know.' He had said it without thinking and blushed furiously, then blushed more when he felt the flaming warmth of his round cheeks. But she had laughed.

'Of course you do. Everyone knows everything around here.'

He'd shrugged, an impish grin on his face, raising his hands as if to say *what can you do?*

'Did you grow up here?' she'd asked.

'No. Bradford.'

And normally he'd have stopped there. Most of his conversations here have stopped there. It's not a town for talkers, this one. But yesterday he was emboldened. He risked peering out from under his shell.

'Still an outsider, me. Even after six years.'

'Six years.' Could he call that look impressed? 'We've no hope then.'

'And you're . . . getting out of the city, are you?'

'Yes, London. I mean,' she had tucked a strand of hair behind her ear, looking for all the world as if she was correcting herself, 'it's for weekends, mostly. Not permanent, necessarily. Not yet, anyway. But the city is so overwhelming, it's such a treat to get away from it all.'

Dev had nodded, as if he himself had been to London, as if he knew all about it. 'It's good for that here. Quiet. Space.'

And Dev had needed space. Eight children in a three-bed

terrace. The endless parade of aunties and uncles, cousins and second cousins and people who weren't really cousins at all but you called them that because you'd always known them and they'd always known you, and there's not an English word that does that. Seven sisters, all getting married one by one, popping out grandchildren. And every auntie coming over, teacups rattling against saucers as they asked, 'When are you going to find yourself a nice girl, Dev? Settle down?'

But girls aren't really Dev's cup of tea. Nor noisy terraced houses quickly filled to capacity by one baby after another. He wanted quiet. Space. The end of his course presented what he's started thinking of as a *rum bunch* of offers (a phrase he picked up from Heather).

'Take the best you can get,' his father said quietly while his mother bawled into a clump of tissues, shouting over the garden fence to the neighbours about her son's achievement. 'Take what you can get.'

'Hmm.' Heather's suspicious hum brings Dev back to the present.

'You didn't like her, then?'

'Not a question of liking her – I've hardly met her. I just wish folk wouldn't come up here wanting to rake up the past.'

'Two Houses, you mean?'

'Aye. What good does it do, digging all that up?'

Dev hasn't heard about the builders, the plans. He doesn't know that there is both literal and metaphorical digging to be done. 'It was a long time ago though, Heather, wasn't it? The ghost, the way they cut up the houses. Surely it can't do any harm?'

'It's not a question of time. Something bad happens in a place and it stays that way. Lingers. That's always been a bad house, you don't go near that house.'

Dev wriggles in his seat, ill at ease with the gritty determination in her voice, the way she is wringing and wringing her hands. 'But it must be seventy years, Heather . . .'

'No matter the years, Dev! We've more secrets than rain, up here.'

He is about to ask her what she means, but as Heather leans forward to take her mug from the desk something slips and the mug rolls across the floor between them, milky liquid seeping into the carpet.

'Damn and blast!'

'Don't worry, I'll—'

'I can clear up my own mess.'

And there is that hardness in her voice that gives him pause, stops him mid-leap towards the kitchen counter and its roll of paper.

'OK.'

'A stupid mistake.'

She bustles past him, and for a moment he wonders if she is talking about the coffee, or this mysterious to-do with Two Houses. She is not in the sort of mood where he can ask.

21

One rainy morning – much like the other rainy mornings when the world turns monochrome and the clouds roll in – the builders arrive to survey the site. There are three of them, tall and scrawny and visibly reluctant.

Simon could not believe how hard it was to persuade them up to Two Houses. His phone calls were answered quickly, desperately, with what he could only read as longing in the other voice – and who would not long for work, he reasoned, up here, in this economic climate? They didn't falter when he explained what the job was, only when he explained *where*.

'Oh, it's a bit far up the valley for us . . .'

'Can't be sure we'd be able to fit you in . . .'

It was on the third attempt that Simon managed to prevail. A scratchy, softly spoken voice, thick with decades of cigarette smoke. A pause that hovered for long seconds before agreeing, 'Aye, alright then. We'll take a look.'

That was Neil, a beanpole of a man who looks like he's been put through the wash too many times; limp, wrinkled, his skin almost entirely without colour. He brings with him two younger men, all angles and elbows, it seems to Simon; so sharp and drawn their faces are little more than skin pulled over bone. Grudgingly, they stand in the garden and look at the site.

'So, it'd be laying foundations here, then.' Simon feels rather foolish, pointing at the space between the houses. The wind rips through his shirt, makes a mockery of his city-boy gilet. 'Or it might be enough to shore up what's been left behind.'

One of the younger men scuffs at the ground with the toe of his boot. They are, Simon realises slowly, Neil's sons. What a thin family business this must be, to be this hungry and yet this reluctant.

'Aye.' Neil's voice is even lower now than it was on the phone. Simon strains to hear it. 'You'd need planning permission though. Have to take it to the council. Might take months, that.'

'Oh, no, the house came with all permissions.' The other man's face falls. 'Besides, as it would just be putting back—'

'Aye.'

There is a long silence, during which the wind surges around them in its customary rollercoaster, spattering the rain that hangs unfallen in the air. Simon tries not to shiver, even as his flesh pricks up into goose pimples. He wishes again that he had worn a jacket.

'So . . .' Enough of this standing around in the cold. 'Do you think you'll be able to do it?'

The response is a defeated yes. They can start unloading their equipment tomorrow. Start the preliminary work over the next few days.

People came from miles around to see the great un-doing. To watch Hestle Hall be torn asunder.

The sound of unmaking rebounded off the hillsides, as mallets came down on stone and hammers smashed through unwanted windows. Things built for permanence, how quickly they dismantled. The bedroom floor went first, before the walls. Before the roof was ripped open to the sky. They took great creaking saws to the beams. Took off their shirts to haul the great iron fireplace away.

Such hooting and hollering, and they were allowed to keep what they could salvage. Horrid, greedy little men, revelling in their own sweat and in our destruction.

*

Simon thanks them, waves them off. He returns to the house, which is only marginally warmer than the wet day outside. Alone in the hallway, he lets the weight of silence settle on his shoulders. Or rather, the not-silence, for there is always the wind, the rain, the creak of the house, the patter of ghostly footsteps, and alone in bed in the navy-blue hours, he cannot tell if it is his sleepless wife or the estate agent's supposed ghost who haunts the house, who treads its floors. Mornings, when the light finally rises over the opposite hill, Simon stands bleary-eyed in the kitchen, inhaling the strong scent of coffee, reminding himself that his fears are unfounded. Yet he sees everything through a glass darkly, in the tint and taint of the silvered mirrors that Jay has hung around the house; antiques whose age blooms across their surfaces in dark, metallic cankers, and how much less threatening they were in London, where nobody spoke of ghosts or hauntings.

The living room has furniture now – their low-backed London sofas, the sleek lines of the reclaimed wood coffee table – but not his wife. Jay is nowhere to be seen, and Simon resents the twinge that flickers over his heart muscle, the tang of disappointment that he feels each time he realises she is absent. The rain has started properly now, staccato beats against the windows, and the familiar mists have rolled in, shrouding Two Houses in white. White outside the windows and white objects on the mantelpiece, too; Jay's collection of found things. Alone, Simon dares to touch them. To hold skull, seed, thimble, button, and he is unnerved by this mantelpiece shrine, this private altar. What do these things mean? Why is she so secretive with them? Simon peers into the filigreed bone of the rabbit skull with its hollows and cavities, strangely jealous of this private devotion to which he is neither part nor privy.

'What are you doing with that?'

'Oh,' Simon's hands clutch the mantelpiece, his heart battering against his ribcage. 'You're here.'

He reddens, colour flooding his cheeks as he tries to replace the bone beneath his fingers as gently as possible. Though even as he does so, his brain asks *why?* Why this deference, this distance? This is his house too.

'The builders agreed,' he says, moving towards her, willing her to move towards him, away from that world of ghosts and shadows. 'They're going to start the work.'

Jay takes herself to one of the sofas, a clutch of books and papers in her hands. Simon bats away the gnawing sensation of his hard work going unnoticed. It buzzes insistent in his ears, a mosquito on the perpetual verge of pricking his skin. When she replies, it is these documents she speaks to, barely raising her eyes to look at him.

'Oh? That's great.'

Simon bristles. 'It is great, actually. It was bloody hard finding a firm who'd come up here.'

Bella, who has followed her mistress into the room, creeps out of the space between them, out of the firing line. Even in her distracted state, Jay recognises a challenge. 'Really?'

'Really.'

'Why?'

'Why what?'

Her turquoise eyes pierce him. 'Why is everyone up here so wary of us, of this place? You saw what it was like in the pub the other night. Now these builders. Why? Why all this fuss about this house, the houses, the ghost –' a shiver soft as a fly's breath runs down Simon's neck '– when the Brathwanes—'

'The who?'

It is her turn to blush now, blood creeping into her pale face.

'The Brathwanes. The people who lived here before.'

'How did you find their names?'

Jay looks down at her papers. 'Someone told me the story. And I went to the library to check it out.'

'You didn't tell me.'

Simon's words hang between them, sharp and accusatory. Why would she keep something like that from him? What value is it, a name? What benefit in hiding it? This whole place was his idea, his project, yet here he is being crowded out of it by ghosts and secrets.

'The Brathwanes,' she continues slowly, 'died seventy years ago. How can people still be frightened of them?'

For as much as he jumps at his own reflection in the mirror these days, Simon has to admit that she has a point. He has felt the stares in the town, in the village; heard the whispers swirling around them like the leaves that have fallen from the spindly trees.

'I don't know, Jay-bird. But the past is past. Maybe it's better left that way.'

For once, it is he who turns from her. Looking out on to the blanched world, he realises with a jolt that it is Thursday. They live up here in a blur of days, out of time, out of space, and he had nearly forgotten that he is meant to be in London next week. The weeks have raced by like the clouds overhead, slipping seamlessly one into the next. He'd mentally allotted four weeks to get things started up here, to get things straight. It has been five, almost six. It had seemed so distant, when they set out, this far-off meeting and yet it is just a few sleeps until he has no choice but to return to the crash and rumble of the city, Two Houses relegated to weekends, as they were always meant to be.

'London next week, Jay-bird.'

'What?'

'We're going back to London. I've got meetings. You're meant to be seeing Jenny, Podge.'

'Oh, I don't know.'

He turns back to her. 'What do you mean?'

'I don't know if I'll come.'

She looks at him, wide turquoise eyes, as if there's nothing untoward in what she's saying at all. As if this is what they agreed when he first brought it up. As if he hadn't said *weekends weekends weekends* until he was blue in the face, and he'd just handed her the keys as carte blanche to live here without him.

'Jay, this is a weekender. It was always going to be a getaway, a bolthole. You've got to come back sometime.'

'I'll come back when I'm ready,' she replies, unfolding herself from the sofa. 'I'm not a child, you can leave me alone for a few days, you know.'

Simon goes into the kitchen, makes another cup of coffee that he doesn't really need to drink. He thinks of his wife and sees her as she was this summer, a pale shadow in the whiteness of the bedsheets, as white almost as this mist that swirls in front of him beyond the window, its stinging nettles once again trying to grow through the crack in the wood. He remembers her, mute and distant, and a ball of dread plummets through his stomach at the thought of having to leave her in this blanched, half-peopled place.

What a crash it was when the last wall fell.

22

With the mist and the threat of separation, a new silence descends at Two Houses. New things unsaid float between the half-furnished rooms, between the creak of the wood and the call of the wind. The builders come with their equipment, and for a time there is the sound of spades and diggers biting into earth. The great reuniting begins.

But at night, Jay and Simon drift further from each other, within their pale, expensive marital bed. Jay tosses and turns with wild, distracted dreams. For the first time in years, she sees her mother as she sleeps, as if her mother, finally, has come back to haunt her. She sees Isobel, grey and listless, returning to her rooms.

And even in sleep Jay's mind is a whirl of questions. Why would she have *met demise by her own hand*? Was her loss too great to bear? Was this place too wild, too lonely? Without the son counting the painted riders galloping across his walls, was it not worth the pain of waking? She remembers her own summer and wonders if Isobel took to her bed, too? If Sir Edwin hovered on the threshold, watching the pale limbs against the white sheets? Did she, too, simply want to turn away from it all?

He died and I was turned out. Turned out of my own home. Girls don't inherit, they said. Not by the terms of this will. There's nothing here for you.

They packed me off down dale to second cousins. Poor cousins. Cousins who had to work for a living and who had no interest in me. No interest in another mouth to feed.

That's when they came. Farmhands, they said. Molemen and labourers, fallen on hard times. They were no more than squatters, bringing their poverty and squalor with them into my home. Dirt everywhere. I remember their stained teeth. The way they spat tobacco on the floor. They lived off what they poached, sucking the bones dry, warming themselves over peaty fires. At first they were polite: oh please miss, we've nowhere else miss. But then the menfolk got ideas, leered at me with their stinking mouths.

They had no rights to the years they had in these houses. But I, a girl, had no rights either.

Heavy with tiredness, she is surprised to come down one morning to find Simon working in the kitchen; their scrubbed wooden table awash with plans and documents, his laptop whirring.

'Oh,' she says, before she can stop herself.

'It's a major presentation, Jay.' How sharp he is; no *Jay-bird* today. 'I have to work on it.'

He pushes her phone towards her across the table top.

'Here, this has been buzzing.'

She takes it without looking, knows already who it'll be. Podge, Hélène, Gavin, wanting her news. Jenny, wanting to know about her work, wanting to know when they can next pitch the retrospective. A gallery in Bloomsbury seeking a commission. The ceramic curator in York hoping for a residency.

She puts the phone to one side, one hand on the kettle, the other on the tap. Simon looks at her not looking at her messages, and his silence says more than words.

Jay slips quietly into a seat at the other end of the table, blows on her mug of tea, fiddles with the sleeves of the giant blue jumper she's pulled on over her pyjamas. Outside, there is the faint rasp of metal against earth, and in the hush, the warmth, with her head gently nodding above her mug, Jay can almost reclaim some of the rest she lost in sleep. Suddenly a shadowy face appears at the window. She jumps, heart hammering.

'What the—?' Simon looks up, annoyed, but she sees him flinch too. For the faintest of moments she thought it was Isobel, come to seek them out. But opening the kitchen door, letting in the roar of wind and moorland damp, her heart settles to see that it is Jacob. Relief and, if she is honest, a hint of disappointment.

'Jacob.'

The morning air is fierce and sweet. Jacob is huddled in his cagoule again, half-turned from her. Jay stands back.

'Do you want to come in?'

'Your wall's fall down.'

'What?' Simon is up now, bustling towards them. For whatever selfish, childish reason, Jay moves into the doorway to block his path. Jacob repeats his claim.

'Your wall's fall down.'

'Which wall, Jacob? Where?'

'Down by the road.' He winces, looking over at the gap between the houses, as if it hurts to stand this close to them. 'Thought I could fix it for you.'

'Of course.' Stuffing her feet into her boots, Jay steps out to join him, pulling the door shut behind her. 'Do you want to show me?'

Jacob is happier away from the house, she can tell it instantly. His shoulders keep their slant, his fists their grip, but he does not seem to be in such pain talking to her when he can look out at the fellsides or let his two-tone eyes wander to the high horizon.

'You just happened to notice the wall?' she asks, but there is no response. They stride on, whipped by the wind, feet sinking into the sodden ground.

'What're they doing?' Jacob asks, pointing back at the

houses and the equipment that moves slowly between them.

Jay pushes the hair out of her eyes. 'We're putting the houses back together. They're preparing the ground.'

'No.' He says it quietly, splattering mud up his trouser leg as he stamps his foot. Jay feels just the edge of fear in her stomach. 'Some things should be left as they are. Some things,' he repeats more to himself than to her as he strides off again across the fields, 'should be left as they are.'

Down by the road, she sees it. The drystone wall has crumpled, its rocks tumbling out towards the tarmac; a landslide in miniature. Jacob stops suddenly, but her foot catches on the wet grass and she is almost falling when he grabs her by the arm. His grip is strong, righting her, and when their heads emerge above the wall, his hand still clenched around her arm, they see a car approaching them along the road.

Tom steps out of the car, his eyes fixed on his brother's hand. 'What's going on?'

'Wall.' Jacob utters his reply before turning his face to the fellside.

'What?'

Jay recovers her step, moves closer to Tom as if to placate him. 'Jacob noticed the wall had fallen. He brought me down and I slipped . . .'

'Oh.'

Tom nods but his eyes are guarded. They bore into hers with strange intensity. For a moment, they pause, looking at each other while Jacob taps some unknown rhythm out on his leg, looking desperately towards the hillside and his escape. Eventually Tom breaks their gaze. He keeps his usual economy of words.

'You'll fix it, Jacob?'

''Course.'

'How much,' Jay pats her pockets uselessly, remembering too late that she is in her pyjamas, that her purse is on the kitchen table, 'how much will we owe you for that?'

Jacob shrugs, turning away from her again. When he speaks, it is to the wind.

'What did you say?'

'Twenty pound.'

'Oh, no, we'll pay more than that.'

'No, twenty pound, it's not a big job.'

Jay looks at Tom as if to say, *please, we can pay more*, but it's a sentiment that Tom finds just as hard to swallow. He, too, looks off into the distance, his face darkening as he sees Two Houses, the yellow digger crawling between them.

'What—' He stops himself, slamming a fist into his thigh as she has seen his brother do. She steps back, startled by the force.

'Twenty pound,' Jacob bleats again.

'Look, you can see when it's done, Jacob, alright?' Tom's voice is sharp, his legs swiftly carrying him swiftly back to the car. 'Come now,' he barks. 'Get in.'

Jacob folds himself into the passenger seat like an unwilling child. Nothing more is said. They drive off without word or wave, and Jay is left at the side of the road, the skies gunmetal and bruised above her. The wind snatches the noise of the engine away, and, watching the car slow as it passes Two Houses, passes the digger she can see but cannot hear, she has no doubt that Tom also thinks that things should be left as they are.

23

Down the dale, Heather's knees creak as she lowers herself into a folding chair. She gives the grass an affectionate pat.

'How are you, you old sod?'

Sod, noun, the surface of the ground, with grass growing on it. Each night is a foray now into words old and new, a habit to keep the time passing, to keep the panic from rising in her chest. Joss sits fat and panting at Heather's feet, ears pricking up in excitement as Heather fishes out her sandwiches.

'Getting too cold for this, Harry,' Heather tells her husband's grave as she tears a sandwich and tosses half to the dog. 'Too old, too cold. Have to come back in spring.'

And what will spring bring, she wonders? What for the folk at Two Houses? What for Tom and the village, for poor Jacob and his awkward ways? What for her and these godforsaken hands, how far gone will she be then?

Chewing on her cheese and pickle, Heather reads the headstone for the thousandth time.

HAROLD ELLIS

1942–2005

Father and Husband

Twice a week she comes down to town to visit the graveyard. Three times if she can. Jackie tells her she needn't bother, offers platitudes about 'moving on' and 'getting your life back', but Heather is bound to this sense of obligation. It is a way to return that long ago favour.

Harry never asked questions. That wasn't his nature. He was a quiet man, in his own world. Birdwatching, when he could get up on to the moor with his binoculars. Fishing, though rarely with the thrill of catching anything. It's his fishing chair that Heather brings now to his graveside. They only ever had one. Harry was a solitary man.

Jacqueline was born five months after their wedding. Harry must have been able to do the maths. He was a deliveryman, for heaven's sake, forever totting up people's bills for fish and veg. But he never said a word. Never treated Jackie as anything other than his own. Even when he turned that awful grey colour in the hospital bed, when the doctors said there was no hope and that anything that needed to be said should be spoken, Heather said nothing. And neither did Harry; ashen, wizened, eaten up by the rot inside him, but still Harry.

They had a window at that end of the ward. Heather was grateful for that. She remembers taking his hand, so frail, suddenly, at the end.

'Harry . . .'

Ever so gently he smiled at her, nodding his head at the tree outside the window. 'Nice robin, that.'

And she'd looked, and said, 'Yes, Harry. A nice robin.' Two hours later, he died. That was the closest they ever came to talking about it.

Heather catches herself wittering on at him, when she comes down to the grave. It is in death much as it was in life.

'Door needs fixing. Can't do it with these hands. I still haven't told our Jackie. You know what she's like. Gets hysterical soon as you'd open your mouth about doctors. And there's the folk at Two Houses.' Heather shifts in the fishing chair, restless as the wind.

'I never . . . We never talked about that, Harry. I don't know if you knew, about Two Houses. And I don't know if you know now? I . . . I don't know what to do. They say they're digging and I—'

But here she stops herself. Gives up her voice and lets the wind do its roaring. It's always been the strongest voice up here, drowning out these little lives in their little cottages. Heather gives the cold earth another pat.

'It'll be right, isn't that what you used to say, Harry? It'll all come right?'

Funny sight I must make, Heather thinks to herself, staggering back towards the car. An old woman with a deckchair, a dog and the remnants of a picnic. Not your usual cemetery-goer, with the sad expression and bunch of supermarket flowers.

At the gate, Joss decides to tangle herself around Heather's ankles.

'You daft dog.' She smiles, but it's getting harder for her hands to undo these knots, to coordinate the untangling of them both. She's almost succeeded when her phone starts ringing. She is so long in the fumbling of chair, basket, lead, dog that it rings off. Just as she finds it, deep in a pocket, it starts again.

'Hello?'

'Mam, it's Jackie.'

'Everything alright, love?' Heather's hands are shaking. If she could just sit down a minute, just set all these things down a second.

'Where are you?'

'Visiting your dad.'

'They've found a body.'

'What?'

'They've found a body. Up at Two Houses. Sarah just called from the village.'

Heather can't think straight. 'Who has? What do you mean a body?'

'A body, Mam! Them new folk were having building work and they've found a body. Police and all sorts are heading that way now.'

Heather forgets where she is standing. 'Jesus Christ.'

'You'll see it as you go back. Police and everything going that way.'

The wind whips around her, slicing into her cheeks, turning the world on its side.

'Mam?'

'Yes, love?'

'You'll look as you go by?'

Heather cannot seem to catch her breath. 'Yes, love. I'll look.'

In the end, she cannot help but look. The cars start before the houses even round into view, pulled up on the roadside, nosed into hedgerows. They are all there. John. Tom. Angela and her horrid boys. The Olivers, the Drydens. The manager from the Co-op drowning in her own flesh. Dev, in his multi-coloured hat and scarf. No sirens, now; just the lazy, circular flash of the emergency lights going round and round, the hiss and crackle of police radios as the day starts fading.

By the time Heather reaches the gathering of people the drizzle has turned to rain. A young policeman appears, his high-vis jacket crinkling and squeaking as he gestures towards them.

'Move along now, please. There's nowt to see.'

But Heather can see a white tent being erected in the space between the houses. Police dogs straining at their leashes as officers make them walk loops of the property. A smart-looking car crawls up behind the crowd and a sharp, educated voice calls out, 'Hilliard, forensics', before being let through on to the site.

No one moves. Instead they watch in silence as the man takes a large case out of his car, shakes the hand of a police detective, and marches into the house. The wind carries the whispers of moorgrass on the air, but the twenty people gathered stand in perfect silence. Gradually the sky darkens, and the blue lights of the emergency vehicles take on a more ominous hue. The plain-clothes officer appears at the door again, gestures to some underlings to move them on.

'Please, we can't have you blocking the road.'

'Sir, madam, please move along now.'

'There's nothing more to see here.'

But sometimes, Heather thinks, cradling Joss under her jacket, it doesn't matter if there's nothing to see. Sometimes the mind sees all it needs to, and the act of being there, standing there in the dark and the rain, is enough. Sometimes you don't need eyes at all to know exactly what's going on over the other side of a wall.

Rupture

24

There's all manner of dirty little secrets here.

A curious intertwining of time and space on this hillside, its cold clammy air caressing her face like an unwanted hand. One of those rare moments where time is no longer linear, and to crouch, waiting, on a damp and desolate patch of ground is no different, really, to waiting at the school gates in spring; sunshine dappling, apple blossom drifting in the breeze, waiting, waiting, for the car that will not appear.

Every seven years, someone told her once, all the body's cells regenerate. Every seven years, everything is made anew. And whose cells are these beneath her fingers? For how many turnings of the earth, how many regenerations, have they been here? What otherworldly lifeline is this that splices through time and space, to bring them together, Jay and Isobel, flesh and bone? For it is *Isobel* she hears in these long moments; that name throbbing insistent in the reedy grasses, on the breath of the wind.

Above them on the moor a curlew calls. *Peewit, peewit,* high and mournful. In the scraggly trees, the crow stares down in eerie silence, walking his feet back and forth along his branch. He knows carrion when he sees it, and God made man from clay, that is what Jay remembers now; the teacher's voice droning on, splintery chairs beneath her legs, dark graffiti inked deep into the desk, bleeding across the wood. God made man from clay, and when the wind picks up again it is as the whir of her wheel, the whir of the wheel, thumb and forefinger pinched together, teasing, coaxing clay to form.

She has talked, sometimes, of clay giving up its secrets; of material that, no matter her effort, would not do as it was bid. Clay with a mind of its own, its cells already decided on its course. Porcelain has memory. If you bend it one way, and then another, it will revert in the kiln to that first bend, to what it first knew.

Jay closes her eyes but still there is bone bursting out of land. Her mind races as the clouds; is this what it was like in France, in Belgium, on the battlefields? Bodies splintered into nothingness. Jagged bone thrown into the earth like branches in a storm. A few years ago, in the studio, she heard a programme about the Iron Harvest. She had actually paused to listen to it, the pot on the wheel collapsing slack and limp between her hands. The way these things stick with you. The presenter's soft r's. The audible hush of the Belgian fields through which she walked. The farmers she talked to still today finding bullets, ordnance, bone.

Her ribcage. Suddenly it is extraordinarily present, tight, encircling, the fearful, avian battering of her heart beneath. 'Men blown to dust,' the presenter said, and her mind had run through all those iterations of dust: children pulled from earthquake rubble; grey powdery people walking away from disasters. But what if you are not blown? How long, then, the return? *Ashes to ashes, dust to dust.* The creaking priest at her mother's funeral, his parched lips, liquorice-scented.

Rain hangs mist-like in the air. The wind flutters, whispers, a gossip on the sidelines of this earthbound, unearthly moment. Dark clouds roll in and though it is early, the light falters.

'They're coming,' somebody behind her says.

And all the while she keeps the bone in her hand, reaching out, keeping it warm, as if it has called to her, out of space, out of time, and she must not let go.

25

It's a long drive for that first little police car, up the lonely valley road.

London folk, the constable thinks. *Won't be anything more than a sheep bone left in the dirt.*

It fell to him for there wasn't anything else doing, and he is one of the few they've kept on in town as skeleton staff (a phrase they will rethink over the coming days). Easy job, he thought. Nothing to it. But the further he gets up the dale, the more his mood changes, until even he is unnerved by the abandoned farms, the ancient phone box, the deserted fields bare of their livestock.

'Like the Mary Celeste up here,' he murmurs, remembering a thing on telly about the ship that was found without a soul on board, dinners ready on plates, a spoonful of medicine ready for the taking. He heard about Two Houses as a lad, about the ghosts and the haunting and the middle rooms missing. But he's never been, and as he pulls off the road, the two houses and their ominous space between looming over him, he can't stop his flesh from pricking into goose pimples, nor his grandmother's phrase from tripping off his tongue: 'Somebody walking over my grave.'

'Bone white.'

'What?'

Jay turns to face Simon. The mug of tea the kindly police constable has just made her dances wildly in her hands. It is otherworldly, shock. Inside, she feels strangely calm. And why shouldn't she, sat on their London sofa for all the world as

119

if everything is ordinary? As if everything is ordinary, even as more and more vehicles pull up into the drive, as the police cars send blue lights looping across the living-room ceiling, radios whirring and crackling on all sides, more and more pale faces appearing at the doorway.

Jay speaks again to her husband. 'Bone white. That's what they say, don't they? It's a colour. A hue. Bone white. Bone china.'

Actually, the bone was nothing like white. It was steeped with yellow moorland, stained with years of wet, brown earth. *Bone dry*, you say in ceramics. That absolute, parched fixed-ness before firing. But it wasn't dry at all, chill and sodden with rain, this never-ending rain seeping down into the land.

Mr Wigmore!

Jay replays the scene in her mind, for it is strangely fugitive, the detail of it slipping away from her with every second's passing.

Mr Wigmore! The builder's voice, high and loud, rattling towards them through the half-filled house. *You should come and see this.*

They went out. Only one of the lads working with him today, his face drained as if someone had switched him to black and white. His hands gripping the sides of the digger tightly, pale knuckles bulging. Neil's hands hanging loose by his sides.

'What is it?' Simon, pushing his glasses back up his nose as usual, business-like, practical, and Jay was hit with the rich, mineral tang of soil that has spent decades unexposed to air. The ground between Two Houses was churned, ploughed, as if they were about to sow their seed, plant a crop.

Neil pointed at something protruding from the dark earth. 'There.'

'What?'

'There, bloody there!' The lad was shouting now.

Jay moved towards it. Bella let out a low whine.

'Jay—'

Simon's voice from somewhere behind her.

'—maybe you shouldn't . . .'

But she didn't listen. She brushed the dirt away, unable to stop, to move backwards. And there was no doubting its solidity, the ivory mass of it, faint cracks running like seams up its sides.

For long seconds, no one moved.

'Is it—' Simon's voice faltered. He and Neil looked down over her shoulders into the dirt.

'That doesn't look animal to me,' Neil murmured. His boy staggered backwards, clutching his stomach, the sound and smell of retching carrying on the autumn air.

'Jay?'

Simon's face, bone-white, swims back into focus.

'Yes?'

'This is D.I. Mosby.'

'Of course, hello.' She puts down the tea, puts out a hand.

The man who meets it is gruff and stubbled. Fifty, perhaps, or perhaps the years have not been kind to him. He clasps Jay's hand in a firm grip, then immediately resumes rubbing the side of his bristled jaw. It is the habitual action of someone who has both toothache and a fear of dentists. Mosby comes with a whiff of whisky, a whiff of a man who is out of his depth.

'Mrs Wigmore, I am sorry about this.'

'It's not your fault.'

He falters. 'Well, no, but there's going to be disruption to you, to you both, over the next days and weeks.'

'Weeks?' Simon's eyes bulge behind his glasses, which he takes off and cleans on his shirt. It's the third time he's done it since Mosby walked in. 'I mean, this really is a weekend place for us.' He looks at Jay, who does not look back. 'My work, our work is based in London, we can't stay up here indefinitely. We're needed elsewhere.'

'At this stage, I can't say how long or short, but there will be disruption, yes, and you will be needed, at least for part of it. We have to complete our forensic investigation first, then there will be questions for you—'

Jay cuts in. 'For us?'

'Yes, ma'am.'

'Why us?' Jay looks at Simon. 'We've only been here a few weeks.'

Weekends, weekends, it was only for weekends, Simon thinks to himself.

'It's all procedure, Mrs Wigmore. Nothing to worry about.' Mosby winces. The dagger pain in his tooth is definitely getting worse. 'Look,' he places a palm down on the table in front of him, leans towards them conspiratorially, 'cards on the table. This doesn't look recent, odds are we won't find much. You'll be back here carrying on as if nothing had happened before you know it.'

Jay and Simon stare back at him, blank-faced.

'But we won't get into that tonight. Do you have anywhere you can stay?'

'Stay?' Jay doesn't understand.

'Yes, Mrs Wigmore. I'm afraid you can't stay here tonight.'

'But this is our house.'

'I know.'

'Our home.' She ignores Simon, who has raised his eyebrow.

'I appreciate it's difficult, but—'

'Look,' Simon puts his hand over Jay's as if he is putting a hand over her mouth. 'We don't have anywhere else to go.'

'There's a pub in the village. Does rooms and that, for the walkers.' Mosby stands, straightens his tie, buttons his suit jacket. 'I suggest you stay there for the time being. I'll get someone to drive you down.'

26

There's no denying it this time, Simon thinks as the police car slows on its approach into the village. Everyone is looking at them. Faces at windows, watching them arrive. Not even the twitching of net curtains: just faces staring blankly out at them as they pass. He looks across the back seat at Jay, who has Bella clasped on her knees, just as she did when they arrived, and he sees that she has seen it too. The blonde woman who spilled her drink is standing opposite the pub, smoking. A man with a sagging belly stops still in the street; a group of teenagers sit on the wall that runs along the river, craning their necks towards the car. It is, to Simon, like some awful dream.

The shock. The disgust. The physical revulsion of the thing, and he is filled with the urge to wake up, to shake this nightmare off. Mixed in with it all, a vague, unwanted sense of triumph. He had felt as if the houses were being taken from him – his brilliant idea, his great plans subsumed by Jay's all-encompassing obsession with the place. *Typical Jay*, he'd caught himself thinking, the imagined words sharp and acrid on his tongue. *To win just by dint of feeling things more, feeling them better.*

Now this, this thing, this discovery. But it is a hollow triumph, and though Simon presses his palms hard against his thighs, he can't stop his hands from shaking. *Shock*, he tells himself, *plain and simple.* But in the dark on these bumpy roads, in the back of a police car, he knows that there is nothing simple about it. Nothing simple about bone appearing in earth, and all that it implies; that the ghost stories are true, that it is a haunted, unhappy place. It is shock and fear and guilt, too, hot and creeping over his skin. These eyes staring at him as if it was somehow his doing.

The pub is empty of customers. There is the same musty smell of sweat and age, the faint citrus whiff of cheap cleaning products. There is no fire tonight, and the electric lights are bright after the dark police car; they are unkind to all the brass tat that hangs on the walls. Simon can't tell if the empty tables and vacant seats are the pub's natural state, or if it's been cleared for their arrival, or if all its customers were in that clump of people that gathered at the bottom of the drive, craning their necks up at the houses, shooed on eventually by the police. Something bitter, bile-like, rises momentarily in his mouth.

Tom greets them awkwardly, his teenage daughter all in black by his side. The police officers had rung ahead. They were expecting them. The constable who drove them down seems the most uncomfortable of all, shifting her weight from foot to foot until she announces that she just has to radio in for something from the car. No sooner is she out of the door than the lanky teenager breaks off from chewing the ends of her hair to ask: 'Did you bury it, then?'

'Zoe!'

Is it just the lights, or has Tom also taken on a chalky pallor?

'Only asking.'

'We've only been here a few weeks,' Simon replies, his voice weaker than he'd like it to be, wishing they'd stuck to his appointed schedule, wishing they were hundreds of miles away in London right now. Jay stares off into the distance, one hand absent-mindedly rubbing Bella's head.

'Means nothing, that. Could've done it when you got here.'

'Zo, get upstairs! I'm sorry—'

'No,' Simon cuts in, calling to the girl who is trudging off towards the staircase behind the bar. 'We didn't bury anything. We had no idea that . . . *it* was there.'

Tom, wide-eyed, tries to cling to some sense of normality. 'Come into the kitchen. Do you want a brew?'

'Jay?'

His wife looks pale, exhausted. She shakes her head. The words, when they come, seem born of some gargantuan labour. 'No, thank you.'

They stand for a moment in the empty pub, three adults and a dog trying not to catch each other's eyes. There is nothing to say, nowhere to run, so they stand motionless, rabbits in headlights, the pub's stale air crowding in on them, too thin, suddenly, for all these lungs.

The police officer returns and stands by the doorway, fiddling with her hands; an awkward wallflower at an un-wanted party.

'Is everything OK?' she asks eventually.

No, Simon wants to reply, *everything is not fucking OK.* But it is Jay who speaks first, turning back towards the door.

'I need some air.'

The officer puts her hand on Jay's arm. 'I'll come with you.'

'I'm fine.'

'No,' a firmer hand this time, one that stops Jay in her tracks. 'Actually, I really need you all to stay here.'

It is Simon who moves first, trying to defuse the situation, not liking the way that Jay's eyes flare, nor the way the land-lord stares blankly towards his wife.

'We'll just go to bed, then, if that's alright? It's good of you to put us up.'

Tom snaps out of his trance, waves a hand. 'No trouble.'

They walk in single file behind the bar, leaving Bella in the kitchen before climbing a tiny, wonky staircase whose steps are uneven, their carpet peeling.

'Mind your heads,' Tom calls, just as Simon's knocks into the ceiling with a low crunch.

He shows them to their bedroom. An ancient double bed,

visibly sagging beneath the weight of blankets. Yellowed wall-paper, its trellised roses sad and brown. A sink in the corner of the room. A bedside lamp with velvet trim.

'It's not much,' Tom mutters.

'It'll be fine. Thank you.' Once again, Simon looks at this man who cannot help, it seems, but look at his wife. Jay has sat down at the edge of the bed, head in hands. Her long hair falls forward, a dazzling auburn waterfall in this faded room, and Simon is possessed by the urge to slam the door, to shut this man, this village, the whole damn world out of their life together. 'Goodnight,' he says firmly, and Tom and the police officer who still hovers at the bottom of the stairs retreat.

'It feels awful to talk about it as an *it*,' she says quietly, once they are lying in the dark. Simon doesn't need to ask what she's talking about. The body may as well be lying with them in this bed, so real and all-consuming is its sudden, unwanted presence.

'Not when you've touched the bone,' she continues, 'and felt it, and that bone was person once. Flesh and blood, and they felt things. They were known, they were loved. Are most people loved, do you think?'

Simon doesn't know. 'I don't know, Jay-bird.' For the first time in ages he feels her inch closer. He reciprocates, each seeking the other's warmth. 'In the balance of things . . . maybe? I hope so.'

'Who is it, Simon?'

'I don't know.'

'How can a person end up there? Beneath that earth? *Why* would they? It can't have been an accident, they must have – someone must have put them—'

'Shh.' Simon makes the sound as much to soothe his mind as hers. 'We can't solve this yet, we can't possibly know.'

The sheets rustle as they nestle more deeply into them.

This mattress is like sleeping above a void, a sinkhole that has yet to be sunk. The boxspring is surely about to give way, their feet creeping higher than their heads as they sink and slope into the bed's abyss. Her fingers reach tentatively for his.

'Simon . . .' She teeters, as if on the edge of apology.

'Yes?'

'Nothing.'

No apology, then. In the darkness, London. London, and meetings; the friends, colleagues, clients expecting their return.

'Jay . . .' His turn to be tentative.

'Yes?'

'I know you weren't sure about coming down this week, coming back home. But now, with this . . .' His tongue is fat and stupid; he cannot find the words he is looking for. 'I don't want to leave you up here.'

He waits, but she does not offer to accompany him.

Eventually he tries again. 'Do you want me to cancel?'

'You can't, Simon. It's a huge client, you have to be there; you're the managing partner, the one they want to hear from.'

Pragmatic, practical. It's unlike her. There are times he's wished that she would have more of these qualities. And yet tonight, in this strange room, in this sinking bed, he would have loved for her to have said *yes, stay with me.* He would do anything, right now, to feel wanted, needed. Downstairs, Bella scrabbles against the kitchen door, whining to be let up into the bedroom.

'We'll see,' he whispers, clasping Jay's hand just a little harder in the dark.

27

High up on the fellside, Jacob has been watching. Watching the streams of cars and lights. Watching the others watching. Watching as the police car drove off into the village, and he is certain that they are being taken, the offcomers, to his brother's pub, and Tom will watch them there, he knows it.

Night has closed around him soft as velvet, but Jacob doesn't mind. He knows this land. In the dark, he sets off towards the abandoned mine workings.

Jacob knows there are many ways of speaking to the earth. Many ways it speaks to you. It might be in the way the long grass licks the air, or in a sudden rush of silence on the moorland. He knows that there are messages whispered in the trees, in the way that saturated ground holds water on its surface and reflects the star-freckled night.

Jacob never knew his mother. She died as he was born, her eyes closing as his opened. Some people told him she was funny. A witch, some said. With potions and spells and ways of knowing what other people didn't want you to. They say the same things about him now, even though he never knew his mother. And Jacob does know things that other people don't seem to. Special, they called him at school. Stupid. But how can you not hear the voice in the wind? What would it be if the rabbits didn't come to you as you stood in a field at dusk, or if the robins in the village didn't land on the palm of your hand? It is unfathomable to him that others don't share in this rich, message-laden world. It would be like turning the radio on and hearing no voice, or going back to black and white after seeing telly in colour.

It is not long before the fellside trails lead him to the deserted workings. Old mine buildings that have slumped and tumbled against the ground, victim to the weather's endless onslaught. Their roofs caved in long ago, some even before the metal ran out, but Jacob knows the corners where you can go to get out of the wind; the spaces where the slanted rain does not fall.

In what was once a manager's office, Jacob lays his fire. The chimney is open now, half its bricks crumbled away, but there's space enough to get a fire going. Carefully he unzips his jacket; he has carried sticks and kindling next to his jumper in order to keep them from the wet. He mutters encouragement to the flames, and as the flare of the match subsides and the tiny tongues of red and yellow creep over the wood, he thinks of the village, and all the people in it; he thinks of them, and their secrets, and the secrets lying beneath the earth at Two Houses, the things that he wants to stay as they are. Slowing down to the crawl of the flame, the purr of the wind on the night air, Jacob mutters his prayers, his incantations.

Down in the valley, other people say their incantations, too. Outside Two Houses, Mosby leans back in the driver's seat, still rubbing his jaw. 'Bloody tooth,' he mutters, as the infection slices down into the bone like a knife. He takes a surreptitious swig from the flask he keeps in his inside pocket. 'Just a touch, just to take the edge off . . .' he says, again.

His officers wander bleary-eyed around the house, startled by the lights, by the sparse London furniture, the interminable hours stretching in front of them before anything actually happens. They wish that they could be in bed, and Hilliard, forensics, who's travelled almost two hours to get to this godforsaken back of beyond, would also rather be at home with his wife; needs to be at home with his wife, for it is their fifteenth wedding anniversary today, and he for one is finding marriage harder the longer it goes on.

Outside, the onlookers have dispersed; have wound their way up the treacherous black ribbon of road to the village or down towards the town; but for all the officers wishing they could be asleep, there are plenty who find they cannot close their eyes tonight.

As Jacob tends his fellside flames, Heather, too, is lighting a fire. It is fiddly, and twice she drops the matches, but tonight she wants to sit in a fire's glow; to feel its warmth in her cold bones, to hear the gentle snap and crackle of its flames. There is something almost spiritual in its light, turning all the living room to gold. She cannot think how long it has been since she went to church. Years, must be. Strictly Methodist up here, but as the wind whistles around her cottage and the flames leap, the dog grunting gently in her sleep, all Heather can remember are the Catholic words she has heard on telly and in films. *Hail Mary, full of grace, the Lord is with thee . . . pray for us sinners now and at the hour of our . . .* The wind rattles the windows in their frames, and try as she might, she cannot rattle her brain to remember what comes next. Trembling, she crosses herself, in case this might be her hour.

Around the street and down the alley, Angela listens to the rumble of her sons' snores. What does it mean, this discovery, this body? She, too, stood in the road tonight, looking up at the houses and the rain and the police going secretly about their business, giving nothing away. Why have they come, these Londoners with their fancy car and their posh accents? What do they want from them?

'No one'd want to live at Two Houses,' she mutters to herself, and yet they do and they are here, and they are digging, digging into a past that has nothing to do with them. In a small voice, a voice Angela hasn't used in years, not since her ex was coming at her, she pleads with them, these strangers who have wandered so violently into the village. 'Go,' she whispers, clutching the sheets. 'Just go.'

In the pub, the strangers drift towards uneasy slumber. In

130

the next room, Zoe's face is illuminated by the blue light of her phone, her thumbs busily tapping out their messages, and in the room beyond that Tom turns his face to the wall. Screwing his eyes tight shut he, too, longs for the warmth of a fire, the dancing of its kind, coppery light. He tenses the muscles in his legs against the urge to run, to rush up onto the hilltops or far down the valley, away from this ghost town and all its ghosts, their fingers clawing at him every which way he turns. He reminds himself of his duties. Father, brother, daughter, wife – he still thinks of Lisa as his wife, despite the stranger she has in her bed, and Tom drives his thoughts from the woman in his guest bedroom, just two walls away, and that hair that glitters as sharply as her eyes. He drives those thoughts as he used to drive the sheep, strong and resilient over the fells, and in the dark he finds a half-sleep retracing the fell routes that were once his haunts: Old Pike, Great Bedeburn, Usha Top, Low Biggin . . .

And up at the farmhouse that is no longer a farm, up at the apex where the fells of Usha and Bedeburn meet, Tom's father, too, is still awake. Ned sits in a house that sags under the weight of memory, heavy with inheritance, thick with things said and unsaid. The news from Two Houses has made its way to him even here – at the very end of the valley, the very end of the world.

But you would not know, to look at him, whether Ned is troubled by it. One of a line of great stoics, he sits, clamping his pipe between his dentures. Ned is no spring chicken, no lamb born under frost. He knows from nights caught out on the fell that it is always darkest before the dawn. He for one will wait for the light, though there are those for whom this dawn takes a long time coming.

28

It is still early when D.I. Mosby knocks on the pub door. He looks rough as anything, Tom thinks. Shirt hanging out, stubble. But then, maybe he himself looks no better. They're of an age, him and Mosby. They go back.

'Morning Tom.' Mosby winces at his own greeting, and Tom wonders if it's the toothache or the hangover that's done it for him this time.

'Detective Inspector.'

'Wanted a word with your guests.'

'Don't know that they're awake.'

They roll their eyes at each other.

'Let's see, shall we?'

Jay and Simon appear at the kitchen table, still warm and fuzzy with sleep. Tom can smell the slumber on them. Mosby pulls up a chair. Tom concentrates hard on making the tea.

'I don't suppose you have coffee,' Simon asks, wrinkling his nose at a Yorkshire brew. Mosby tuts. Jay rubs Bella's head and the dog collapses in gratitude at her feet, relieved that the night's fears are over, that her mistress has not abandoned her.

'So . . .' Mosby is rubbing his jaw again. 'I've just to go over a few particulars with you both.'

'Maybe I should—' Tom makes to go, but Mosby holds up a hand to stop him.

'You're alright, Tom,' and Simon, who is already feeling territorial, wonders about this. 'Bit of grub wouldn't go amiss though.'

Tom obliges as Mosby flicks through his notebook.

'So, you took ownership of the property on . . .'

'September 15th,' Simon replies curtly.

'Right.' Mosby notes it down, his writing painstakingly slow. 'Sep-tem-ber 15th. And you came from London, yes?'

'Yes.'

'Lon . . .' the pen inches laboriously across the paper, '. . . don. And why did you decide to come up here?'

Simon and Jay look at each other.

'To get out of the city . . .' he begins.

'We needed a break . . .' she finishes.

'Right.' Mosby raises an eyebrow. 'But why here?'

'It was just for weekends,' Simon blusters. 'A few weeks to start with to get things settled, yes, to do some work on the house, but we're going back to London. We'll be going back to London,' he says again, sounding slightly less sure of himself.

'Long way from London for a weekender,' Mosby replies lightly.

'We wanted space, quiet . . .' Jay proffers, the colour rising against her will in her cheeks. The privilege of it – how ridiculous it sounds. Over by the cooker, Tom can't bear to look at her, but he can't bear not to either, the hairs on his neck rising at her very presence. With renewed vigour he cracks eggs into the pan, sets to buttering toast.

'Space . . . and . . . quiet.' Mosby finally finishes writing. 'And did you have any idea about the . . . *remains* when you bought the property?'

Simon snaps. 'What?'

'I said, did you have any idea—'

'Are you suggesting that we bought a house deliberately for the body buried underneath it?'

'I'm just asking, Mr Wigmore—'

Jay interrupts. 'We knew about the death.'

Tom wheels around. Mosby looks up from his notepad. 'Sorry?'

'We knew about the death,' she continues, turquoise eyes clear and fierce, a damn sight clearer than Mosby's. 'About the Brathwanes. Isobel and Edwin, the house cut out in between.'

For a second, the very room seems to sigh with relief, its walls breathing out before contracting in again.

'But obviously we never dreamed,' Simon cuts in haughtily, bristling at these secret details of his wife's spilling forth, 'that there was any truth to it.' Banishing, even as he speaks, the spectres that have haunted his dreams; that have run their cold fingers along his skin even in his waking moments.

'Right.' Mosby nods.

'Is it her?' Jay asks bluntly.

'Is it who?'

'Isobel, Isobel Brathwane.'

'Who's that, then?' Mosby's rubbing his jaw again, his eyes narrowed.

'The woman, the ghost.'

'It's not her.' Tom's voice is strong and sure. They all turn to look at him. 'She's buried down dale, in the graveyard. Everybody knows that.'

They didn't know, though, and it takes a moment for the air to settle itself around this new information.

'But it is . . .' Jay turns back to Mosby, tentative for once. 'It is a body? Human?'

Mosby clears his throat and looks down at his tea. 'Oh yes, it's human.'

Simon shudders, his shoulders turning in on themselves.

'Female?'

'Jay—'

'I have to know, Simon.' She touched it. She felt its weight. The first to lay eye or finger on that bone since . . . And she has to know to whom it belonged.

'It's early days,' Mosby says hurriedly, as if hoping to get off this topic. 'Obviously there'll be a full report.'

'But you have an idea.'

'Our forensic investigator, Dr Hilliard—'

'He must have spoken to you.'

And yes, Mosby remembers the tap on the car window this morning. Waking up into biting air, wiping a pool of spit from the corner of his mouth (and his suit), stepping out to meet the imposing Dr Hilliard, six and a half feet tall and the poshest accent Mosby's ever had to contend with. Until he met this lot, any road.

'Yes, we spoke.'

Mosby squirms in his chair. This is the old Jay, Simon thinks.

'He believes,' Mosby starts, for Jay's stare has wheedled it out of him, 'he believes that it's a woman. Been there some time.'

Tom places the plate of bacon and eggs on to the table with more force than he intended. The clatter of it cuts the air, brings a new sharpness upon them.

'Sorry.' He looks up and into Jay's eyes. 'Can I . . .?' He scoops up egg and bacon and passes them in her direction.

'Oh, I'm vegetarian.'

'Vegetarian. *Vegetarian*.' Mosby rolls the word around his inflamed mouth as if he'd never heard it before. Tom, mortified, wishes he would not. Jay picks daintily at an egg, as if to please Tom, who's turned ketchup red above his stove. She doesn't even like eggs, Simon grumbles to himself, fed up with this bizarre tableau of domesticity as the officer investigating the body found beneath their house tucks into a full English, wincing in pain with every bite, and the pub landlord he doesn't like butters his wife's toast and refills her tea.

'When will we be able to go back to the house?' Simon's voice cuts sharply across the domestic patter.

'Three days,' Mosby replies through a mouthful of egg and beans. 'Four at most, I should think. Can't promise, mind, but obviously we'll keep you informed. Seems unlikely it'll be a big case, long time and that. If it's been there that long, not much chance of finding anything.'

'I assume we're free to come and go as we please?'

'Sorry?'

'That we're not under any suspicion?'

'Oh right, yes, no, no worries there, Mr Wigmore. You and your wife can do as you please, though I would ask you to keep us informed of your movements, give us any contact details.'

'Good, because we'll be going to London tomorrow.' Jay looks up, but if she's surprised by the certainty of Simon's statement she covers it well. 'Obviously I can give you a number, but my firm has an important pitch this week and I really can't miss it. The best line is 020 – should I write that down for you?'

Mosby, struggling with a bacon rind caught in his bad tooth, nods. Simon takes the notepad and dashes off the number.

'Where can I stay?' Jay asks quietly.

'Ahh!' The rind comes free. 'Sorry, Mrs Wigmore what did you say?'

'I want to know where I can stay.'

'Aren't you . . .' Simon falters '. . . why don't you just come down to London, Jay-bird?'

She shakes her head.

'So.' Simon tries to cover his embarrassment. 'Where is my wife to stay while your investigation is taking place, your officers tramping through our house?'

'*Houses*,' Jay chips in and he wishes to God that for once she wouldn't. For one moment no one needs to think about that one house made two, the pain and division, the crack and crumble of it.

Mosby takes a slurp of coffee through one side of his mouth. 'Have you any family in the area?'

Jay shakes her head. 'We don't have family.' She watches Tom and thinks there might almost be a pang of envy in him.

'Well.' The Detective Inspector wipes his mouth and rises to his feet. 'I should think your best bet would be to stay on here, if Tom'll have you.'

'We can't do that,' Simon says.

'Of course you're welcome here.' Tom's reply is simultaneous, and suddenly Simon is feeling less enthused about his loudly vaunted London trip.

'You might want to see about some payment though.' Firing his parting shot, Mosby leaves the kitchen. Simon's ears burn, his mouth blusters. Humiliating not to have thought of that first.

'Of course,' he flounders, cleaning his glasses again, 'you must tell us, Tom, what we owe you.'

'Don't worry about it.'

'I insist.'

'Neighbourly kindness.'

'No, you mustn't be out of pocket.'

Jay watches this exchange with blank eyes. Two men facing off across a battered kitchen table, over what, the price of a bed and a cooked breakfast? She does not understand it. But, she thinks with a sigh as the now-familiar spattering of rain begins to fall against the kitchen window, perhaps, with everything else that there is to be understood this grey and solemn morning, perhaps it is better not to. She rises.

'I'm going to take the dog for a walk.'

'Don't forget your coat,' Simon urges.

'Oh.' She stops. 'I left it at the house, at Two Houses.'

'Here,' Tom is already stepping into the hallway, opening the door for her. 'Borrow this.' He holds an enormous battered overcoat out for her and slips it on to her shoulders. 'I can drive Simon up to the house now to get your things.'

Simon, emasculated, smiles weakly, and Jay, cocooned in a coat made for someone twice her size, steps out into the rain to walk the dog.

29

'Folks shouldn't go sticking their noses in.'

Jay is vaguely aware that this is aimed at her.

It is no good: she has walked as far out of the village as she can without seeing Two Houses, and the whole way her fingers twitched and tangled themselves, desperate for a cigarette. Four years without, but who's counting? How often are fingers faced with bone, anyway?

'A pack of Marlboros, please,' she says to the blonde woman in the village shop.

The *please* is not reciprocated. Just a grumpy *'Ten pound'* as the pack is slammed down onto the counter.

Fumbling with her purse, three notes flutter down to the floor at Jay's feet. She bends to gather them up and, righted again, meets the cashier's eye. Jay has seen how carefully others count their change here, how meticulously they gather each penny up.

'Must be nice to have money to throw around.'

There is nothing to say to that, and she is out the door before she realises she needs a lighter.

'Oh, a light.'

Angela takes a lighter off the shelf, clasps its neon-pink case tight in her hand. For a moment she stares Jay right in the eye, her gaze so fierce that Jay feels a tremor somewhere at the back of her knees. When Angela speaks, it is almost a whisper, low and gravelly, with a bitterness that makes Jay's breath catch in her throat.

'Why did you come here? Why won't you just leave us alone?'

The lighter shoots free from her grasp, spinning across the counter and bouncing onto the floor. Angela is on her feet, stilettos marching towards the break room at the back of the shop.

Dazed, Jay calls after her. 'Don't you want me to pay for this?'

A shrug from Angela's departing back and the break-room door slams shut.

Out in the damp air, Jay is grateful for the cigarette's sweet hit, its sharp reverberation in her lungs. *It's just the cold*, she tells herself. She does not want to admit that her hands are shaking. Who is that woman anyhow, to tell her where she can and can't go? They bought the houses fair and square.

She drags Bella along the back streets of the village – too narrow for even the smallest car to get through – furious with everyone: with Mosby and his stupid questions; Simon and his pretensions; the body, for appearing; Isobel, for having haunted the house in the first place.

Isobel.

She stops within sight of the Methodist chapel, sitting up above the village on a rocky outcrop, long out of use by the look of its crumbling facade. Was it here, Tom said, that Isobel was buried? Is it here that Jay will find a trace of her? *Surely not, surely not, surely not*, she tells herself, because if Isobel is here, then who is it, lying stained and decayed beneath their land? How many ghosts can one place hold?

The chapel steps are high and steep, slippery with months of rain and little footfall. There doesn't seem to be a grave-yard, just a tight ring of discoloured metal fence posts, a door locked with a great eroded chain, overgrown with lichen and rust. Peering too far ahead of herself, Jay slips, slamming her shin into the stone's sharp edge.

'Damn it!' she cries, momentarily dazzled by the pain, and in this moment, with stars flickering in front of her eyes, she is furious with herself, too. This was supposed to be her escape. Her haven. Her rebecoming. Instead she is sitting in mud, hunting for ghosts, knee-deep in secrets she does not understand, as far away from her work as she has ever been. Livid, she grinds her cigarette into the dirt.

'You looking for ghosts, missy?'

It is Heather, from the library, coming up the steps towards her. She is not scowling today; an almost-smile dances over her lips, creeps around those perfect hollows in her cheeks.

'I don't know what I'm doing.'

'Isn't that the truth of it?'

Jay's mouth hangs open as the old woman lowers herself down on to the step beside her.

'It's wet—' she goes to say, but Heather waves her words aside.

'Can't be minding a little bit of wet. Never do anything up here if you're afraid of a bit of rain.'

On the grass below them, Bella and Joss circle each other, tails wagging.

'Why can't we be like that, eh?' Heather points at them. 'This village hasn't been too friendly to you.'

'Not really.'

'It's not easy. We've not a taste for offcomers . . . *Newcomers*, you'd say. We've not had much practice.' Heather's boot noses at the dirt in front of them. 'Even those born and bred up here get shut out, sometimes.'

Overhead, the clouds are the colour of pigeons' wings, gunmetal and grape, heavy with their approaching burden.

'You shouldn't let folk like Angela bother you.'

'Angela?'

'In the shop just now. I saw.'

'Oh.'

'It's difficult for folk. You're not like us, with your money, education—'

'That's not our fault.'

140

'No, not ours neither, that we haven't had that up here.'

'Angela . . .' Jay murmurs the name, as if its syllables will help her wrap her head around this stranger's vitriol.

Heather smiles. 'I doubt she likes you being down at the pub. She's a soft spot for Tom, has Angela.'

Jay doesn't argue. Instead she watches a group of sparrows swoop down over the village roofs. They must be some of the last of the year, readying to make the long journey south.

'I was meant to be able to work. I came up here to work.'

'Lucky you. Some of us never had the chance to work.'

'It's too much, it's . . . overwhelming.'

She who'd thought London was overwhelming. She remembers mornings in the Tube, her eyes aching with all the different posters, adverts, tatty newspapers, free magazines; when the world seemed so *saturated* with words that she couldn't read anything any more. It all became one giant meaningless blur and she couldn't wait to get out, to get away.

The wind picks up, the clouds scud suddenly faster overhead, and as if in rhythm with them Heather makes a sudden change of tack.

'Were you looking for her?' She nods at the chapel looming behind them.

'I was looking for Isobel.'

Heather shakes her head. 'She's in the graveyard down dale.' And then, more quietly. 'It's not her, your body.'

'It's not *my* body.'

Heather shrugs.

'Who is it then?'

'How should I know?'

'Because everyone knows everything up here.'

Heather fixes her eyes on the dogs in front of them. 'We're too much looking back.'

Jay doesn't know what she means by this.

'Need to be looking forward. Leave what's past to the past. But it's hard.' Heather sighs. 'Not much future to look to, for most us.' She holds out her hands. 'I've to do something about this, you see.'

Jay watches as the wrinkled hands spring and jump in front of her, entirely of their own accord.

'I'm sorry—' she begins.

'Don't be. Comes to all of us in different ways.' She draws a more serious look across her face. 'I've told no one, not even my daughter. Others, too, who have a right to know things . . . You're not to go blabbing—'

'I won't.'

'No, I know you won't. I only tell you to . . .' Heather struggles to find the words. 'To tell you to keep going forward. It's no use, this looking back, this digging into the past.' For a moment, Heather looks her straight in the eye. 'It is what it is, this life. Can't change it.'

Joss comes bounding over, a bundle of fur and muscle that nearly knocks Heather off her seat. 'Alright Jossy, hometime.' Heather starts to heave herself up.

'You're not going to tell me who she is, are you?' Jay asks, helping Heather to her feet.

'You should be getting on with your work,' is the firm response.

Jay cannot help a frustrated smile escaping from her lips at this surreal conversation. 'This is a strange corner of the world.'

'I imagine most corners are strange once you start looking at them.' Heather descends the steps, lead in hand. 'On with your work. Leave things be.'

And for a moment, on this strange outcrop above the village, Jay is seized by the urge to put her hands to use again. To slap the clay on to the wheel, to lose herself in its endless revolutions, its infinite possibilities. For the first time in months, her fingers yearn to be wet and cold, to be guiding a tool along a pot's lip.

But she can't, of course. She remembers all too suddenly

the police cordon at Two Houses, the blur of sirens and the flashing lights, all her studio still in its boxes. She relives with a shudder of revulsion that cold, wet bone, the way it felt in her hand. Out of nowhere, tears smart in her eyes: for the bone, the houses, the last year and all it has flung at her. The summer in her bed. The doctors. Her work. Her mother; still, after all these years, her mother.

'It's just the cold,' she tells herself, rubbing her eyes with the edge of her sleeve. 'It's just the cold.'

30

Tom drives Simon to Two Houses in silence. After much conferring among the officers in their high-vis jackets, they are waved up to the front of the main house.

'Do you need a hand?' Tom asks.

'I'll be fine.'

So Tom waits. Tries not to let his eyes stray to the space in between, the tent, the white-clad investigators with plastic over their shoes. Farming was a hard life; it had its own proximity to death, especially up here, on these hills, but even Tom cannot help but shiver as the tent flap opens and closes, revealing only a snatch of rough, incriminating earth.

A hand lands on his shoulder.

'You alright?'

It's Mosby – Tom could smell the sauce on him a mile off. He remembers Mosby from school, football, going out on Saturday nights, and even then, twenty years ago, there was something manic in the way he clutched a can of lager, something that didn't let him put a drink down.

'Fine.' Tom is quiet, aware that any number of eyes could be looking at them. 'You?'

'Fine.' Rubbing his godforsaken jaw again only makes the smell of booze worse. 'Want this done and dusted.'

'We all do.'

At that moment, Simon appears from the house clutching an armful of belongings. Wide-eyed, he's a sheep before shearing, a ram before market. And as Tom grips the wheel on the drive back to the pub, he wishes that he was in the shearing pen again; wishes he could grab Simon by the fleece and shake him, tell him to get out of here.

But he doesn't. As always, the rain sets in and the heavy drops of it against the windscreen stand for conversation. By the time they are back at the pub, and unloaded, and Tom has a moment to look at his mobile, he has amassed three missed calls from Lisa. Following his guest in from the rain, he decides that today is not the day to face that music.

There is a different music today, faint strains and strums of it drifting across the village. It is the noise of things whispered, of breath exhaled. The percussion of fingernails tapping nervously, or the soft, insistent picking at skin around a cuticle.

Tom hears it, even as the wind catches his ear at a roar, even as nothing – from the outside – looks any different. He didn't know there were so many ways to lower a voice, to put sound to things you'd rather leave unsaid. There were the officers at Two Houses murmuring into their radios, waiting for the static grumble to murmur back at them. There was Mosby, and the way he'd tried to quiet him in front of the crowd. Now, within the close confines of the pub, there are the discussions between Jay and Simon that he does his best not to overhear; voices heated then rapidly cooled, volume diminishing into whisper as they remember where they are, that walls have ears, especially when they're paper thin like these ones.

'You're really not coming?'

'I don't want to.'

'They've just found a body beneath our house.'

'You think I don't know that?'

'This was only meant to be for weekends, Jay-bird.'

'What difference does that make?'

'Christ, why would you want to stay here with all this going on?'

Below them in the kitchen, Tom flinches, then, at the intimacy of it; wishes there was somewhere he could go to be away from this, even as his feet stay firmly rooted. Their voices drop to murmurs now, but still Tom can make them out.

'I just don't want to come this time.'

'I don't like the idea of you staying here by yourself.'

'I'm not by myself, I've got Bella.'

'But I'll miss you.'

At this, Tom drops the washing-up cloth and strides through into the pub. The constable is back again, the same mousey-looking one they had before, sat in a corner scrolling through her mobile.

Pulling his coat on, he tells her: 'I'm going out.'

She raises an eyebrow in return, then turns her eyes to the ceiling overhead where they can hear Jay and Simon pacing.

Tom stops, one arm of the jacket dangling. 'What, I'm not allowed anywhere either?'

Her voice is whiny, somehow petulant. 'I was told it's best if everyone stays put. If you all just stay here, like.'

A thundering of feet on the tiny staircase.

'We're off for a walk,' Jay announces, Simon a step behind her.

'I was just saying to Mr Outhwaite, better you all stay here, if you don't mind. Better just for the time being, like.'

Jay and Simon look at each other, then back at her.

'Really?'

The policewoman crinkles her nose into a sort of helpless smile. It makes her nose look even longer somehow, her two front teeth more prominent, as if she might be about to nibble off a hunk of cheese. Simon reaches out to take his wife by the arm, as if he might be holding her back from something.

'I'll go and pack then, love.'

Released, Jay throws herself down into a window seat and settles in to watch the freely moving world outside.

The day passes in a twitching of curtains, in slow steps made deliberately meandering along the village street. People stare

146

at the pub, at each other; when they drive down the dale they stare at Two Houses with its incident tape and police flood-lights, and, somewhere inside that tent, a body being dug up from the ground.

By afternoon, when the minibus has wound its way up the valley road, even the handful of kids it drops in the village have heard of it. They bounce around in the usual fizzing excitement brought on by penny sweets and cans of Coke, but news of a *body* adds an extra frisson to their shouting, faces pressed to the window as they pass.

'My da says it's a witch!'

'A witch? I heard it's an old man what got battered in a fight, buried there so they don't find him.'

'Maybe it's the ghost!'

'Ooh, the ghost, the ghost!'

They tumble out in front of the library, the last as always in the long list of drop-offs, hurrying excitedly up towards the path that leads over the hills to Two Houses. Stevie Metcalfe, Angela's boy, is the last one out, as always. Little Stevie Metcalfe, not so little any more, tall and stocky as his brother, pimple-dotted. On the pavement, he bumps into Heather.

'Stevie Metcalfe, you're meant to be in after-school club till your ma gets back.'

Stevie squirms apologetically before his feet join the clatter of school shoes running up the alley. 'I'll be right back, Mrs Ellis!'

Heather shakes her head. Inside the library hall, Jacob is setting out rows of tables and plastic chairs for the after-school group. He likes to help her with this, and Dev likes to let him, but today Jacob's face is dark as thunder, the plastic chairs quivering as he slams them down.

'Steady on Jacob, how many do you think we're having today?'

'Want to have enough, Heather.'

His brows are knitted into a frown. His lips, when she gets closer, are gnawed almost to bleeding.

'Jacob,' she says gently. 'Everything OK?'

'Fine.'

'I don't think we'll be getting many today, love. They're all off up to, well, you know.'

But if he hears her, Jacob shows no sign of it, inching along with his uneven arms and his gammy leg, setting his chairs out one by one. She lets him alone, lets him get on with it. A couple of girls trickle in, setting their satchels down on the tables.

'Hello Mrs Ellis.'

'Hello dears.'

They go to the furthest end of the tables, as far away from her and Jacob as they can. Pausing on the threshold, Heather looks back at the man in front of her.

'Jacob?'

He looks up.

'How's your da?'

A shrug. 'Same.'

Same, of course. Same as always. Save that suddenly, on this damp, mizzly evening, standing in the library doorway looking down on the village, nothing feels to Heather that it will ever be the same again. Suddenly, she is transported back through all the times she's stood in this doorway, all the women whom she's stood here with. Jennifer Reed, with the lazy eye. Annie Binkley, who had two sets of twins. Sally, married the same week as Heather was. Jennifer, Annie, Sally; Elsie, Marjorie, Maryanne. Elizabeth from the farm at Top Riding; Lucy at Souse End. Gone now, all of them. Died or left or drifted away, and just her left here, hanging on. In the distance, she sees a flash of neon against the murky dusk; another police car rounding the corner towards them.

No, she thinks, resting her weary head against the doorframe as her hands dance and jitter. Nothing will be the same again.

3 1

Simon gets up in the dark to ready himself for London. He felt useless, yesterday, when Tom drove him to Two Houses; watched him struggle to gather up the things they might need with a mind wiped blank of any practicalities and a police officer trailing him through the house, even as he delved into their underwear drawer and stooped to find a missing sock in the laundry basket.

Back at the pub, they ran out of things to say. There was simply nothing to talk about. There are only so many times you can circumnavigate the same scant set of details.

'A woman.'

'A long time.'

'God.'

They had a brief update from Mosby and his team. No active missing persons, nothing real to go on. There'd be the usual procedures, the usual checks, but the forensic search was, for now, concluded, though few conclusions had been reached. He and Jay went to sleep on opposite sides of the sinking mattress and now, already, he is up again.

Trying to dress without knocking into anything in the tiny pub bedroom is hard. Simon looks at the lump of his wife, curled up in the bed. He can't help but feel that she is going away again. Closing herself off from him. She spent hours walking the village yesterday morning, before the police officer curtailed their movement; returned having turned back in on herself.

A flash of white from her eyes, and he realises she is awake.

'I don't have to go.'

'You should.'

'You should at least call Podge, Jenny. They're expecting you.'

'I will, I will.'

'What are you going to do up here?'

'Wait,' she replies. 'Go to the library. Read.'

But you won't find this story, he thinks sadly. This is just going to hang over us forever, a miserable, unhappy, wretched cloud – for Simon cannot see how anyone happy could have ended up beneath that sodden turf.

King's Cross jangles with a thousand different noises: the pounding of feet along platforms, the *ding ding ding* before the announcer's voice, the breathy exhalations of train doors opening, and the long, slow screeches as engines come to life, start up, start off.

'Tickets please!'

'*Standard*, get your free *Standard*.'

Everywhere, people, and Simon is temporarily dazed, thrown, before he remembers himself. Head down, feet shuffle, and he makes his way out of the concourse. Six weeks can't have made you one of those gormless tourists already, he chides himself as his momentary lapse is righted and he sets off at a stride down the Gray's Inn Road.

But the city is deafening after such extreme silence. Vans and motorbikes jostle for space, buses the size of cottages thunder along beside him, and the air sticks, grey and claggy, in his mouth. He looks at the people around him, their pinched faces drawn as tightly as the sensible black coats they pull around themselves. The smells, too, so inescapably urban: exhaust, kebabs, perfume, vomit.

The office, though, is an oasis. Bright, quiet, and yes, Simon remembers why he travelled here every day for fifteen years. Exposed beams and brick walls, city light trickling down on them from the skylights, and he has to do a double take to realise that, here, it is not actively raining. There's not even drizzle.

'Simon! Welcome back, stranger.'

George, his second in command, beaming at him. Tall, blonde, in her early thirties, she walks towards him as one big smile. Is it netball she plays in her spare time, he tries to remember, or lacrosse?

'George, great to see you!'

'Well, how is it?'

Simon runs a hand through his hair. Her smile is contagious. 'It's good, it's . . . it's bloody quiet.'

'I bet.' She glances down at her watch. 'Dom's not going to be back until four. Do you want a coffee?'

And so they traipse back out into the street that is already losing its light, the yellow street lamps flickering on with that ominous buzzing, the way a bulb sounds when an insect lands on it. Their usual café is twinkling with fairy lights, and Simon is momentarily breathless to remember that it is newly November; that, in London terms, Christmas is just around the corner.

'So, what's the house like?' George dips into the froth of her cappuccino with a spoon. 'Let me guess: you've taken out all the non-structural walls. It's big and rambling, and at the back, a wall of glass, one giant window. Am I close?'

'Not even.' Simon shakes his head and takes out his phone. It feels alien to carry it here, where it rings and buzzes. It has not had much use in the rural north. 'Here, look.'

He shows her his photos, tells her the ghost story, explains the missing wedge, the strange space just floating in between. George's eyes grow wide.

'Wow! Beautiful stone.'

He won't, he realises, tell her about the body. There is something magical and intriguing about a ghost story. Less so a real-life body – once flesh, now bone – lying putrid beneath your earth.

She leans in and he cannot help but breathe in the fresh coconut-scent of her shampoo. *What are you doing?* he tells himself. But it is nice to be the centre of attention, for once. To have someone ask how *you* are, listen to *your* stories without their eyes sliding off to some unknown middle distance that you are silently but forcefully barred from.

His thumb swipes over a photo of Jay and Bella on the moortop. Jay is windswept, laughing, her hair russet against the green-gold sedge grass.

'She looks happy,' George says.

'Yes. It suits her up there.'

And does he imagine the slight stiffening in George's shoulders?

'So she's . . . It's better?'

'Yes.'

'Paintings, right? She's an artist?'

'Ceramicist.'

'Oh, yes.'

The conversation falters here. George sits back in her chair, Simon folds his arms. Obviously George had known that something was wrong this summer. She'd covered for him, helped him out in ways for which he was infinitely grateful but unable, in his awkward, quiet, ever-so-British way, to thank her for. Because to thank her would be to acknowledge what was happening, and the days that he did manage to make it into the office last summer were easier for not having to explain that his wife was lying at home, deathly silent; for not having to take people's questions or sympathy or prurience. And throughout, there was George – even when he announced that they were heading up north, finding a weekend place to do up, an escape to the country. The indefatigable George with her smile and her competence and his utter faith that everything would be alright in her hands.

'We should get back,' she smiles, and he, smiling, follows her.

*

That night, Simon cannot sleep. He tries ringing Jay, but her mobile does not connect, the landline just rings and rings, and it takes him full minutes to remember why she would not be answering, that she is not at Two Houses. He hadn't thought to take the pub's number. He could look it up, of course, but he doesn't fancy hearing Tom's voice at the end of the line, having to ask him politely, patiently to speak to his wife.

Their London house is cold, filled with that stale smell of windows too long unopened. The doormat was piled high with letters when he arrived; the forgotten fruit in the fruit bowl shrunken and covered in white fuzz. With no bed, sofa, table, the rooms he gravitates towards are strangely empty, and the flat pack boxes in the hallway (replacement furniture, unopened, untouched) offer little comfort. The whole place has the feel of a half-house, a half-home. It is the same feeling that Two Houses has, with its bare minimum of furniture.

The red light on the answerphone is flashing and Simon listens idly to its messages. Friends, mostly, wondering when they'll be back. Repeated messages from Podge, growing increasingly irate that their mobiles won't connect, that he's had no news from them. Finally an estate agent calling to say he's found their dream property, no strings attached. *Yeah right*, Simon thinks.

It takes him a little while to work out where to sleep. In the spare room? But Jay has commandeered the spare bedding for Two Houses. On the pull-out bed in his office? In the end, he takes a duvet down to the living room and folds himself up in the armchair in front of the television. Some mindless TV show, but it makes no odds for his mind is far from here, far from this dazzling screen and its bright lights; it is up on the fellside, in the quiet and the cold. He thinks of Jay, and Bella. Of them in the pub. In that sagging double bed without him.

He lied when he left the office, told his colleagues he had

plans, was seeing friends. That was easier, somehow, than admitting that he was on his own. That he knew, already, that he would be lonely. This does not feel like their home any more, no more than the big, dark, haunted houses on the hillside, with their secrets and ghosts and bodies (and *dear God*, Simon pleads silently, *please let there be only one body*).

In the early hours his eyelids finally flicker towards sleep, and he wonders, in that brief moment of lucidity before the fall, how this will all resolve. How these tangled skeins will unravel.

32

After Simon left, Jay slipped back into the sinking bed, her eyes half-closed, halfway between waking and dreaming as the rain – predictable as breath – tapped out its clockwork rhythm, its persistent steadiness, against the window.

In half-sleep she had wild half-dreams, of felltops and bodies. She was back at Two Houses, trailing a translucent Isobel through its empty rooms. But it was not Isobel in front of her, it was not, and in a moment of horror the weightless woman paused before one of the silvered mirrors, and it was her own face that Jay saw in its glass. Her own bones sunk beneath the earth, taking root in the dark ground.

Later, she dresses. Descends. Meets Tom in the kitchen. They move strangely through the pub, she and he, their limbs awkward and uncoordinated, their eyes lowered. The space is smaller, somehow, with just the two of them in it. The policewoman has finally been stood down, but still it is a dance not to step on the other's toes, not to collide in the narrow hallway.

Jay picks up a battered paperback and sits by the fire, Bella at her feet. Tom stands at the bar, totting up figures. The lick of flame, the scratch of pen on paper, the quiet juddering of rain; these are, for a time, all that is said between them as the clouds shift and the world turns.

Jay turns the pages of her book, but she is not reading. Her mind cannot string the printed words together. Its wires have come undone, and in waking as in sleep all she can think of is that bare ground between the houses.

For the first time, she misses Podge; Podge in his utter devotion, who'd sit with her through anything, listen to anything. She feels a hot flush of guilt at how she has ignored him. It's always been easy to tease Podge, with his ability to get drunk on two glasses, his endless name-dropping. How warm and proud she'd felt at her first opening to hear him brag that he was her *best friend*; how, later, she'd found pleasure in the weariness of it. 'Uh oh, Podge is at it again' with a knowing smirk and her bright turquoise eyes rolled at his expense. But these last weeks have been a total withdrawal, a cutting off of all those years of friendship. She's known it even as she's done it. But how could she tell him this? Where would she begin?

If she closes her eyes, she is back in a basement studio at Chelsea, the floor tacky from years of students splattering paint and clay up the walls. 'It's *Untitled*,' twenty-year-old Podge says with great authority of the twisted metal shape in front of him, and she remembers even then her horror at the idea of untitled work. Podge has stuck with it – *Untitled 24*, *Untitled 372* – but she, she has sought names, needed nomenclature, given every dish and bowl, even those first hideously wonky pieces, a moniker. *Mood*, in a dark Prussian glaze. *Hen*, a dish speckled like an egg. It gnaws at her, this namelessness of the bone she held within her hand, the way she has always felt sad to run her fingers across old grave-stones, lichen-laced, and see their identities crumbling before her.

'Morning, Tom!'

Angela appears from nowhere through the doorway, her pink jacket glittering with rain. Launching herself towards the bar, Angela is clearly about to say something – *are you alright?* perhaps, or *how are you?*, there is something tender in her bearing – when she sees Jay sat in the corner. 'Oh.' She comes to an abrupt halt. 'It's you.'

Tom looks up from his accounts. 'Jay and Simon are staying

156

a while, Angela. You know. With Two Houses and that.'

'Of course.' Angela eyes Jay suspiciously. 'Well, you know me,' she says, as if by way of introduction. 'Folk tend to have a lot of jobs, up here.'

She turns back to the bar. 'Tom, I hate to ask, but can I come tomorrow instead? Shazza's in bed, ill she says, and she's no one to open the shop.'

Tom is already waving a hand in acquiescence. 'Of course. No bother.'

'You're sure?'

'Aye, it's just the two of us today.'

The phrase hangs awkwardly in the air.

'Right, fine. Good then.' Angela bristles. 'See you tomorrow.'

With that she storms back out again, and Jay and Tom are left in silence, each to their own business, and to the business of not looking at each other across the newly empty room.

Around noon, the door opens again with a gust of wind and weather that shears the precarious peace they've created. It is D.I. Mosby, still grey, still sleepless. He plants himself at the bar.

'Give us a drink, Tom.'

He does not see Jay, tucked in her corner.

'A half pint, is it?' Tom's voice is measured.

'Yeah, and the rest.' Mosby waves him towards the taller glasses. 'This bloody case. Wind, rain, mud. Never thought I'd miss my bloody office. And for what, eh? Not like we're going to find owt.'

Tom clears his throat.

'Why won't you find anything?' Jay asks, closing her book. Mosby chokes on the foam of his pint, jumping to hear her voice behind him.

'Mrs Wigmore. You're a quiet one. Didn't see you there.'

'Why won't you find anything?'

Mosby mops the front of his suit.

'Thing is, Mrs Wigmore, it's what we call an *historic* case. No one reported missing. No effects with the body. No sign of anything recent like – odds on, we won't find anything.'

'But you are looking?'

'Aye, of course we're looking. Whole point of the job is looking.' And there is an edge to his voice now, like running her finger along a knife. 'But if there's nothing to find, we won't find it, will we?'

Jay lets this sputtered illogic pass, but the silence that falls is less easy than that which came before. It is taut, as if they are all holding their breath. Eventually Mosby loses heart and leaves, half his pint still languishing in the glass.

No one else comes in, and without new coal to stoke it the fire has dwindled to mere embers by the time that Jay asks, softly, 'Do you know who it is?'

Tom looks up at her.

'Why would I know that?'

'Because everyone knows everything round here.'

'Not me,' he says, retreating from her.

33

Unlocking the library door, putting the milk in the fridge, the biscuits in the tin, Dev thinks about the post, the next round of bills, the next council meetings. He dreads the arrival of the postman these days. Libraries are falling faster than the rain, dropping like dead cattle, sudden and heavy. He knows that, hears all about that from the friends from his course. But he's stuck. He doesn't have anywhere to go if this place fails.

All at once, the kettle rumbles to the boil, the chapel clock strikes, and there is the flutter of letters landing on the doormat. Dev's mouth is in his heart as he leafs through today's post. Nothing official-looking, thank god. He does not pretend to understand whatever magical alchemy is keeping this place open, but he knows it can't last.

Idly dipping into the biscuit tin, Dev wonders about magic. Remembers his mum's various insistences upon it, filling the house with coloured crystals, poring over the tealeaves at the bottom of her mug. They'd all had to switch to loose leaf during that particular fad; black tealeaves endlessly caught between their teeth, and for what? Prophecies that bore no more truth than a tabloid horoscope.

And yet, staring out of the window on to the steep fellsides, almost purple today beneath these bruising clouds, Dev wonders about magic now. He thinks of Heather, and her dark warnings about Two Houses. Bad places, bad land.

Dev's never seen a body. He can't even watch crime dramas on telly, and he cannot fathom what it means to have a body found at Two Houses. Can't fathom how it got there, either, because it's not the Wild West, up here. He's never seen so much as an argument, let alone a fight, which is more than he can say for Bradford; Minnie and Dina from number thirty-three tearing each other's hair out over some bloke, drunk white kids pummelling each other at the end of the avenue. But folk are quiet up here. Resigned.

It must be ancient, he decides, settling down at his desk with a cup of tea and a pile of custard creams. An ancient body, ancient history. And yet even he, in his shy, peripheral way, has felt the tightening of breath in the village; the worry, the quiet, the whispers.

'Don't be daft,' he tells himself, settling down to separate the first biscuit from its creamy innards. It is just gone ten. If Heather's late, he might have a moment to give Gareth a ring.

The library was built for grander days than these. Its vaulted ceiling rises high above the metal shelves of battered books, the stained-glass windows decorated with poets most people in this place have never heard of: Spencer, Dryden, Donne. Most days Dev loves the faded grandeur of it, but as Jay enters he feels suddenly embarrassed. This woman – this *artist*, so they say – brings with her a whiff of the big city, of a world more glamorous and cosmopolitan than he could ever dream of, even as she's shaking the rain off her waterproof and smearing mud-caked wellies into the doormat.

'Hello.' Dev catches her looking at her own reflection in the window, as if seeing her own pale face were to see a ghost. 'Was there . . .' Dev gestures to the bookshelves around him, as if giving a royal tour. 'Were you looking for anything in particular?'

'I wondered –' she is standing right in front of him now, long red hair in mesmerising ringlets, eyes wide '– if you could help me?'

'Yes, of course, I mean – I don't know.' His words come

out a cringe-making stutter. 'Can I help you? What do you want help with?'

'I want to find out about the body.'

At first, he thinks he hasn't heard her correctly.

'What?'

'I want to find out about the body.' She crosses her arms. 'The body. At Two Houses?'

'The body?'

'I don't think the police are going to do anything about it.'

'What . . . I mean, why not? They're investigating, aren't they?'

'They say it's an historic case.'

'Meaning . . .?'

'Meaning they don't think there'll be anything to find.'

'Really?'

'Yes.'

'But, I mean, that can't be what they mean. That they're not going to look.'

'All they say is that there won't be anything to find.'

'And you want to instead? Find something, I mean.'

'Yes.'

The rain drums down on the roof above them, steady and insistent, much like the way Jay stares at Dev, much like the beating of his heart in his chest. Outside, the dark is gathering. Soon, the school bus will be here, the faithful few of the after-school club trickling in. And Heather – he does not know where Heather is today, but how she'd scold him for even thinking about investigating this. His hands turn clammy, his cheeks red at the very thought of her.

'What makes you think,' he says eventually, licking his cracked lips, 'that I'd be able to help?'

'You know about research. You have all this.' It is Jay's arms, now, that sweep expansively across the space around them. 'There must be records, archives—'

'Not archives of people who were . . . *murdered*!' He lowers his voice, blushing at the word, despite the fact that the library is empty.

'No, of course not, but there must be . . .' She gestures, weaving her hands in front of her as if she can't quite put her finger on the words. 'People talk here, don't they, about Two Houses? About the village. About all these places being unhappy, about bad things happening.'

Dev nods, tentatively.

'So I thought, maybe, you know, perhaps there's a trace of that somewhere?'

'But it's not . . . I don't know if that's the kind of thing people write down.'

'But we can't know that until we look.'

Dev nods again, before he realises quite how smoothly she's brought him in on this search. How seamlessly 'we' tripped off her tongue, how already – even against his will – the cogs in his brain are turning. And wouldn't it be interesting, for a change, to look into the past? To have a project more substantial than re-covering children's books in sticky-back plastic?

He teeters, not wanting to rock the boat, to put himself in a position more precarious than the one he habitually occupies up here, with his books and his brown skin and his long, solitary hours. And yet, he is magnetised, mesmerised by this woman standing before him with her expectant eyes.

'Alright. I'll do some digging.'

His agreement is quiet. Even as he gives it he wonders if it is a mistake. Visions of his father talking to them as children. *Don't make a fuss. Don't stand out. Don't put your hand up. Don't give them anything they can use against you.* Well, he thinks, what of it? Maybe it's time he stood up for himself in this strange, grey place.

34

Lisa Mackey didn't grow up in the village. She didn't even grow up in the town. Her parents moved there when she was seventeen and, not having anywhere else to go, she moved with them.

Tom remembers their first meeting as if it were yesterday. Down the Kings Arms, in town, Christmas music blaring over the ancient sound system, the pub a crush of drunken teenagers and tinsel. He noticed that she was also on the sidelines. Quiet, on her own. He'd asked if she wanted to go outside. She did.

They must have walked six miles that night, twice round the town and then up on to the fell to look down at the houses and their lights sparkling.

'Prefer those lights from up here,' Tom had said, and Lisa, shivering in spite of the greatcoat he'd loaned her, leaned into his side in agreement. He had always read it as agreement.

For years, they were happy. 'We were happy,' he mutters to himself now as the car thunders down the narrow road. 'We were happy.'

Except that, somewhere down the line, Lisa stopped being happy. And Tom didn't see it, didn't notice the creep of it until it was too late, and total. She didn't love the land. Didn't love him waking up at four in the morning to feed the flock, nor the long hours alone while he was out on the farm. Said she'd rather die than move up into the farmhouse, even though he promised her they could do it up nice. She wanted a change, a fresh start, and even at the eleventh hour, when Tom was on the verge of agreeing to move to town, move completely away if she wanted it, he didn't realise that her idea of a fresh start didn't involve him at all.

Nineteen months, it's been now, and still the burning in his throat, the clawing panic around his lungs if he thinks about it too long. His vision blurs, and it is as he is wiping his face with his arm that the car swerves, and a figure swims into focus in front of him.

Jacob stands on the verge at the roadside, hands thrust deep in his pockets.

'Christ alight,' Tom is out of the car, breathless, heart pounding. 'Jacob, what are you doing, man? What are you doing in the road?'

'Meant to be fixing the wall,' his brother replies, uneven eyes screwed tightly shut.

'What wall?'

'Two Houses.'

Even as it hammers, Tom feels his heart plummet. 'You can't be doing that now, Jacob. Not with the police.' Tom opens the car door for his brother. 'This is their land now. You can't be going on it. That's trespassing.'

Jacob shrugs again, his fists clenching and unclenching in his lap. It terrifies Tom how little his brother has changed over the last thirty years. 'Probably don't even know it's trespassing,' Jacob counters. 'Probably don't even know what they own and what they don't.'

Tom can't argue with that. He who knows boundaries like the lines in his palm, who could recite unaided where every plot of land meets and divides in this valley – it pains him to think that these people have just bought a slab of earth unthinking. That the joins, the boundaries, the water courses don't matter to them.

'Any road,' he continues, his eyes in front of him. 'Leave them alone, alright?'

This is met by Jacob's habitual silence.

*

'Where we going?' Jacob finally asks as they arrive at the outskirts of the town. He has become fidgety over the last few minutes. Tom knows he does not like the town. Memories of school buses, school bullies, years of crowded, jostling incarceration in classrooms and hallways when all Jacob wanted was to be out on the fell.

'Dropping Zoe's stuff back.'

'Back where?'

'At Lisa's.'

'Thought she lived with you.'

'She does a week with each of us,' Tom says. It is the hundredth time he has explained it. 'A week with me, a week with . . .'

He doesn't finish his sentence. They pull into a newish housing estate, all red brick and sharp corners and everything touching the next: all the houses joined together, joined to their garages. Even the cars are almost touching. It is claustrophobic, Tom's lungs tightening at the thought of it.

Tom switches the engine off. 'You stay here, alright?'

It is only a few feet up the garden path to the doorbell, and with long legs like his Tom should cover it in a stride or two. But he hovers, debates, girds himself, fiddling with the car keys as if he's doing something important, all the while wishing he didn't have to ring the doorbell, praying it's not going to be Mike who answers and who'll make him ask for her.

'Tom.' His ex-wife appears in the doorway, wrapping her pink cardigan around herself as if to protect her modesty.

'Lisa.' No need to protect her modesty; he can hardly bear to look at her.

'Where is she then?'

'Out with friends,' he says. 'I brought her stuff.'

'Brought her stuff, but not her. Oh, very good Tom.'

There it is, Tom thinks, the first of Lisa's vicious little stab wounds. Dagger-filled, his wife, like one of those martial artists he saw at the circus once, throwing knives and miraculously missing his beautiful assistant each time. Except that Lisa's daggers never miss.

'Here.' He hands over the two rucksacks he's brought. 'I'll be off then.' He turns back towards the car.

'And you didn't ask?'

He wheels back to her. 'What?'

'You didn't ask where she's going, who she's with.'

'She's a teenager, she probably wouldn't tell me.'

'I can't believe you. She's fourteen.'

'I know how old she is, Lisa.'

'How can you not know where she is? She could be anywhere!'

'Listen, I'll call her later, check she'll be back on time.'

'Oh, sure, if it makes you happy.'

'None of this makes me happy, Lisa.'

For a moment they look at each other, and Tom is astonished at how hard her stare is; how utterly it erases the decade and a half they spent together. Surely she thought some of it was good? Or she'd have left him sooner. Again those eyes bore flint-sharp into his chest.

'Listen Tom, as you're here . . .'

Already he is on alert, his hackles rising like a dog tasting attack on the air.

'. . . there is something I wanted to talk to you about.'

'Oh yes?'

'Mike's got a job up on the rigs.'

Mike, the man who sleeps in his wife's bed, who takes his daughter to school in the mornings.

'Bully for Mike,' he replies, arms folded tight across his chest, as if it is he who needs protecting now.

'And I'll be going with him.'

'What?'

'With Zoe, obviously.'

'What the hell are you talking about?'

The blood is pounding in Tom's ears. He can't see straight,

166

can't speak. It's as if she's thrust her icy hand through his ribs and is squeezing it around his heart.

'It's a good job, Tom, a good opportunity, for all of us.'

'I don't care if it's a job running the United fucking Nations.' His voice is low, coursing with anger. 'No way on earth are you and that lump taking my daughter up to Scotland.'

'He is not a lump.'

'Oh come on, Lise.' Tom almost laughs. 'Actually, you know what, I think it's *great* news, a *great* job for Mike. One that requires no thinking at all and one that keeps him a hundred miles away from my family.'

'You can stop right there, Tom Outhwaite, if you think I'm leaving her with you!'

'Well you can stop right there if you think I'm letting you take her. Joint custody, Lisa, joint custody. What part of "joint" does rural bloody Scotland play in that?'

'She's my daughter!'

'Yeah and mine too.' Tom slams back towards the car, not caring how many neighbours are peeking through their net curtains. 'I'm not letting you do this.'

'Well I'm not letting you spoil any more years of my happiness!' Lisa shouts at him.

'Oh yeah, go on, Lise. Believe what you like. You *were* happy, we *were* happy – until you went and shagged someone else and messed it all up.' Finally his voice has caught up with his heart, and he yells at her as if the force of his words might knock her down and change her mind. 'You are not bloody taking her!'

He doesn't hear the final things she shouts, out on the pavement in her slippers, banging her fist against the passenger window so that Jacob cowers in his seat. Tom is pure animal: rage and breath and blood, all charging through his system, dumb to anything besides fury.

'What was that about?' Jacob asks, as the car veers at speed out of the estate.

Tom doesn't answer. Instead he waits until they are out on the Nelder road. With no one in sight except his brother, Tom gets out of the car and roars.

'Bloody woman! That bloody . . .'

The wind snatches at his words, the rain hides the tears on his cheeks. At the roadside, doubled over against one of Jacob's recently repaired walls, Tom fights for breath. For anything that he can cling on to in this subsiding world.

Eventually, wet and breathless, he gets back into the car. They drive in silence back up the dale.

35

Night falls, and there are no twinkling lights in the village yet, just yellow smears against the dark cottage windows. The evening, cold and damp, is tightly drawn, the rain falling steadily on roofs and windows. Heather's daughter is paying an unexpected visit.

'You didn't have to come up, love.'

'You haven't been down.'

'I've been busy.'

'Have you?'

'Keeping busy.' Heather pulls the sleeves of her cardigan down to cover her trembling hands. They've been bad today, the worst yet. She couldn't have kept them hidden at the library, so she hid at home instead. 'The library, after-school club, you know.'

'I don't know why you spend so much time there, Mam. Not like they're paying you.'

'I'm just doing my bit.'

'Mmm.' Jackie is standing by the window, twitching the net curtain as she casts an eye out over the village. 'Lot of big readers up here, are there?'

That you also wanted to get out, Heather thinks. Get away from all this. Generations of them, tied to these sorry square miles, like the bloody sheep on the fells. Good for breeding and nothing else. Not that there's even sheep any more.

'Well,' she smoothes out the blanket on the sofa, 'we don't do too badly.'

Jackie turns to her. 'What of this body, then?'

'Haven't heard anything.'

'Must be some news.'

'Quiet as the . . .' Heather plumps the cushions instead of actually saying *grave*. It would be distasteful, somehow.

Jackie lights up.

'Why are you sitting here in the gloom? Don't mind if I smoke, do you? Turn the bloomin' lights on.'

Heather hasn't turned the table lamps on because it can take minutes, now, to actually get the switch flicked, and between Jackie's hammering at the door ('Bleedin' hell Mam, hurry up would you?') and opening it she had to hide the packs of pills she's been stockpiling from the chemist. Reluctantly, she starts fiddling with the lamp, her fingers hot and sweaty and even more useless than usual. 'Oh, blasted thing.'

Luckily, Jackie lives in her own little world. Sees only what she wants to see. Heather watches her daughter watching the street, and wonders how this tall, dark-haired woman, with her broad shoulders and wide, cat-like eyes, could have sprung from her. And Jackie looks even less like the Ellis clan. Little Harry, with his fair hair that already at nineteen was beginning its speedy canter backwards across his head. Harry, small and slight, with his big nose and small, twinkling eyes, quiet and beaky as one of his beloved birds.

'What's the goss, then?'

With the interest her daughter takes in any kind of gossip – the faintest whiff of rumour, the fanning of cinders into full-blown flames – Heather cannot understand how her own heritage, her own blood secrets, haven't crossed her mind. But the mind is a strange beast, Heather knows that well enough. And sitting day after day in her three-bed semi with her husband and two kids, all eyes glued to a widescreen telly, maybe that doesn't lead the mind to enquiry.

'There's really not much to say,' Heather murmurs.

'What do the Londoners make of it?'

'Oh, I don't know. They must be used to excitement in London.'

'Mmm.' Jackie stubs out her cigarette. 'Well, best be getting back. Back to the kids.'

Nothing changes. Heather frying up those square potato things for Jackie's tea; Jackie in her kitchen frying them up all over again; and Kirsty, seven now, how long before she's at the handle of a frying pan? She wanted to be a ballerina last year, and they'd all smiled and nodded, but already that dream has faded and Heather is not convinced that any other will take its place.

'Alright, love.' Heather wraps her arms tightly around herself, relieved that Jackie is not the sort of daughter who'd go in for an embrace. 'Thanks for stopping by.'

'You should go over to the pub.' Jackie cocks her head in that direction. 'Get the news.'

Heather does not go to the pub. That night, she wakes with a shout, loud enough above the radio to startle even deaf old Joss, who's taken to sleeping at her feet. And in the suffocating minutes afterwards, she thinks back to the junior doctor's room, after the shock of the consultant's words. The low hum of his computer and the disinfectant smell and the way the plastic chair creaked beneath her.

'I'm sorry, Mrs Ellis.'

She said nothing. There was nothing to say.

'Is there someone I can call?'

No. There was no one.

'I do think . . .' the doctor leaned forward in his chair at that point. He was a kind man. Young-ish. Not attractive by any means, but kind. Kinder than his silver-haired colleague who spoke the news as if it was incidental, as if she was just one of a long list of fatal diagnoses (which she probably was). 'I do think you should be in touch with people, if there are people to tell. A person, perhaps.'

And Heather wondered, afterwards, about that revision. Was it just a sort of political awareness, a knowledge, in his line of work, that there are many who have no one or just one, a whole generation of old people left on their own? To her, it felt prophetic. Because there is a person she needs to tell things to. And how much worse with this news from Two Houses; that body dug up and all these secrets finally coming up for air just at the moment that she needs to tell hers.

'Distance can be hard,' the youngish doctor said, showing her back into the waiting area. He must have thought her family was far away. But Heather knows that distance is not just a matter of miles. Sometimes the people nearest to you are the ones from whom the most is concealed.

Finally, her heart settles, fluttering still, but only as branches in wind, feathers in flight. Joss, exhausted, lays down her head, and Heather tries to do the same. But there is this question of loose ends. Of things to be tied up and ironed out. Slowly, heavily, she hauls herself out of bed. The dog squints at her through one half-closed eye, pretending not to notice as Heather pulls on jumper, trousers, boots.

'You coming, Jossy?'

Reluctantly Joss plops down from the bed to join this night-time escapade. She is nothing if not loyal.

Gone midnight, and the air outside is still, knife-cold, like metal pressing against the skin. For once, the rain has paused – a brief hiatus – and a near-full moon lights her path along the village street. She has not said to herself where she is going, but her feet are taking her there anyway. Up out of the dark village, out on to the hillsides.

'Funny,' she murmurs, as they pass the pub. A glimmer of light from one of the windows – the only sign of life or wakefulness. Joss snuffles along beside her as Heather opens the gate and directs them up towards the tops.

36

In the pub, other secrets are finding their light.

'How long have you had this place?' Jay asks.

''Bout three years.'

Tom, she is realising, rarely says anything that doesn't need to be said. They are sitting across the table from each other. Between them, the remnants of a fishfinger dinner. Two half-empty pint glasses. A pink table lamp, its frilly trim totally at odds with the rough-hewn man sitting opposite her, all in the glow of the light from the oven.

'And before that?'

Tom takes a long draught from the glass in front of him. He sets it firmly down on the table, letting the seconds and the beer suds slide before he answers.

'A farm. Family farm. Up on the tops.'

Jay, too, holds her words in her mouth before letting them pass.

'Why'd you leave it?'

'Forced out. No money in it any more.'

Two sips from their respective glasses. Jay thinks back to London, to Simon's suggestion of getting out and the lacka-daisical privilege with which she'd stuck a pin in the map. The interview with D.I. Mosby floods like hot light into her mind, and Jay is ashamed to think how easy it was. How complacent they were. How they joked about the house prices – that you could get a weekend home, do it up and pay a mortgage and still have more than enough to comfortably live on. Tom is looking at anything but her – how like a painting he is, by lamplight – and she wonders if he has ever felt the urge to stick a pin in a map. To start driving and not look back.

'Did you think about leaving?'

'We did leave.'

'Going further than here, I mean. Really getting away.'

He shrugs. 'Got my da, my brother. They still live up on the, in the house. Got my daughter.'

'Of course.' Her cheeks glow like the pink velvet lampshade. She thought the dog was a responsibility. 'Your mother's not around, then?'

'She died. And my stepmother. Twice widowed, my da.'

'Oh.'

Time passes, marked only by the murmuring of the wind and the ponderous ticking of the kitchen clock. Eventually:

'Can I get you anything else?'

'No, thank you.'

The awkward formality of it. Their polite sallies to and fro, each treading so very carefully. He goes to lift the dishes, but she stops him. Without even thinking about it, she places a hand on his wrist. He jumps at the touch.

'What was it like up here?'

'What?' He can't seem to think, not with the heat from her hand on his.

'What was it like? When you were growing up?'

He moves away, places the plate back down on the table. Sinks slowly into his chair. No one has ever asked him this before – has ever asked him anything like this before. It takes full minutes to formulate his reply, to sift through the memories flashing before his eyes.

'Harsh. It were a harsh life. Difficult weather. Well, you know that. Hard graft to make a success of it. That made the people hard, too. Not bad, mind. Not all of them. But hard. No time for tea and sympathy when lambing's on and the snow's coming.'

Jay learned, after her mother's death, how not to speak so

174

that someone else will; how to hold breath secretly, tightly to yourself, so that their lungs can expand, their secrets spill slowly, unwillingly forward. In front of her, Tom is unfurling, a bud that has kept its petals tightly to itself, and she, perhaps, the sun, coaxing it out.

'It was mining and farming, here. Farming way back to Viking times, like. Then the mines came. That was all done with long ago – when my da was a lad. Almost everyone went back to the farms, and it were good, for a while. Hard work but you could live on it. But that changed. No one wants wool any more. Costs more to shear it than you get to shift it.

'And people changed, too. There was a community then. Pitching in, helping out. But purses got pinched and faces too, and the farms started to fold. Affected folk differently. Some moved out, moved to the town or the council estate, or wherever they had that they could go. Others stayed, but they got hard, bitter. We were the last, in these parts, to give it up. Stupid, maybe, but when it's been in your hands, your blood . . . You feel it's in you, you know? That you are *meant* to be there. Without that . . .'

His words trail off, his eyes with them.

'So the village wasn't always this quiet, then?'

Tom laughs, a short sharp laugh that sends his head backwards. 'No, it wasn't always empty. There were people here. And they were happy, happy enough.'

And of course, he thinks of Lisa, who he'd always thought of as happy enough.

'What about . . .' Jay hesitates, the words on the tip of her tongue.

He meets her eye for only the second or third time all evening. 'What?'

'What about Two Houses?'

Even in the half-dark, she sees a change come over his face. Something cold, incalculable; it closes him off from her, even as he had just been so open.

'Tom?'

'What about it?'

'What was it like?'

He whistles breath through his teeth the way the wind rushes through the long grass.

'It weren't a happy place,' he mutters. 'I'm sorry to say it, but it's true. Maybe it'll be different now, you, and your –' there is the slightest hesitation before he says it '– husband. Maybe you'll make it happy.'

'But the ghost story? That wasn't recent?'

'No . . .' Tom's eyes shift towards the window again, out towards the impenetrable night. 'Forties, I think. After the war. But these things leave their marks. Their traces. Even if us folk can't see them.'

Jay waits for him to continue, the weighted seconds of silence compelling his words.

'The old man died, long time ago, before I was a lad, even. Place fell to rack and ruin. Families passing through, farm-hands and the like who couldn't make a go of it on the farms any more. They weren't meant to be there, but they'd nowhere else. Turfed out eventually, poor sods. It became . . .' and his words are almost indistinguishable from breath now, so quietly do they come. 'It became somewhere to go. Teenagers to drink, or to do whatever. Kids to go as a place for dares. But it was . . . Bad things happened there.'

Jay is at the edge of her seat, the limit of her lungs. 'What things?'

He shakes his head.

'What things, Tom?'

'I don't know.' He is up again, and the full height of him startles her. He starts gathering the dishes. 'I don't know. I shouldn't have said anything.'

He turns from her, his jutting shoulder blades sticking out as he plunges his arms into the sink. When he speaks it is without turning back to her.

'It's different for you. Maybe you can change things. Maybe you can make it happy. You have money, and each other. You chose to come here.' He laughs and it is bitter now, and horrid. 'Why did you choose to come here?'

It is an interrogation, an accusation, flying sharp and vicious across the room.

'I don't know. We needed to go somewhere.'

He snorts. 'That sounds ridiculous to someone like me.'

'Me too.'

He turns back to the dishes.

'*Anywhere*.'

'What?'

'You could have gone *anywhere*.' And it is only when he says it that she realises how vast that *anywhere* is; how infinite its possibilities, how open, unbounded.

'Daft as houses,' he says. 'Isn't that what they say?'

'What?'

'Folk are daft as houses. And now you've got two of them.' He chuckles to himself, but there is a hardness to it, an edge that catches in his throat and on the air.

'What about your daughter?'

'What about her?'

'Does she want to stay here?'

He shrugs, trying to loose himself from the memory of Zoe in her bedroom, the declaration that this was all just so much shit, and her mother's promise that she was going to take her, going to make her move away from him.

'Don't know. She's a teenager. Wants everything and nothing.' Tom turns back towards their sparring match. Fists up. 'What about you? Didn't you want kids?'

She stares at his moorgrass eyes. 'Maybe. Maybe not. Wanting something doesn't mean you get it.'

'True enough.'

'Besides, we met late. We'd both been busy with our careers.'

Oh, your careers, he thinks, and she watches the thought pass across his face.

'What about you? Your wife, is it?'

'Ex-wife.'

'Was she from here?'

He gestures into some unknown distance.

'Down the valley.'

'Is that where she is now?'

'Yes.'

'What happened?'

'She found someone else who made her happy. I was trying to save the farm, the family. I didn't have time to make her happy.'

The wind rattles the windows in their frames. Bella stirs at Jay's feet and for a second she is back in London, in the summer heat, Simon teetering unwelcome in the doorway, and it is so unpleasant that she shakes her head to sift away the memory of it.

'I don't think you can make other people happy.'

'You're maybe right about that.'

'I'd like to see your farm,' she declares.

'It's not a farm any more,' he counters.

'Still.'

'OK.'

'Good.'

They stare at each other across the kitchen, two combatants at pause, taking stock, taking breath, something electric crackling between them.

'Well . . .'

'Yes.'

'It's late.'

'Yes.'

They each make their preparations for going to bed. Jay pours a glass of water. Tom folds the tea towel over the back of the chair as his grandmother taught him to do so it dries by morning.

They meet, awkwardly, in the doorway.

'You should . . .' It is he who reaches to touch her arm this time. He stops himself just short of contact but she feels each of his fingers anyway, warm on her skin despite the distance of millimetres. '. . . You should show me your work sometime. Pottery, is it?'

'Ceramics.'

'Yeah, that.'

'How did you know?'

'Jacob told me. Told me you did things with your hands.'

She turns her palms to face him, callouses faded after all this time away from the wheel.

'It's been a quiet year.'

'New house, new start, maybe.'

'Yes. Maybe.'

He nods.

'Thank you for the fish fingers.'

'Any time.'

37

Angela couldn't help herself. Down the pub to do her customary clean and hoover, she couldn't resist spending a few extra minutes in Jay's room, poring over the few objects scattered on the bedside table: a ring with a great lump of amber in it, a fine gold chain, an expensive-looking hand cream that gave off the faintest, cleanest floral scent.

She was careful not to get caught, but returning home to her cottage, she raged. What was that woman thinking, trespassing on Tom's hospitality like that? And after her husband had gone to London, too? Sitting in the corner of the pub by the fire as if she owned the place. As if she had some kind of hold on him. Typical Tom, stepping in to save the day even when he didn't want to. Typical bloody Londoner, taking advantage.

And yet, just for a moment as she's applying her lipstick – Fuschia Dream tonight, one of her favourites – Angela has to acknowledge that there doesn't seem anything typical about this stranger, Londoner or not. That a typical Londoner would have been better for all of them; would have come, played the country life for a few months, then buggered off again. This woman's digging into the earth. She's putting down roots, and what kind of harvest might she reap?

But enough of that. She stands up from her dressing table and straightens her dress. Little, lilac, with push-up bits under the bust. Digging in her handbag, she pulls out for the umpteenth time the profile she printed off secretly at work while Shazza was out having a fag with the deliveryman. *Kevin James, 48, accountant.*

A little thrill runs up the back of Angela's legs. She likes the sound of an accountant. On telly they drive nice cars and have detached houses with neatly mown lawns and tumble dryers. And he seems nice, this Kevin. Tall, with dark hair, and in his picture he's wearing a suit with the collar of his shirt open. She likes that. She's been saving up for petrol money. She has a good feeling about this one.

The rain has hardly stopped these last few weeks. By the time Angela gets to the restaurant, excitement bubbling up in her like a fancy drink, it is bucketing again. She wonders, not for the first time, how there can be so much water in one sky; how come so much of it ends up in this corner of the earth.

The restaurant is Italian and candlelit. It looks much fancier than when she'd looked it up. Fifteen quid for a plate of pasta? But it's too late now, by the time she's looking at the menu inside the main doorway the waiter is upon her, all smiles and a folded towel held over his arm, and 'oh yes, miss, your friend is waiting for you.' And she is swept up on it, his manners, his smile, his stiff white shirt and the way he presents the table to her with a flourish, even stopping to pull out her chair.

Kevin, though, is not quite as advertised. He is heavier now, thickset in a way his photograph did not acknowledge. His hairline has travelled back a good three inches. But he kisses her hand, tells her to sit down, sit down, *have a bloody drink.*

Trying to be demure, she chooses a glass of the house white.

'Oh, you don't want that bloody stuff! Get a proper glass, the Chardonnay or something.'

It's only four quid more, she tells herself. 'Alright then, Kevin,' she smiles.

He downs his beer, orders another for when her glass arrives.

'Cheers!'

They clink glasses and get down to small talk.

'So, Kevin, you're an accountant.'

'God yes, most boring job in the world. And you, Angela? You manage a shop?'

'Oh, yes,' she lies evenly, smoothing out her napkin.

'What kind, then?'

Oh why not? she thinks.

'It's a little boutique shop for ladies. Evening wear, wedding dresses, you know the type.'

'Oh I know the type alright!' he guffaws, throwing his head back so that she can see the rows of dark fillings in his teeth.

'It's lovely, actually,' she hurries on, carried away on the dream now. 'Ever such pretty dresses, and we get lovely ladies coming in to try things on.' (Of course, who pops into her mind but that ancient Agnes who comes into the Co-op every day for a tin of beans, stinking of cat's piss?) 'It's such a pleasure, Kevin, to help lovely ladies pick out their special dresses.'

'Well, I imagine you'd be very good at that, Angela.' He finishes another pint and burps over his shoulder. 'And what about you? Not married? Always the bride's outfitter, never the bride, eh?'

She stretches her face into a smile. *Brittle*, her mother's insult rings in her ears. *You're just so brittle, Angela.* 'Something like that.'

The food comes with another beer – his third? Fourth? – and she is sipping her wine ever so slowly, trying desperately to eke it out.

'And what about you, Kevin? Never married?'

'Oh, I was married alright,' shovelling wet forkfuls of food between his lips. 'Bloody nightmare. As soon as the ring was on her finger, she let herself go. A right slob, she was,' as a thick glob of steak sauce falls slowly down his napkin. 'Not like you, Angela. Not nice-looking, in nice shape.'

182

'Thank you.' She is trying not to look at the stains on his napkin, trying not to acknowledge the lump in her throat. All her excitement, all her hopes. All the petrol money she saved to get here.

As the main courses are cleared away, she gets up to go to the toilet. Of course, she goes the wrong way, towards the door, and she can hear her 'date' laughing at her as the waiter, ever so politely, points her back in the opposite direction. She hates herself for it but there are tears in her eyes, and she can't quite see straight, not with all the candles. As she turns, she bumps straight into the village librarian.

'Oh my god.' Her jaw drops open. His, too, seems to gape a little.

'Sorry.'

'What's that then, Angela?' Kevin yells across the restaurant, turning the heads of the other diners. 'An old flame is it?' he chortles.

'No,' she stammers, trying to recover herself. 'We hardly know each—'

But Kevin is up, more belly than anything else as he waddles towards them.

'I'll just—' Dev makes to go, but Kevin is upon them now.

'No, don't be running off young man. I'm no racist, I'll shake anyone's hand as long as he's a real bloody man. You from the same village? Angela's just been telling me about her shop, lovely dresses and all that.'

'Dresses?' Dev looks confused.

'Yes, her dress shop!'

'Oh,' Dev looks at Angela. Her insides crumple. 'Her dress shop. Of course. Well,' he smiles uneasily, 'it was very nice meeting you, seeing you, Angela.' It is the first time he's used her name, and with that he retreats to his friend at the corner table.

'Eh up, he's not a nancy, is he?' Kevin says loudly. 'Two blokes having dinner?'

'I expect they're just friends.' Angela hardly hears him. 'Let me just powder my nose.'

Sitting on the toilet, Angela hangs her head backwards, trying to persuade the tears to sink back into her eye sockets.

'Bloody man, bloody, bloody, *bloody* man,' she spits between gritted teeth. Of all the people, it would be him; dirty, smelly, horrible him.

Back at the table, there is another beer and Kevin is slurring his words. People are beginning to look at them now.

'Is your companion alright, madam? Would he care for some coffee, perhaps?' the waiter asks.

'No coffee, no coffee,' Kevin waves his hand around, shooing the waiter like a fly. 'Just the bill. The night is young, eh, Angela?'

The bill arrives, discretely folded.

'We'll split it, shall we?' throwing his credit card down.

'But . . .' His steak was three times the price of her pasta, not to mention the beers.

'Oh come on, Angela, you don't want to be a kept woman, do you?' That roaring laugh again, bouncing off the restaurant's walls. 'You can't assume I'm just paying for your dinner – you're not that pretty!'

The restaurant falls silent around them. Even Kevin, in his haze of Heineken, seems to hear it.

'Come on, now,' he puts his hand on her forearm, trying to make amends. 'I just meant with your business and everything, you're a successful woman!'

Shaking with rage and humiliation, she throws two twenty pound notes down on the table. Blinded by tears, she hurls herself towards the restaurant door, catching her bag on another's diner's chair as she does so.

'Have a good evening, ma—'

But she is out in the driving rain before the waiter can finish his sentence. She stands disorientated on the pavement. She has never been so humiliated. The rain slams down in the darkness, cold on her bare arms, and it is hard to see her way to her car, to find the keys in her handbag, to get the bloody, ancient bucket of metal going again. It is only once she is inside that she realises she is sobbing, for all that she wanted the night to be and for all that it so resoundingly was not. And all of it witnessed by that man, that *bloody Paki.*

Smearing mascara over her cheeks with the back of her palm, she hurtles off back up the dale. She is going to make him pay for seeing her humiliated. She is going to make him pay.

38

'Jay?' The line is faint, crackly. 'Jay?'

'Yes?'

'It's me.'

'I know.'

Simon is flustered. 'I was just – I wanted to let you know I'll be back the day after tomorrow. Sorry, I, we – another presentation went in at the last minute.'

'That's fine. Thanks for letting me know.'

There is a silence, and Simon imagines he can hear the wind blowing outside her windows, the ever-present spatter of rain to which he's become accustomed.

'Are you OK?'

'Yes, fine. See you soon.'

Another grey morning, another grey day, and finally, the morning after that, Jay is allowed back to Two Houses. D.I. Mosby stands at the door as she enters.

'Any trouble,' he winces, handing over a business card, 'just call.'

'You think there'll be trouble?'

'No.' He thrusts both hands into his pockets and rocks on his heels. 'It's the ends of the earth, up here, and it were a long time ago.'

'How long ago?'

He shrugs. 'Twenty, thirty, forty year ago, they reckon. It's much of a muchness when you're in the ground. Not much to go on.'

'So you haven't found out who she is?'

Mosby coughs. 'Like I told you, an *historic case*. We've no missing people, no leads to go on. Nowt likely to come of it. So, no. I don't think you'll have any trouble.'

I've found them out, the things that people have been doing here. And the people that have been doing them. Common, vulgar things done by common, vulgar people.

I will not have these houses turned into stables; a place for dark misdeeds no better than what animals do, raw and heaving against the stonework. These walls were made for better than this. I will not have harlots darkening our door, nor children on dares, nor empty philanderers seeking their little pleasures. God help me, I will turf them out myself.

Inheritance, be damned. I turfed out the last lot.

Inside, Jay walks around as if learning the house anew. Everything, for once, is exactly where they'd left it. The same mugs unnervingly upturned on the draining board where Simon was busy washing them; her library books and papers up in one of the empty bedrooms – the empty bedroom that was once a nursery – exactly where she placed them down.

She thinks back to what Tom said. Families passing through, abandonment, illicit teenage activities taking place between these walls, and always, always, the body, the bone, looming towards her down the dark, quiet corridors. It is a new silence now, pointed, after all these officers tramping through the place. It is as if all that noise, that activity, has left a stain on the place, and the hush is fiercer in compensation.

In the upstairs hallway, Jay leans out of the window as they did on that first day, looking across at the second house, at the patch of ground, its earth freshly disturbed, an angry new scar. She braves the wind – ferocious, today, spitting – and goes across to the other building. Bella stays close at her heels as she drags back to the main house the pile of boxes she's been so studiously ignoring. Her work boxes; the boxes from her studio.

Clay, plaster, powders; glazes, tools, moulds. She drags them out onto the floor, heart hammering in her chest, driven on by the rain driving against the windows, and Tom's words in her ears. *New house, new start, maybe.* The rain is thick enough that occasionally she looks up thinking she sees a face, a ghost staring in at her, but each time she takes the lurch of her heart and pushes it back into her work again.

And not for months has she had this urge to feel wet clay between her fingers; to press and mould, shape and guide. To feel form becoming within the compass of her hands. She'd forgotten the elation of it; the joy in the smell of wet clay, the way it creeps secretly up your arms.

'Bone white,' she murmurs to herself, looking down at her pale, ghostly hands plunged in their medium. The silence is deafening. The radio – where is her radio? Music to drown out the words in her head, to push her on with its fillips, breath and rhythms. So urgent is the need that she runs, hands dripping, through the rain back to the other house to lug it over, Bella confused and excited, and it is exhilarating to set herself up within these cold walls, to drag out the wheel and set it going while a storm thrashes outside the window, tossing and turning like a body caught in too-tight bedsheets, the clouds contorting, whipping themselves into a frenzy, the wind bending that poor, lonely, determined tree in the garden over on itself again, over and over until surely it must snap. Bella paces, whines, and Jay is unable to do anything, anything, but spin the wheel faster, throw the clay down harder, pinch it into shape beneath her hands.

She is out of practice. The most simple pots collapse at the wheel, her fingers pinch the clay too thin. She has forgotten the forceful bone-ache of it, clunky and out of joint. Time has no dimension as she works, and as the storm gradually quietens, the fierce rush of blood in her quietens with it, and she finds her hands are working by themselves, pulling, pressing, extruding shapes, and there is hardly any agency to it.

The sky turns to ink, and as it blurs between blue and black she hears the sound of a fist knocking at the door. Jay thinks about ignoring it. About letting the hammering go unanswered. But as if outside of her own skin, she finds herself standing up, wiping her hands, pulling back the latch.

It is Tom, his dark hair smeared in wet shapes along his forehead. He is clutching a bag to his chest.

'You didn't take any food,' he says.

Jay lets him in, reciprocates his kindness in offering a towel for his hair.

'Here, let me light a fire,' she says, as his wide eyes take in the white walls, the smart London furniture, the ripped boxes and clay dust settling on every surface.

'I won't stay,' he says, rooted to the ground.

But his eyes wander, and soon the fire is beginning its slow crackle. Jay takes the bag of food – 'Vegetables,' he murmurs, 'for a vegetarian' – and when she has placed it on the kitchen table, she finds him looking at the strange shapes of clay on the wheel.

'Not my best work. Here, these are more . . .'

And she digs into one of the half-emptied boxes, pulling out things she had almost forgotten. A tiny globe, not yet glazed. A plate the green-ground colour of his eyes.

'They're lovely,' he whispers, as if her having made them was enough to warrant whispering. He looks for a long time, runs his fingers along the edge of the plate in a way that raises the hairs on the back of Jay's neck. It is she who is rooted now, watching him, in the hush, in the firelight.

He turns to the mantelpiece, to her strange altar of discovered treasures. Thimble, skull, stone, but it is a new feather – the most recent addition, placed there the day that they made the discovery – that he picks up in his hands.

'Peewit, is this,' he says, turning the emerald sliver between his fingers. 'You know it?'

She shakes her head.

'Beautiful. Great big feather on its head, like a headdress. And it makes the noise, *peewit, peewit*. Sad noise, actually.'

'Sometimes the sad things seem the most beautiful.'

He doesn't seem to know what to say to that, for they stand for a minute and let the fire do the talking.

'Well,' he says eventually.

'Thank you for the food.'

'Thank you for showing me.'

He nods at her and walks out into the night.

39

Simon stands alone and shivering on the platform. It is not the welcome he had been hoping for.

Jay knew what time he was coming. He'd called her, told her. *Yes, yes,* she'd said in that way of hers, when he annoys her with his insistence on details. *I'll be there.* But it is late and cold, and she is emphatically not here. The hours of his journey have seeped into Simon's skull; he can still hear the dull roar of the train in his ears, feels its vibrations within his bones. It's not what he needed, actually.

Simon wraps his arms around himself, partly for warmth, partly out of petulance. London was London – gritty, grotty, dazzling and wonderful – and he needed the return here to outshine it, to dazzle him with the calm, quiet beauty of the place, the majesty of the hills. He needed to want to be here, in this place that has somehow slipped away from him between his fingers. To want to return, and to be wanted, returning. Which is difficult, anyway, on a cold, rainy November night when the world has been shrouded in darkness since four o'clock, but Jay turning up at the right bloody time would have helped.

He takes a few steps along the platform, trying to decide whether pacing or a taciturn stillness will best convey his displeasure. Eventually, the creaking Volvo pulls up, his wife as pale and ashen inside it as a spectre. He can see that her clothes are covered in clay dust.

A final phone call before he left, one that he'd been dancing around for days but that finally could not be avoided.

'Podge, it's Simon.'

'*Simon!*' That high-pitched squeal that Simon has always found difficult. 'How *are* you? *Where* are you? *Where* have you *been*? Is she there? How is she? Put her on, put her on.'

Simon rubs his hand across his forehead, feeling out its furrows. He knew this barrage of questions would be coming, but even so . . .

'She's not here, Podge. I'm at the office.'

'Is she at the house? I'll go round.'

'No, no . . .' trying desperately to curb Podge's enthusiasm. 'She's still up there.'

'*Alone?*'

'She's fine, Podge. She's better.'

Even as he says it Simon is haunted by the image of his wife sat on the floor of one of the empty bedrooms, her red hair fanned out behind her, books and papers spread across the floor. He remembers the curve of her spine as she leaned into them, as if tracing runes or fault lines across the floor-boards, in the house's very bones. The curve of her spine as she reached down to touch the bone, and he's discovering, now, how often the word 'bone' pops up in everyday conversation, carrying none of the horror and repulsion of that thing they found sticking up from the ground.

'I thought this was for weekends, Simon,' Podge continues, his voice heavy with recrimination. 'I didn't think you were taking her up there *permanently*.'

Simon is close to snapping now. 'I'm not taking her anywhere, Podge, she's her own woman. She loves it. Loves it up there. I don't know, she'll hardly leave the place. *Anyway*,' his turn to stress his words now, carrying on before Podge has the chance to interrupt him, 'I just wanted to let you know that she's OK, that we're OK.'

Lying through his teeth. Her smile as wide as ever, George waves goodnight at him through the glass wall of his office.

'Maybe she'll come down with me next week.'

*

Back up north, in the chill dark of the borderlands, they make bits of conversation as she drives. She doesn't mention her work, though it's obvious that she has been working. He talks a bit of London, but finds silence better suited to these unlit, winding roads. Already, his stomach is tense with return. He has not been at Two Houses since Tom drove him over.

'I made dinner,' she says, as they pull off the main road.

'Lovely,' he replies, all the while thinking of London, and sanity, the dirty streets that make sense in their own, convoluted, polluted way; the noise, disorder, chaos from which you understand exactly who you are and what you're meant to be doing.

As they enter the main house, he is stopped in his tracks by the mess. Throughout the living room the boxes from her studio, ripped open, gaping. The newspaper he'd used to pack her things crumpled and tossed aside. Bags of clay, bits of objects, things from London finished and in progress still – every surface covered in them, even the work papers he'd left neatly in a corner, even the jumper he'd left unthinkingly on one of the armchairs. An animal marking its territory could not have done so more clearly.

Jay has wandered off into the kitchen. He can hear her singing to herself, stirring something on the stove. Standing alone in the doorway, Simon feels utterly rejected. His idea, his great plan, and there seems to him no greater way for Jay to make this place hers, to squeeze him out of this space that it was his idea to come to, his idea to rebuild. It is clear to him, in these moments, that she has not missed him. That she does not want him here at all.

He takes a few steps into the room and, by the wheel, finds strange long shapes, white extrusions of clay. He picks one up, idly, before recognising what it is.

Bones. She has been making bones.

'Simon?' she calls from the kitchen, for all the world as if everything is ordinary. 'Dinner?'

The recent horror surges up in him again, sharp and rancid at the back of his throat. Four days, he left her; little more than a week since the thing was found, and here she is making dinner for the first time in months, and he, he is holding a porcelain bone in his hand. He thinks of the office, and meetings, and how ordinary those few days were. He thinks of the police and the earth and that awful afternoon, how abnormal everything in this corner of the world seems. His architect's plans, chucked in the corner, dumped under a pile of junk – and wasn't it her who wanted a studio in the first place? Who picked these godforsaken houses of all the others they had to choose from?

'Simon!'

He replaces the bone at the edge of the wheel. Tries to calm his breath, the panic that beats beneath his ribs like a summer moth, lured inside by a candle's light. Crossing the threshold into the kitchen, he tries to smile, and George rises unbidden, unwanted, in his mind.

40

Bloody Paki. That's what she calls him. *Bloody Paki.* And the rest of it, he's heard her saying that, too. *There's something funny about him.* Or, *he's not right, that one.* Or, *he should go back where he bloody well came from.*

Waking up into a chill morning, the first frosts knitting their webs across his windows, these are the words still running through Dev's mind. He knows the kind of things she'll be saying about him, has spent days worrying over them. He's heard those words before. Heard them that night walking home from school when three skinheads came running at him, pasty and violent, leaving him in a puddle on the floor with the rusty taste of blood in his mouth. Heard it on the bus in Bradford, where old white people would shout it for no good reason. Heard it from the Bangla boys, too, because there's no such thing as not fitting in with just one group of people. Dev's an outsider wherever he goes.

He gets up, makes tea. Thinks about calling Gareth to apologise again for ruining their evening with worry and panic, for only picking at his spaghetti and his tiramisu, terrified that she'd come storming back in to shout at him. But he's too late. Gareth will be at work by now, and Dev should get a move on too. Worrying into the small hours, he's slept through his alarm the last few days, snoozed its warnings, and once again he is running late. He leaves his tea to stew on the counter.

Locking his door, Dev looks up at the grey fellside, dark and foreboding above him. He pulls his knitted jumper up around his neck against the morning's bite. The worry, the secrets – he came here to get away from all that. Not that he expected tolerance, understanding. Dev's learned the hard way to expect neither. But he thought he might be far away enough up here, quiet enough, nothing enough, for people not to care. He's tried the city, all its people supposedly self-involved, but in fact knitted imperceptibly together, neighbourhoods, ganglands cheek by jowl, the endless friction and fracture of people who weren't supposed to give a damn about each other.

He walks the village street with tentative steps, ducking his head from the cold, but also from whatever vitriol Angela might be about to fling at him. The Co-op is quiet, though; to his great relief, she is not smoking her usual cigarette. Climbing the stone steps to the library, Dev realises there's very little that separates his mum with her net curtains on a Bengali street in Bradford from Angela with her net curtains here. Skin colour, yes; one head of hair silver, the other bleached, but the prying eyes are no different. The same stuff, they're made of.

Trotting up the library steps, he jumps to see Jay standing in the doorway.

'Hello.'

'Oh! You scared me.'

'Did I?'

'No, it's . . .' Dev feels his heart resume its normal place in his chest. 'We don't usually have people queuing up to get in, is all.'

'Ah.' They stand for a moment looking at each other, the beginnings of rain pattering down on to the stone doorstep, before she says 'Can I come in?' and Dev feels like an idiot.

'Of course.' He fumbles with the keys.

She is here, he knows, for news of Two Houses. News of the investigations he was to have undertaken. What is it, a week since they spoke? And he has idled, dawdled, twiddled his thumbs, for Heather has been in every day this week, and how can he look when Heather is so vehement in wanting him not to?

'Have you found anything?'

'Not yet . . .'

'Have you looked?'

'It's been a busy week.'

Jay looks around her at the flaking paintwork, the empty returns trolley. 'Has it?'

'Heather, my colleague . . .' Dev squirms under the intensity of this woman's gaze. 'She didn't want me digging anything up.' He feels a blush creep over his rounded cheeks.

'It's already been dug up, Dev. The body. It's real. It's here. Everyone knows about it.'

'I know, I know.' And where is Heather this morning, he wonders, scanning the street for the dog and duffle coat. 'Come in.'

They sit on opposite sides of Dev's narrow, cluttered desk, covered as it is with biscuit crumbs and unopened letters, papers curling up at the edges and marked with sandy rings of tea.

'How do I find her?' she asks.

Dev fiddles with the multicoloured buttons on his multicoloured waistcoat. 'I'm thinking, I'm thinking . . .'

He thinks and the rain slams against the windows. The already swollen river strains at its banks, bulges just a little wider.

'There are censuses,' he says suddenly. 'But they'll be too old. There are parish records. The parish newsletter here, we have them all – who went to church, who baked what for the church fête.'

Jay's stomach sinks.

'But where do I start? I've nowhere to start from.'

Dev marches into the kitchen, retrieves a pack of Hobnobs, offers her a biscuit and starts nibbling.

'You found out about the haunting, the cutting of the house in two,' he says through a mouthful of biscuit.

'But that was easy. That was in a book. This is . . .' She trails off. This is like nothing else.

'No . . .' Dev's buckteeth break into a second biscuit. 'But you know when that happened, roughly – the cutting out of the rooms, I mean. When was that?'

'The forties, I think.'

'So look from then. Who lived in the house then? Who's lived there since? Who's lived in the village since then?'

'The whole village?'

He stares at her, eyebrows cocked and lips pursed. 'It's hardly a major metropolitan area.'

She concedes.

'I'll look at the newsletters, the village documents,' he says. 'People leaving, maybe. Coming and going. They might have mentioned it.'

'They might,' she nods, but he can see her mood sinking in her stomach. This is clutching at straws. Neither of them have a clue.

Dev finishes his tea, relishes the sweet, oaty crumble at the bottom of the mug.

'You have looked *in* the houses, right? Cupboards? Attics?'

41

But you cannot teach people. Cannot unrot the apple, cannot remove the taint. Pull the maggots from the wound, but still it festers.

They say children are innocent, but children are the worst. Drawn to dirt and misbehaviour, they see what they should not see, step where they should not go. They know how to wound, with their teasing, with their questions, dagger-sharp. Their words are like pinches, but no amount of pinching draws the badness out.

The one thing I know is that you cannot teach that which is already corrupted. If a dog is lame, you shoot it.

And is it madness, Jay wonders, to be crawling up into a dark attic? To be a hound with scent, a beast in heat? All day she has paced, fidgeted, waited for Simon to be busy doing something so that she can crawl up here, her fingers scrabbling over bare boards towards strange half-shapes and objects she cannot see, and she has never liked the dark.

But Dev was right. There are things up here. She holds a torch between her cheek and shoulder, heavy and cold against her skin. Boxes of books, it looks like. Papers. Things. Belonging to the Brathwanes? Or the families who came in afterwards? In all that abandonment and decay, who paused to leave their things up here? Unwilling to venture too far from the warm square of light offered by the attic's hatch, she claws at them, hauls them towards her.

The first box offers her a selection of parcels, painstakingly wrapped in yellow newspaper. *One man's trash is another man's treasure*, her father would say. Another woman's, maybe. There seems to her something feminine about these scraps of things so carefully parcelled up. Perhaps that was just in her family. Her father couldn't wrap things, couldn't coordinate the tear of tape and snip of scissors. They didn't have wrapping after her mother died.

Jay shakes herself. This isn't about her mother. And look – between clouds of breath made thick and white in the cold dark air – this is a child's tin soldier, his paint worn so thin that his proud chest juts out in a square of gunmetal, his gun snapped off long ago. In the next package, a tiny bracelet: a gold loop for a child's wrist and, dangling from it, a golden heart. Jay's heart is in her throat as she turns to another, bulkier present. A child's knitted jumper, dark mud of ages past encrusted down its front. Who would have kept these? Why would they have kept them here? She thinks briefly of *Jane Eyre*, of mad Bertha in the attic, and prays – to the god she does not believe in – that a mad woman does not live in her attic. Perhaps she is the mad woman.

A second box yields paper. Letters from the 1970s: wafer-thin sheets curtly typed, and (she squints) are these messages about the local school? Jay didn't know there was a local school. And yet each letter carefully preserved in date order: 12 September, 27 September, 3 October. She digs deeper, her fingers reaching the sharp edge of a photograph. Women lined up in front of the chapel: pelmet skirts and thick plastic glasses, each face as dour as the one before it. *Mothers' Fun Day 1979*, someone has written out in stilted script on the back of the picture. It looks anything but fun.

Jay brings the photo up close to her face, the torch wavering precariously beneath her chin. She is so close that her breath fogs the ancient photo paper. Names, too, written out here. Marjorie, Maryanne, Heather – she gasps, for it is Heather, staring back at her, sad and sepia and so much younger.

Already the beginnings of those hollows in her cheeks, that fierce, guarded look around her eyes.

'Jay?'

Simon's voice makes her jump out of her skin, heart hammering against her breastbone.

'What are you doing up there?'

'Just looking,' she lies.

'Why don't you look in our boxes instead?' he asks, a flinty edge to his voice.

She stashes the photo under her jumper, returning to the light well and the ladder.

'I'll look where I like, thank you.'

'We're living in a sea of cardboard. You're so busy with your head in the past, you've hardly touched a thing—'

'I have!'

'Tipping things out on to the floor doesn't count.' Finally, weeks of bitterness are finding their voice. 'Why drag your boxes over to this house if you're just going to leave them festering?'

She slips the last two rungs of the ladder, its thick metal clanging into her side. She struggles for breath, unwilling to admit that it hurt. Not that Simon seems to have noticed.

'Where has this come from?'

'I'm just saying, there's enough stuff to do without you clambering around up there.'

'I'll clamber wherever the hell I want to, Simon.'

'And what about your studio?'

'What about it?'

'Well,' he blusters, slamming down the stairs, 'why are we going to all this trouble to build it, why am I designing it, if you're not even going to use it?'

'I am not going to apologise to you for ghosts and bodies, Simon!'

'I'm not asking you to!'

'Well what are you asking of me? Always something!' She's

shouting now, and there is something brutal and good about spitting these words into the suffocating air. 'You're always there! Always watching me, always wanting something!'

He turns and walks away, but she is too far gone now.

'I'm sorry, Simon, if this isn't your idea of the idyllic family home! Not that we're the idyllic family to begin with!'

He wheels around. 'Don't put that on me.'

'No, I know, I know perfectly well that the lack of children is my fault.'

'The lack . . .' Simon splutters, unable to get the words out. 'You never even asked if I wanted them! You never even mentioned that you did!'

'I don't know if I did!'

'Then why the hell are we fighting about it? Why the hell are we here?'

'You just, I can't . . .' She teeters on the brink of losing it, of losing all the thousands of things her raging mind wants to throw at him, just for the sake of it, just by dint of having ammunition. 'You just want me to create all the time, to make things to entertain you, to provide some kind of endless enlightenment!'

He slams his fist down on the kitchen table. 'This suffering artist bit has really got old Jay, you know that?'

For once it is Simon who grabs his coat and slams out on to the dark hillside.

They never argue, not like this. Silences and heavy sighs, things oh-so-pointedly unsaid – that has been their way, not violent words thrown out into the frigid air; anger, frustration and need made heavy, thick as ice, great sheets and floes around which they now must navigate.

Simon stomps down to the road. He is shaking, though he cannot tell if it is with cold or anger, or both. Overhead, the stars whirl in their firmament and he would pause to watch them, were it not for the crow cawing menacingly from the dark trees behind him, the sound of branches creaking in the wind, and, suddenly, footsteps coming up behind it.

It's Jay. He knows it, doesn't need to turn around to see her. The unthinkable has happened and they have fought, and she has come down from the house to fetch him, to apologise. She, for once, has dismounted her high horse. Secretly pleased, Simon leans back against the wall, waiting for the tap on his shoulder.

It doesn't come. Instead, something rustles in the under-growth. A creature – rabbit? Vole? – shoots across the road, knocking the breath out of him.

'Jay?'

He turns now, but in the dark there is no one, nothing, to be seen, just the steep land leading up to the main house, where an uncurtained window spills out its light. Shivers convulse down Simon's back. He heard it, he absolutely heard it. *Heard what?* he tries to reason with himself, but his heart overtakes him. Again, there is footfall, someone walking close by him but he does not wait to see who it might be. Who knows what spirits are walking on a night like this? Tripping, trembling, he rushes back to the house, his mind making ghouls out of the country air.

They set up camp on opposite sides of the living room. Jay curled in a chair in front of the fire, poring secretively over her attic finds. Simon, his teeth chattering, at the table with the laptop whose light casts no warmth. Bella knows that something is wrong; looks from one to the other, wiggles her eyebrows. The house settles into silence, slipping back into its long years of hush like muscle memory; easy, auto-matic.

In bed, cold air fills the space between them, and Simon, clinging to the edge of the mattress, feels like one of the Two Houses, drifting away from its other half in the night.

42

Morning comes, grey and drizzly, as if the skies know that they are arguing. In the middle of the living room, Jay plants her hands on her hips.

'Where are my things?'

'What?' Simon looks up from his laptop and his mug of coffee, extra strong this morning.

'My things.' She gestures at the bare floor in front of the fireplace. 'The things I was reading here.' *The things I lugged down from the attic*, she adds silently, *while you were making your grand gesture standing out in the cold.*

'I haven't touched them.'

'Yeah, right.'

Jay storms out of the living room and up the grand turning staircase. In one of the empty bedrooms, she finds what she is looking for, along with the books she borrowed from the library. The books, her notes – but they have been ruffled, rifled through. The photo album is missing. Back in the living room – the room in which they live because it is one of the only rooms they have furnished – she confronts Simon.

'There are things missing.'

'What?'

'Things missing, from my books, my papers.' She dances warily around what it is, exactly, that has been lost. 'I've found where you put them. I just want the other things back.'

'I haven't touched anything.'

'Bullshit!'

She can feel the furrow in her brow, the blood pumping in her chest. Those were *her* things, these are *her* secrets. She is the one guarding them. Simon, his cheeks reddening, scrapes back his chair.

'If you're going to be like that,' in his most devastating, clipped, professional voice, 'I would appreciate it if you didn't move *my* things. My *work*.'

She sees the cheap pleasure he takes in emphasising *work*.

'I haven't touched your stuff. Why would I be interested in your *work*, Simon?'

'Oh yes, I forgot. Real jobs are so boring when you're a creative artist.'

Wordlessly, she leaves him.

Tramping her way across sodden fields, she meets Tom on the outskirts of the village, looking down from the bridge that takes the road over the river.

'It's high,' he says, by way of greeting.

'Higher than usual?'

He shrugs. 'Won't be good if it gets much higher.'

'Does that happen? Does it flood here?'

Tom pushes back off the bridge's stone slabs, wiping chalky sediment from his hands.

'Has done. Might do.' He stares at her, eyes guarded, as if he wants to keep her, too, at arm's length.

'I'd like to see the farmhouse.'

For once, he does not correct the term. He nods, and they walk silently into the village to his car.

They do not say much as the car winds its way up the rough-shod road towards the isolated farmhouse. Tom concentrates on the road, Jay concentrates on looking out of the window. Soon, the village is just a grey cluster of roofs set amid the enormity of the valley's head, its hillsides moss and pewter beneath the clouds.

'Must be hard,' Tom says eventually, as they rattle over a cattle grid, 'for you to see what we see in it up here.'

'I don't think that's hard.'

She thinks back to those early exhibitions, the Chelsea shows. Podge in floods of tears because someone had mocked his work within his earshot. Callous – no, *careless* – visitors wandering idly up and down the aisles, not knowing that their jokes, their mockery, were audible. It happened less, later. Her own exhibitions had been blessed with a good response, but even then you caught the sliver of critique, the whispers between old women. *But what is it? What's the point?*

'Is that so?' Tom raises his eyebrows.

'Yes. Plenty of people come to my exhibitions and don't see what I see in it. The work, I mean.'

Tom nods slowly. 'Fair enough.'

'You might, when I showed it to you, have wondered why on earth I'd bothered.'

'I didn't.'

He pulls the car up into the yard. The farm is long and low, its stone almost black with age. Jay feels a shiver of trepidation as she steps out into the blustery air. There is no shelter up here, nothing to blunt the wind's force, and she is nearly knocked over by the ferocity of it, falling back against the car door. Tom looks as if he might be stifling a laugh.

Above the howl of the wind, he points behind her and says: 'Don't fall off the edge.'

Sure enough, a few metres beyond where she stands the ground seems to just fall away; a rocky escarpment plummeting beneath them. Below, the village, the whole dale stretching out before them.

'They call it dale head, up here. Head of the dale.'

Swearing beneath her breath, Jay hurries away from the edge and towards the house.

As the door slams shut behind them, the wind's roar is quieted to a kind of consumptive breath.

It is dark inside, the air close. It takes a few moments for Jay's eyes to adjust, to make shapes out of the murk in front of her. Smell comes before sight, a wave of mould and earth sharp enough to graze the insides of her nostrils. Cat pee and food gone bad, then thick, cloying clouds of pipe smoke. Faintly, somewhere, gas, and by the time she has identified all these different assaults on her senses, Tom has guided her into the kitchen.

Jay struggles not to say something. Struggles, too, with what is clearly a horrified silence. But if they thought Two Houses was bad before they moved in, this is another world. She did not know that people lived like this; she could not have imagined people living like this.

Wallpaper hangs like curtains from the walls. In some places, the plaster beneath blooms with damp – green and blue – while in others it has crumbled away to bare stone. The floor beneath her feet is filthy, thick with grime, and overhead loose wires are slung like fairy lights across the low ceiling. The table is covered with dirty plates and papers, odds and ends of farm machinery, and among it all, over by the gas cooker, is an old man on a battered armchair, wires and stuffing falling out on to a rag rug beneath his feet, looking at the air above her.

'Jay, this is my dad, Ned. Da, this is Jay.'

Ned nods.

'I told you about her,' Tom continues. 'She's moved in down at Two Houses.'

'Oh aye,' Ned murmurs, pipe clamped between his teeth. Jay wishes she could meet the cloudy eyes with her own, but his are fixed firmly on the wall behind her.

'Hello,' she says finally, making as if to shake his hand and then wishing that she had not as she ineptly navigates the various obstacles in her way. Ned's hand is hard and cold. It makes her think of the hillside. The decades he must have spent out there working on it.

She tries to fill the silence.

'Tom's been very kind to us. He let us stay with him at the

pub, after . . . well, after we had a problem at Two Houses and . . .' *Why, why are you prattling on?* she thinks to herself, desperate to stem this tide of words escaping pointlessly from her mouth. She stutters about how grateful they are, how comfortable the pub is, before faltering to an uneasy halt.

For long moments, Ned and Tom keep their counsel. Like father like son. Jay's eyes range over the hearth, whose long black mantle is decked with faded ribbons, horse buckles rusted into nothingness, and a few photographs, frameless, leaning against them. One is a double portrait, and she strains her eyes to try and see the faces.

'I'll wait in the car,' Tom announces, leaving the house as fast as the wind slams into it. In the fresh silence, his father seems to find his voice.

'Bad place, Two Houses.' He smacks his gums together. He only has two or three teeth, as far as Jay can see.

'Everyone says that.'

'Bad things happen.'

Inching closer to the hearth and the photographs on top of it, Jay is emboldened. 'Why do they say that? What things happened?'

Ned tries to whistle through the gaps in his teeth, but with a mouth more gap than tooth, it comes out as a strange gurgle.

'Wasn't always like this,' he murmurs.

'Pardon?'

'This.' He gestures, arthritic and angular, at the room around him. 'Wasn't always like this. But place has memory. Unhappy things stay, places stay unhappy.'

Jay feels her brain rattling around inside her skull, trying to wrap itself around this statement. 'Like Two Houses, you mean?' she asks cautiously.

'Aye.'

'And this place?'

'Aye.'

208

'What happened?' she asks again, but Ned has turned his milky eyes away. They flicker for a moment, as if watching figures from a past to which she is not privy. Finally, they alight on the photographs on the mantelpiece.

'My wife.' He raises a trembling arm and points.

Jay follows his gaze towards the photograph. Like the others, it is unframed, leaning wonkily on its curled edges. The woman is square and heavyset, the corners of her chin forming almost perfect right angles. Perhaps the sun was shining when she posed for this; her forehead is scrunched into a frown, her eyes narrowed to serpentine slits. 'She looks nice,' Jay says, though the woman looks anything but nice. 'Is that Tom and Jacob's mother?'

'No. My second wife. Maryanne.'

And a tingle of something runs along Jay's spine. Hasn't she read the name Maryanne recently? In those letters? On the photographs from the attic?

Ned sighs. 'Been a long time now. Can't make folk happy. My Tom's learning that.'

'Yes,' Jay agrees, without knowing quite what she is agreeing to. 'Well,' she makes to head back to the door, 'it was nice to meet you.'

'Lot of secrets,' Ned sighs. 'Lot of pain.'

He stands, joints creaking in protest, and shuffles off to another part of the house. Almost without thinking, Jay's fingers snatch the photograph, stuffing it in her pocket as she leaves.

43

Heather hauls herself up the side of Usha Top, her lungs squeezing like concertinas, her breath ragged and puffing with the effort like the ancient accordion that used, when she was a girl, to be lugged by travelling Irishmen around the dale's pubs.

'Penny for a tune, lassie,' and the wheezing would start up again, man and instrument, as they kept their side of the bargain.

Heather steadies herself against the stone wall that lines the road. A faint dizziness has set in like a misty rain, barely perceptible above the rushing of her blood.

She did not bring Joss with her today. Their night-time walks have tired the old girl out. She lay resolutely slumped on her blanket, not even lifting her chin from her neatly crossed paws.

'Alright Jossy, I'll see you later.'

Jackie would be furious if she knew about the night walks. Jackie's furious about most things these days, Heather finds. Every time they talk it's something new. No signal on her mobile, the price of food, the fact they can't get the new Sky box up here. Migrants, refugees, the wrong contestant voted off last Saturday night, nothing good to watch on telly. Heather is amazed at the tirades that spill forth from Jackie's nineteen-to-the-dozen mouth.

The whole world is angry, Heather thinks. Angry men on the news; angry voters in America, Germany, France. Protests down near Dover and up in Glasgow. And where will it go, she wonders, this anger? In her experience, anger usually has to find a target.

She knows only too well, beyond that initial burst of outrage, the kinds of things that Jackie would say to her. *Irresponsible. At your age. Out in the wet and the dark. What if you died? What if you fell? We can't be coming up here every day to look after you, Mam; how many times do I have to tell you?*

Heather hasn't seen many people grow old. Her parents' generation died young, much younger than she is now. And her contemporaries. Gone, or dead and gone. Jennifer and her lazy eye. Annie Binkley and the two sets of twins, grown into two sets of strapping men, off to work the collieries and the boats. Harry, taken too young, and the tears smart if she thinks of Elsie, poor battered Elsie, her baby sister.

Hands on her thighs, head bowed in an effort to regain breath, to hold back tears, Heather hears Jackie's voice shouting at her for being so daft, overstretching herself. And Heather knows – in her bones, her waters, however it is that we divine these unshakeable truths – that Jackie would not ask why. *Why* she has taken to the hills, at night, in the day. What *kind* of preparation this is, so different from the neat little pills she counts up over and over. What exactly it is that she is preparing herself for.

Above the persistent rumble of the wind, Heather hears a car approaching. Instinctively, she ducks behind an opening in the wall, the gap where once a gate stood. *No need for gates now*, she remarks sadly, as Tom does every time he drives past. And it is Tom, thundering down the track, and the woman from Two Houses sat next to him. In the split second in which they pass her, unseeing, Heather thinks she sees sorrow on their faces; severity, silence.

'I wonder . . .' she says to the dusty air.

'Mam!'

Her child fingers tug at her mother's apron.

'Mam, I don't want to go!'

The kitchen. Their cottage. The smell of grease and blacking. Her mother dusts off her hands, flour falling as snow onto Heather's face, dusty and tasteless to her tongue.

'We've got to go, duck.'

Folding the apron over the back of the rocking chair. Smoothing her hair down in the small, clouded mirror, too high for Heather's gaze to reach.

'Stop fussing, woman.'

Her father, in the doorway, the dark stain of his presence creeping over the kitchen. The 'fussing' left bits of flour in her mother's hair, but you couldn't really tell among the strands of what her mother called salt and pepper. Heather remembers tasting a strand of it once, quietly, while her mother was dozing. It tasted nothing like salt.

Bundled up in scarves and hats, Richard's nose dribbling as always, Elsie picking at the scabs on her knees, they step outside. Other families, too, appearing on their doorsteps, emerging into this biting winter morning.

'Look,' someone says, pointing up at the fellside. 'It's coming.'

And sure enough, at her eyes' farthest reach, the pony and trap come into view. Two figures sat up front, other stick people walking behind. On the trap, a dark wooden box.

'Mam, Mam.' Tugging at her mother's arm again, pulling on her skirt. Heather needs to go, badly, and it's so cold that the hot release of it between her legs would almost be worth it on this icy day.

'They'll be lucky if they don't turn over,' a neighbour says.

'Mam, I've got to go.'

'You can't go, love. We're to stand here, pay our respects.'

'Respects to who?'

'To old Mr Outhwaite.'

'But where is he? I can't see Mr Outhwaite.'

Richard points at the procession. 'He's in the box, silly.'

'Why's he in the box?'

'Because chapels don't have graveyards, stupid. They're taking him down dale to graveyard.'

Above them, their father growls. 'I'll be taking you both down dale if you don't button it.'

They do button it. It is an eternity of squirming, of pressing her legs together as tightly as she can, before the sad group finally arrives. The men remove their hats as the trap approaches. Heather still can't see old Mr Outhwaite, but she sees Ned on his mother's knee at the front of the trap. She waves.

''*Llo*, Heather.'

Jacob's greeting sends her tumbling backwards against the stonework.

'Oh, Jacob, you gave me a fright.'

'Sorry.'

'Don't be sorry, lad. I was away with the fairies.'

Jacob looks down on the valley below them. 'I saw the car,' he says.

'Yes, me too.'

'Why's he bringing her up to the farm?'

Heather doesn't know. 'I don't know, Jacob.'

And suddenly she remembers him as a lad. Little Jacob. Jackie, of course, full of teasing about his slanted shoulders, his *particular* way of being. It wasn't his fault, poor lamb, not having a mother. Living up on that farm, all three of them, Ned no good on his own. And then the years of Maryanne, the years of farms failing and no one having a bean to rub together. Heather shakes herself, tries to rid her mind of the memories that flash and dance before it. It wasn't his fault, poor Jacob.

'I been doing the wall at Two Houses.'

She tries to smile, but it is a weak attempt. 'That's nice.'

'Fifty quid they give me.'

'Gosh, that's very good.'

He shakes his head, eyes tightly shut, and Heather does not think it is just the wind that makes them so.

'I don't want them here.'

Tears smart in Heather's eyes.

'Oh Jacob . . .' She reaches out to pat his arm, forgetting until he flinches that Jacob does not care for touch; that the proximity of others is worse for him than loneliness. When she herself has spent so many nights alone, so many lonely nights, trying with everything she can – the dog, the dictionary, the radio – to fill them, it is hard to think that there are others who need that cocoon. Need space and air to be.

'Some things should be left as they are,' he says again, moving from her.

And is there truth in that, she wonders, looking down at her own, trembling hands. Should some things be left as they are? She has no answers for him, this young man who isn't young any more, yet who seems too fragile for the truths of the world. Sighing, she invites him to join her, and they walk a ways back towards the village together.

44

Why did you do that, Jay asks herself, *why did you do that?*
She's not a thief, not light-fingered; her whole world is based
on the importance of touch, of making and moulding, and
how can you do that if your fingers slip so easily into someone
else's pocket? To steal an object is not far off stealing an idea;
worse, perhaps, because who is she to say that Mr Outhwaite
with his cloudy eyes and empty gums doesn't while away his
hours staring at that photograph, at the image of a lost wife?
Twice widowed, Tom told her. *Why, why, why did you do that?*

The drive back is excruciating in its silence, the photograph
burning a hole in her pocket, her breath unnaturally high and
fluttering in her throat. And Tom, Tom looking away from
her as much as he can. The occasional flash of his moorgrass
eyes. Tom who invited her into that house, embarrassed
though he was by its decrepitude; Tom who came to her, who
she let look at her work; Tom who seems in his silence to see
exactly what she's done and to find it utterly, unspeakably
predictable.

Down the fell they hurtle, through the gates that hang open
like slack jaws, around the tiny swirl of village, along the
single street, over the river, full to bursting. A flash of black
and white as a magpie dives off the road in front of them,
and Jay's cheeks flush to remember the childhood stories of
the greedy magpie, stealing silvered, shiny things to keep in
its nest. *Jay-bird, my Jay-bird*, Simon calls her, but maybe
there is more of the mag in her; hopping along, stealing
objects and secrets and histories that do not belong to her,
guarding them jealously against her cold heart. Her breath

rises, and Tom's breath, too, is jittering now, as uneven as the raindrops that the wind spatters onto the windscreen.

Eventually she says, 'Thank you, for taking me.'

Tom nods.

'Has he . . .' She can feel the photograph against her thigh as if it is still dripping wet with the chemicals that developed it, hot and corrosive against jean and skin. 'Is it a long time he's been alone?'

She can almost feel Tom's skin bristle.

'Since my stepmother died. Left him and died shortly after, we were told. Long time now.'

It is Jay's turn to nod, slowly, knowingly, as if she might be able to coax his secrets out across the frigid air between them.

'I never had a stepmother.'

'Lucky you.'

'I wouldn't say lucky. I was twelve when my mother died.'

'Twelve.' Tom whistles below his breath. 'That's twice as long as I got with mine.'

'It's not a competition.'

'You made it one.'

'How did she die, your mother?'

'In childbirth. With Jacob. That's why . . . why he's the way he is.'

'How quickly did your father remarry?'

'You're not inquisitive, are you?' Tom runs his hand over his stubble. 'Quickly, alright, he remarried quickly. He couldn't look after the farm and two little ones, not on his own. He remarried out of need; convenience, you'd call it. Not a very nice woman. Couldn't have kids of her own. Didn't like other people's –' Jay raises an eyebrow against the sting of this accusation '– which is funny for someone who spent her time with children. Not much else to it.'

They are out on the road to Two Houses now, leaving the last dregs of village behind. Tom points at a solemn, ramshackle building at the side of the road.

'Old schoolhouse.'

It is a small, squat little thing. With its naked roof, stripped of its slates, and windows half boarded, half broken, Jay had not distinguished it from the other dilapidated barns and houses.

'I didn't know there was a school.'

'Well, there was.'

'Do you know where they all went?' she asks, thinking of all the faces that once peopled this place.

'Some.'

She waits.

'Some went up to the rigs. Some to town. Or they had family some place, or they got themselves rehoused on some estate somewhere. The rest, god only knows. Just upped and left.'

'They didn't keep in touch?'

He snorts, the strong line of his jaw stiffening. 'No. Because it hurts to have to leave. Folk didn't keep in touch, didn't come back to visit.'

'And your stepmother?'

'Upped and left like the rest of them. Like the Martins who got thrown off their farm without a stick of furniture, or them at Top Riding couldn't keep up their repayments. Or Heather's sister, got walloped one too many times, or old Binkley, took to the drink and never came back.'

Tom swings the car abruptly up into the driveway at Two Houses. For a moment, they are still. These are strange intimacies that have passed between them, with his father at the farmhouse, with her work at Two Houses. Jay does not want to move: she is teetering on ice as thin as paper, the web spun between them as fragile as a gossamer thread, and to open the door, thank him, walk away, will risk breaking it.

In the end, she does not have to, for it is Tom's face that clouds over, his hand that reaches first for the door.

'What the . . .'

He is out of the car, and she follows him, scrambling up the last steep bit of drive to the main house. Nearing it, she sees what he has seen. Across their windows, strings of dead creatures have been hung. A parody of festive garlands, their lifeless bodies tremble in the breeze, some long-blackened, some twisted, others fresh and dripping blood.

'Oh god.' Her hands fly up to her mouth, pushing back the horror that convulses in her stomach. She is bent over, her insides cramping.

'Jesus.'

Tom is already at the window, trying to loose the knots that have fixed these little monstrosities in place.

'What are they?'

'Moles.'

'What?'

'Moles. You know, little furry things, dig up earth.' He has succeeded, and one string of dead bodies slumps onto the windowsill. 'Farmers don't like them. Make holes in the ground, cattle get their legs caught, get injured. So they used to string 'em up. A warning to their friends.'

'But . . .' The wind whips at Jay's hair, whips at the limp corpses in front of her. 'But why? Why here?'

Tom looks at her, the corners of his mouth downturned. 'I'd say someone wants you to stop digging.'

Behind them, the door opens. Simon, in spectacles and slippers, scowling out at them.

'What's going on?'

'Someone . . .' Jay doesn't know how to form the sentence. 'Someone's put these here.'

Simon steps forward before recoiling back again. 'Christ alight.' His face turns ashen. 'But I've been here, all morning. Sat here all morning looking out the window. I saw nothing.'

For a moment they are frozen, two men and a woman stood on an empty hillside. The crow calls hungrily from his perch in the tree, as rusty blood drips onto the stonework.

Filth. Rot. Misery.

45

'Dad?'

'Hi, Zo.'

An edge of worry in her voice. 'Is everything OK? I'm at school.'

'Yes, sorry, I . . .' Tom, pulled over at the side of the road, in the opening of what was once Cockett's lower pastures, when Cockett was still farming, leans his head back against the headrest. The farm, the visit, the horror in Jay's face. Those critters strung up and rotting, and he still has the smell of decay on his hands. 'I just wanted to hear you, is all.'

'Yeah?' His girl, not so little any more, sounds unconvinced.

'Sorry to interrupt. What class is it?'

'Maths.'

'You don't like maths.'

'Hate it.'

'I'll keep talking then.'

She relents, offering him a half-hearted, dad-joke chuckle. Tom looks at the clock on the dashboard. Forty minutes to his appointment.

'Zo.'

'I knew something was wrong.'

That same tone of voice as when they told her they were splitting, small, deflated.

'It's not that anything's wrong, love.'

'But?'

How to say this? How to make his mouth form the words that he cannot bear to think about? 'Has your mam said anything about Mike?'

Stony silence, just the wind rocking the car, whistling through the gap where the window doesn't close properly.

'Zo?'

'Said he'd got a job somewhere.'

'Scotland?'

'Yeah.'

Tom squeezes his eyes tightly shut, though it doesn't stop the hot creep of something wet around the edges.

'Do you want to go?'

'Not really.' He can hear her fiddling with something, her hair, the bracelets on her wrists, perhaps. 'My friends are here. You're here.'

'I am.' Wiping his eyes with the back of his hand. 'I am. Look, Zo, your mam can't make you go, legally can't take you, I'm sure of that. I won't let that happen.'

'OK.' That small, scared voice again.

'OK, good.'

A car approaches, slows as it sees him on the empty road. It is John, belly wedged behind the steering wheel. He waves, gestures. *You need help?* Tom waves him on, and soon he is alone again, just his daughter's breathing at the other end of the phone. He remembers her when she was tiny, how loud her breath was then, especially in sleep. They were comforting, the snorts and rustles of it, telling him that she was alright.

'You'd better get back to maths.'

'OK.'

'Zo?'

'Yeah, Dad?'

'Love you.'

'Love you too,' she mumbles, hanging up the phone and leaving him to the grey and empty landscape.

Down the dale, Tom sits in the shabby waiting area at the solicitor's office. More cardboard boxes litter the floor than usual, more teetering piles of cream paper. The clock above him ticks slowly on, rain taps against the grimy window, and it is a while before Helen – six feet tall, ruddy-faced, white-haired – comes out to meet him.

'How do, Tom?' She claps a hand on his shoulder and Tom can't understand how someone of her stature has spent her life cooped up in this paper prison.

'Alright, Helen.'

'You're not though, are you? Else you wouldn't be coming to see me.'

She ushers him into her office, where he can just make out the outline of a desk beneath mountains of paperwork. She clears a way for him, sweeps thick buff folders off a chair so that he has somewhere to sit. At his feet there is a binbag full of shredded paper.

'Having a clear-out?'

He wants, in some perverse way, to delay their conversation as much as possible.

Helen drops forcefully into her seat. 'I'm clearing out. Clearing off. Giving the whole thing up.'

'Retiring?' Tom asks, wide-eyed.

'That's the one.' Helen runs a hand across her chin. 'Had enough, Tom. Enough of paperwork and people's problems. Not yours, mind. I'm off somewhere new. But any road,' she leans forward now, like a strict headmistress, 'what's your business, Tom Outhwaite?'

And finally, there's no more avoiding it.

'Lisa's new man.'

'Aye?'

'Got a job in Scotland, up on the rigs. She wants to go with him. Wants . . .' his throat tightens until he can hardly get the words out '. . . wants to take Zoe with her.'

'She can't.'

'That's what I said.'

'Legally, she can't. Joint custody. She's bound by that, and there's no moving a child without due process.'

Tom looks down at his hands. Softer now, since the farm went. 'I'm worried she's going to go anyway.'

Helen takes this in for a second.

'Look, I know you Tom, and I know Lisa. Knew her at least. I'd be lying if I didn't tell you I think she's a flight risk.'

'Flight risk?'

'Flight risk – risk that she just ups and goes, does it anyway, to hell with the consequences.'

His stomach shrinks into itself, his mouth turns to desert. 'So what do I do?'

'Nothing.'

'What?'

'You can't do anything, pet, not until she tries it.'

'But how . . . if she goes . . . what if I can't find them, what if I can't get Zoe back?'

'Listen, don't panic.' Helen is up again now, clapping her great manly hand down on his shoulder again. 'I don't think it'll happen. She's not daft, Lisa, however much she likes the new fella. But you keep an eye out, ear to the ground, anything odd that Zoe says, anything changing in her behaviour. You tell me. And we'll go from there, right?'

She doesn't let him pay, and Tom emerges dazed into the wet afternoon, light-headed, as if the world has become yet more uncertain underfoot. He drives out of town, up the Nelder road, trying to breathe normally, trying to replay Helen's advice in his head.

But all he can see are the birds overhead: waxwings, winter visitors, swooping down into the hedgerows; the last geese trailing V-shaped towards a warmer south. In the distance, he sees the familiar speck of a buzzard soaring high and ominous above the tops, and his heart beats faster, echoing the way she said *flight risk* in his mind.

46

That night, the winter birds go to roost, but there is a murmur of discontent beating around their feathered hearts. Something more than wind or rain ruffling their breasts. Up at the farm Ned Outhwaite can taste the change on the air, and on television newscasters begin to talk of a storm approaching. There are charts and maps and hastily thrown together animations, meteorologists scrambling for suit jackets and puffing out their chests. In layman's terms, there's big rain coming.

Angela ignores their warnings, flitting instead from channel to channel until boredom drives her to her bed. By day, she keeps what watch she can over the comings and goings; by night, she seethes. The blood boils in her as she plays over the same events in her mind. Tom and Jay; Heather and her snarky ways; but most of all – most vividly – that bloody Dev in the corner of the restaurant, the way he looked at her. *Her dress shop. Of course.* Tossing sleepless beneath the blankets, Angela stews.

'You're in a right stew,' her mother used to say, hand on her ample hip, cigarette dangling from one corner of her mouth. She used to stew apples in autumn, Mother did. Angela and her brothers would be sent out to gather them up, as many as they could. Hours spent peeling them at the kitchen table, digging the worms out, trying to skin the whole fruit in one, unbroken corkscrew of peel, and she'd be made to do it most, because *boys will be boys, Angela, and they don't enjoy that sort of thing.* Angela hates anything like that now; apple crumble, apple pie. Always, always, it seems to her now, a pot on their stove growing up, her mother stirring the sugar in, waiting to turn hard fruit into mush.

Angela stews, yes, but where the apples in her mother's pan got softer, their sickly sweet scent drifting throughout the cottage, Angela feels herself getting harder. In bed at night, her teeth grind together. It is an effort to unclench her fists, to loose her jaw.

The scene in the restaurant runs on a loop in her brain. It's like those Saturday night things on telly, where you watch someone slip on a banana skin once and then they slow it down so you get each jolting millisecond of the shock, the fall, the juddering impact. As a teenager, Angela would creep downstairs at night. She never liked her brothers, was never allowed to watch what she wanted when they were in the house. But late at night into the early hours, with the sound off, the glare of the screen burning her eyeballs and her teeth chattering with cold, she'd sit in front of the television, winding her videotapes through to the final scenes of her favourite films, where the girl runs into the boy's arms, where they kiss passionately in front of a setting sun. A romantic, Angela. Always a romantic.

She learned early the importance of being pretty. It was always the pretty girl who got the boy, not the women like her mother who sat on the sofa and let themselves go, fat and ugly while their men laughed down the pub with the pretty girls. 'I like 'em pretty,' her father would say, through a mouth of beer and rotten teeth. 'You're so pretty, Angela.' And she liked the compliment, even when she knew that he kept his hands on her for too long.

Although she doesn't get out of bed now, although the scenes she's watching fill her with nothing like the thrill she got from those romantic comedies, she feels like she's a teenager again, her finger glued to the video player buttons: pause, rewind, pause, rewind. Dev and his stupid hamster face. The way his eyes bulged at her. *Her dress shop. Of course.* She can hardly remember what Kevin looked like now, but that look of Dev's is ingrained in her memory. Angela counts down the long minutes to morning, plotting ways to make him pay.

Steven and Declan haven't noticed any change in their mother, small though their cottage is. They are teenagers – thirteen and fifteen respectively – passing their days in a fug of hormones. There are embarrassing surges (on their faces, in their trousers) and it's enough to get through a mind-numbing day of classes and fix their gaze on a football match or video game.

They had been seeing their father every few months, but last time he turned up drunk with his motorbike outside the school gates. Declan thought it was cool that he yelled *You can fuck right off* to the headmaster, but Steven was embarrassed. Later, he was embarrassed to be embarrassed, but their mam's said they can't see him any more any road so it doesn't really matter.

When they stay late, they get the school bus into town and slope across the market square to the chippie, heavy bags slung across their shoulders, shirt tails and shoelaces trailing behind them. It's part chip shop, part Chinese takeaway, and Declan always makes a point of glaring at the man who serves them.

'Fucking chink,' he says most days, as they step out onto the pavement with their bags of chips steaming in their hands. Today, Steven says it first, and Declan nods approvingly. A police car wheels slowly into the market square, crawling around the perimeter like a cat on the prowl.

'Dec . . .'

'What?' The reply comes through a mouthful of chips.

'What did they . . .' Steven nods at the car as it passes. 'Down at Two Houses . . .'

'Spit it out,' his brother says, spitting flecks of golden potato.

'Why does everyone care about it?'

Declan chews his chips thoughtfully. It's true. Everyone seems to be whispering about it. His mam. Shazza in the Co-op. The old men in the pub, the kids on the school bus, but they're pretty stupid in Declan's view and don't actually know anything. He knows that they found a body, but so what? Things like that turn up all the time. Cows died in the fields and that wasn't a problem. Mrs Hardy died in her house and it took a week for anyone to find her. And two years ago, bad weather washed seven drowned sheep off the fells so they got caught under the bridge in the village, just rotting there until Tom Outhwaite and Will White had to wade in and pull out their bloated corpses. Just before Will White left, that was. Left to find work someplace else, someplace better. Cows, sheep, old women – Declan can't see what's the fuss at Two Houses. But then, he reasons, some people get funny about death. When their dad's mam died he forced them to go to the funeral even though they didn't know her. Dec was furious; he'd had to miss a big football game at school, his chance to get picked for the county. Couldn't see what difference it made, the three of them sat there in that big empty crematorium.

'Dec?'

'Dunno. Probably to do with that fucking Paki.'

Steven nods. Their mam seems to blame most things on him.

Four o'clock and it is pitch night, but Angela honks the car's horn as she pulls up on the other side of the square for them. Quickly, they chuck the paper wrappings onto the pavement, smearing greasy palms along their trousers.

'You been eating chips again?'

'No.'

Angela rolls her eyes and they head out of town on the deserted village road. In the back seat, Steven presses his face against the window, its glass thick and cold against his forehead. He strains his eyes as they pass Two Houses. No police there now, just lights in the curtain-less windows, so the whole place leers out at him like a strange, misshapen face. He looks back until the road bends, and the light from the windows is hidden once again.

They eat dinner in silence in front of the telly. During an advert break, an Indian man walks onto the screen. Angela tests the water.

'I'm fed up of seeing those bloody faces.'

'Bloody Pakis,' Steven pipes up.

Angela nods. 'Disgraceful what he's been allowed to do up here. Criminal.'

Declan's absorbed in his mobile, but Steven's ears prick up. 'What's he been allowed to do?'

'Come up here, take our jobs. Why's he working in *our* library? Your brother's leaving school next year and chance'd be a fine thing, him finding work. What's a bloody immigrant doing with a job then, eh? Clear the plates, Stevie.'

Steven gathers up the dishes, mulling these things over in his mind.

'And that to-do at Two Houses,' Angela continues, lighting up. 'I'd bet this house on him having something to do with it.'

Declan pipes up. 'Thought they were Londoners, them lot?'

'One outsider's the same as another, Dec.' Angela looks her son in the eye, waves a warning finger at him. 'You better watch out, better watch yourself. He's a threat to you, he is. You boys better watch yourselves.' She stands, shaking crumbs and ash off her jumper. 'Right, I'm off to the pub.'

With that, Declan seizes the remote and turns on the football. Both boys turn to watch it, but there is an uneasiness that settles in the air between them, the beginnings of something that is more than just throwing insults.

47

The passing days do nothing to heal the divide at Two Houses. Jay and Simon pull away from each other, two sides of a wound whose cells refuse to knit together. Their fight hangs heavy and unspoken between them. London looms, too – she will not go, he will not ask her to – and all the while the house creaks with its histories, the secrets that only she is privy to.

Simon buries himself in his work. Jay slams dramatically from one house to the other, trailing clay and porcelain dust, a Milky Way of making in her wake. She has moved, with great ceremony, her wheel and boxes back to the other house. There, between the cold, ivy-clad walls that Jimbo hasn't worked on yet, with the green clouds of mould that creep across the ceiling, she is throwing work again, her pale face made ghostly by the chill and the way she wipes the dust across it.

Her papers, her books sit smack in the centre of the living room, burning a hole between them with their presence. They are pointedly untouched, their secrets quietly starving the room of oxygen. Outside, the first clouds of the storm roll in, dark and velvety, veined like marble. But without a television, in the silence that has grown between them that forbids either to turn on the radio, they do not know that it is coming.

In bed at night, in the blue hours, Simon's chest is so sore that even he – no poet, by nature – can convince himself that his heart is breaking. That it, like the houses, will crack and shear, tearing itself into two irreparable halves.

So lonely has Two Houses become, so inconsequential his

presence, that he seeks refuge in the metropolis. He doesn't strictly need to attend this meeting; it's only a follow-up now that they have won the bid. He has his computer up north, his drawings, his plans. God knows there are enough bedrooms here for him to have an office if he chooses. There is no reason to go, save the fact that Jay will scarcely notice his going. So, with bags packed, he walks out of the main house, past the windows that were strung with bloodied moles, past the space between the two houses, its earth raw with recent violence, and knocks on the door of the second house. Jay opens it, her face pale, bruised circles beneath her eyes.

'Can you drive me to the station?'

Without Simon watching over her, Jay lays out her finds across the whole living room. An attempt to bring order to madness, reason to chaos. Carefully she places the battered tin soldier on the wooden floor, the gold bracelet, the muddied jumper.

She turns to the box of papers she has hauled down. There are newspaper clippings, yellowed and moth-eaten, like antique lace. The old ink smudges beneath her fingers, but they tell stories of farms folding, no work since the mines closed, old houses falling into disrepair.

There are letters, too, on flimsy, official-looking paper. About the village school, which makes her think of Tom and the way he pointed it out to her. Notes from the School District Board to the Parish Council. A financial award here. A change in curriculum there. Why would anyone have kept these? Why would they have kept them here, in the dark, mouldering attic of an abandoned house? Jay's eyes rove quickly, hungrily across their pages, willing them to betray their secrets. It is a long time coming, but there is a hint of something in the neat rows of type. By the end of the 1970s, the letters grow more frequent. They talk of reports. Rumours. A letter of October 1982 notes receipt of a missive claiming that things have been exaggerated, but regretfully informs the

Parish Council that the village school will still be closing.

Beneath these, she finds photographs. Dozens of them, thrown in at strange angles, bent and broken after decades of holding these awkward shapes, some stuck together by time and damp so that she has to prise them apart. Photographs, like that of the Mothers' Fun Day. A church fête. A school fair. A prize cow and here, yes, Jay pulls them closer, photographs of people, too. She squints down at Heather, stood next to a young woman with the same sad eyes. Is this her sister? Beaten so many times, Tom said, that finally she went away. But the photographs are small, and blurry, and Jay can't tell a bruise in sepia. Still, after all these years, they hold their breath.

Then Jay spots it. A photograph larger than the rest, in a brown mount, embossed with gold letters: *Butterfield, Photography, Nelderdale*. Butterfield had evidently been brought in to photograph the school in its last years. Glum-mouthed, dark-eyed, the children stare out of the camera with wariness beyond their meagre years. Brightly coloured knitted jumpers; mauve and mustard corduroy, and the same grey-green fells rising up behind them in the distance. Jay's heart flutters against her ribcage to recognise Jacob, his eyes screwed up against the light. Tom's childhood face, staring solemnly out at her. A puff of white-blonde pigtails that must be Angela, and – she squints – is that the same woman standing next to them all as in her stolen photograph? Yes, that same wiry hair, the same tightly drawn, suspicious eyes – it is Maryanne, Tom's stepmother. The stepmother who did not like children. She stands proprietorial in front of them, the Class of 1982; their teacher.

Jay's heart beats faster. Maryanne was the schoolmistress. But she didn't like children, Tom told her that, just the other day Tom told her that. She scrabbles through another box, pulling at the remaining papers, ripping them even. Are these Maryanne's things? Why would they be here, at Two Houses, and not at the farm? Why, when all anyone can tell her is what a bad place this is, that bad things happened here, why would Maryanne's belongings have ended up, damp and forgotten, in an abandoned attic?

Her hands scrabble towards the bottom of the box. They find a school attendance book, inscribed in an elegant copperplate, as if of another time, another place. *Janet was a good girl. Bethany has learnt to sit in silence.* But this past is not quite the past. There are names she recognises here, and delicate little comments next to them. *Angela Metcalfe was made to wash her mouth out with soap. Jacob – twelve strikes for trouser-wetting. Thomas Outhwaite – given the standing stone.* A chill creeps across Jay's skin to read these names, these beautifully calligraphic punishments. Who would have wanted to keep these books, these litanies of punishment? Why would she have wanted to keep them? Why, next to report cards – *Daisy is a joy to teach* – and lavender-scented notecards, flower-trimmed and still faintly fragrant after all these years?

Jay has never been one for puzzles, clues, the piecing together of disparate pieces of information. It is Simon who adores crosswords, Simon who does Sudoku in the bath, who loves nothing better than to pull his brain apart in search of someone else's logic. And Simon is not here. She has not shared it with him. Bella slumps in front of the fireplace, her wet eyes an accusation that it is Jay who has driven him away.

'I'll be back in a minute, Bell,' she tells the dog as she pulls on her coat.

Already, the afternoon is dark. The sky hangs low, steely and scowling, as Jay digs her chin into her chest and sets out along the road against the wind. Her eyes smart, it is a battle to breathe against the force of air rushing down the dale towards her. She turns her head to snatch at breath, the wind banging against her ears, whipping the plastic of her jacket as she stumbles, as if drunk from the weather, along the road to the village.

There is a strange blankness in her mind. Like porcelain unglazed, paper unwritten. Like bone. Like the pale fields and the grey sky, and the rock faces that lour down on her from the hilltops. The schoolhouse. She has to go to the schoolhouse.

No cars pass as she wends her way. A few fat drops of rain begin to fall, a taster of what is to come. It is not long before, breathless, shaking, she reaches her target.

Pushing aside the scrubby weeds that have grown up in front of it, Jay peers in through a broken windowpane. The schoolhouse is a single empty room, void of any furniture or markings, just nettles growing in at the windows, mud and muck along the floors. The window frame beneath her fingers is rough with splinters, a single jagged nail sticking out of it, on which a wisp of white – sheep's wool? A bit of jumper? – is caught.

Jay inches along, over weeds and rocks and old forgotten beer bottles, towards the next window, wondering if she can get in, wondering if standing within these walls will tell her something, the way that the walls at Two Houses have.

Suddenly, out of nowhere, she feels a hand on her shoulder. She stumbles, screams, knowing even as she does so that the wind is roaring, that there is no one to hear her, no one to stop whoever it is behind her from delivering a swift smack of a spade to her head, like they did to the moles, like they did to the body at Two Houses for all she knows. Simon's face swims before her eyes as she cowers low against the stone wall, fists clenched, eyes screwed shut, until two large hands lift her upright again, and she hears Dev's voice through the rush of blood.

'Dev! Oh, it's you.'

'It's me, it's me,' he repeats, his green anorak swirling around him in the wind, his plump cheeks emerging from the tightly drawn hood. 'I've found something for you.'

She clutches him, and together they lurch out towards the road, towards Two Houses. And hundreds of miles away, away from the storm and the fear that courses through Jay's veins and the troubles that seethe beneath the surface at Two Houses, Simon, too, has somebody almost within his grasp. Caught up in this place and its histories, its sadnesses, its mysterious figures, Jay does not know that she peoples her dreams with the wrong ghosts. That there are spectres more real and more ominous than those she has thought of; that beyond the howling wind and the bitter rain, a storm is coming, and it is not the storm she thinks it is.

Ruin

48

'I love what you've done with the place,' Dev enthuses, bright-eyed, shaking the rain off his coat and on to the floorboards. He drove them up to Two Houses, but even the dash to and from the car has left them sodden. Dev's eyes rove around the living room. The wood is still bare underfoot, the plaster on the walls unpainted, but his eyes are wide as saucers as he takes in the sleek modern furniture, a mustard-coloured painting that Jay brought from London and has finally pulled from storage, a few bits of her finished porcelain dotted across the table. In his admiration, he turns a blind eye to the detritus on the floor, the papers and objects and photographs scattered in front of the fireplace.

'Please,' Jay gestures to the low armchair that Simon insists on calling mid-century modern; she calls it plain uncomfortable, and feels momentarily guilty to see Dev slip and slide on its peculiar, sloping angles. She pokes at the embers of the fire, adds a log to them, before sitting opposite him on the sofa, her heart in her throat.

'What did you find?'

'Well, there's lots of people who've left here.'

Her heart plummets. 'That's all? *Lots?* That's all you found?'

'I didn't say that was all,' Dev bristles. 'I've looked at the people who left – the *lots* of them' (he raises his eyebrows) 'and I've looked at where they've gone. Some to the big cities – Newcastle, Sheffield. Some to the town. Some, as far as I can tell, up to Scotland to work on the rigs, and one lot seem to have gone abroad.'

Jay can't hide her disappointment. It sits, bitter and rotten, in her mouth.

'But no one missing.'

'I didn't say that, either.'

For a moment, she cannot speak. The rain pummels the windows with the steady susurration of blood, the fire spits and cracks in front of them.

'Did you find her?'

'I don't want to say I found her . . .'

'But?'

'But there's only two women, as I can see, who leave here in those years who I can't find again. Anne Smith and Maryanne Outhwaite.'

Jay repeats the name in a whisper. 'Maryanne Outhwaite.'

'I know. She must be Tom's mum?'

'Stepmother. His father's second wife. But, but . . .' Jay tugs at her hair, an old trick when trying to concentrate '. . . there's another woman too, this Anne Smith? And what about Heather's sister? I've been looking at these old photographs,' she gathers a handful up, leafing through them, pointing too quickly at the faces for him to be able to see them. 'Tom said that she went off, too. What about her?'

'Listen,' Dev's voice is calm, steady. 'I found her. Elsie Dinsdale. She died, youngish, in a hospital in Berwick.'

'How do you find these things?'

He shrugs. 'Online. Electoral registers. Telephone directories. Obituaries in old newspapers. But,' leaning forward now, 'here's the thing. Anne Smith's a common name. I found dozens of them, after she'd have left the village, all over the country. She could have gone anywhere.'

The light is dawning, even as outside the sky darkens.

'But Maryanne Outhwaite . . .' Dev leaves the sentence hanging.

'. . . is a much more unusual name,' Jay finishes.

'Exactly. And I can't find a trace of her.'

'She left. Tom told me that. She left, they got word that she died.'

Dev raises his palms. 'I couldn't find her, but that's not to say—'

'Dev, these are her things,' Jay interrupts, looking down at the papers strewn in front of her. 'Her papers. She was the schoolteacher, and look, attendance books, report cards, things that must have belonged to the children.'

'Why are they here?'

'I don't know, I don't know. But if they are, and the body is—'

Dev shakes his head. 'That's not enough.'

'I know.' Jay runs her fingers along the creases of her forehead. 'Wait . . . is there a way, I don't know, a way to find out where someone was born? And when?'

'Well, the census, but each census is kept closed for a hundred years.'

'There's no other way?'

'Well, I mean . . .' Dev's brow furrows. 'We have the parish registers, at the library, in the archive. If it's someone born here, you could look there.'

They set off again, Jay's car following Dev's along the treacherous road, slick with water in the black night. Each drives in grim silence, teeth gritted against the slippery, sliding road, against the nagging fear of what they might find.

'I'm not sure we should be doing this,' Dev murmurs, unlocking the library door, switching on the lights, as Jay stamps her feet, an effort to bring some sensation back to her toes. The fluorescent lights flicker, and with each new gust of wind the bare branches of a tree crack ominously against the window.

'Here.' Dev sets down a pile of leather-bound books. 'What year, roughly?'

'I don't know.' She thinks back to the farm, to Ned

Outhwaite and his ancient, weathered face, impossible to age. She thinks of how old her own mother would have been. 'The forties? Thirties, maybe?'

There is only one volume for those years, and they pore over it together, heads almost touching as they skim the neatly written lines. Births, marriages, deaths; more deaths, it seems, than anything else.

'Wait, is that not—'

They see it at the same time. *Maryanne Brathwane*, born 26 June 1940. Jay's finger runs along the row of ink.

'Dev—'

'My god.'

'She was born at Two Houses.'

Two Houses, before they were two houses, because the book in front of them has *Hestle Hall* written out in painstakingly neat handwriting. Maryanne Brathwane, the child of Sir Edwin and Lady Isobel, christened on the 28th day of June, the year of the Lord 1940. The address given: Hestle Hall.

'But the stories.' Jay looks up at him. 'They mention the death of a son. A son dies, and that's why Isobel takes her life, *rumoured to have met demise by her own hand*. There's no mention of a daughter.'

She pulls the book towards her, flicks back and forth until she finds it. A second child, a second Edwin. A few years younger; only a few years living.

'So why . . .' She can't put words to it. 'Why does Isobel leave her daughter? Why is Maryanne left behind?'

Dev chews his lip. 'I don't know. But it's there, in black and white. Born at the Hall, at Two Houses.'

Jay pushes her chair back. 'We have to go to the police station.'

'Now?' Dev is incredulous.

'Yes, now!'

'You can't drive down to town in this, not now. It's Sunday night. Your detective won't be there.'

'Not even for murder? For the identity of a body?'

Dev puts his hand on her arm. 'Trust me, I've been here longer than you. Don't go on a Sunday night, you'll only make trouble. Go in the morning, catch him in office hours.' He glances at the window, which is glossy with the weight of water sliding down it. 'You sure you can get back in this?'

Jay nods, dumbly, the figures of Isobel and Maryanne swirling in her mind.

49

Far away, Simon is slipping back into a former self. It is Sunday, roast chicken and crispy potatoes thick on the air, and everyone they know is down the pub. The Rose and Crown, once a proper bar for Bermondsey wharfers and warehousemen; now the shabbily chic home of craft beers and bottles of Montepulciano.

'Look who it is! The prodigal son, returned home from the north.'

It is Podge, beckoning to Simon with open arms. Simon bolsters a wan smile.

'You alright, Podge?'

'You know, Simon, I'm *not*.'

'Let's get a drink.'

Simon had forgotten the exaggerated campness of Podge's gestures, the way he flings his hips from side to side and puts his hands on them to make a point of being outraged or flabbergasted. Simon buries his nose in his pint, drinks from it more quickly than he ought to.

'My dearest friend in all the world, vanished off the face of the earth! Disappeared without a trace!'

'She didn't call you, then?'

'No, she did not!'

'Oh.'

'Oh indeed!' Podge leans in more closely, dropping the show. 'Is she alright, Simon? Seriously? I know, I know, a change is as good as a break and all that, but I don't know that I buy that after a break*down*. Everyone's asking about her. *I've* been getting her calls, for goodness' sake!'

Bet you love that, Simon thinks darkly. Podge the gate-keeper, hanging on to the coat-tails of greatness.

'I don't know what to tell you, Podge.' The pub is warm, its lights golden against the outside gloom. There is the contented hum of a Sunday afternoon, laughter and glasses clinking, the final scrapes of spoons in pudding bowls. The beer has settled quickly, fizzily, in Simon's empty stomach and he wishes that he was one of these cheerful people polishing off a roast. 'She picked the house, she's the one who's refusing to leave it. She loves it up there. It's wild and rugged, it suits her, frankly, more than London ever did. I keep reminding her that it was only meant as a getaway, that our lives are down here, but . . .' He shrugs. 'I think, in her own way, she's happy.'

Podge narrows his eyes. 'Is she working?'

Simon tries to push the porcelain bones out of his mind's eye. 'Yes, she is.'

'You look like you're hiding something, Simon Wigmore.'

'I'm not, Podge, I promise.' Simon drains his pint. How cheap words come these days. 'I'll get her down eventually. Or . . .' He stops himself, realising he doesn't much fancy Podge coming to stay. 'I'll get her down.'

And with that he heads out into the dismal night.

Sunday night. The dregs of a weekend. Not the night to meet for dinner, but what else could he do? Simon saw her coming a mile away. In fact, he can replay with picture-perfect recall how George had bounded across the office on Friday after-noon, in the lull between real work and office drinks, to ask about his dinner plans.

'Oh, sorry, already booked in with friends,' Simon had lied, shuffling the papers on his desk to avoid looking at her glittering eyes, her dazzlingly white teeth. 'And tomorrow. You know how it is.'

'Sunday, then?'

And her smile, her smile – he'd had nothing to defend himself with, no lie ready at the tip of his tongue, even as he felt the danger of what he told himself was an unwilling acquiescence, the thrill dancing in the very pit of his stomach.

He'd not told her, of course, that he was not staying at home. That, unable to bear the thought of their half-empty house, he had checked into a rundown hotel near St Pancras, where the surly desk clerk informed him that the privilege of a window overlooking the train tracks required him to 'pay upgrade'. Simon didn't want to 'pay upgrade', so he'd sat in his boxers in a windowless room, eating a kebab in front of the television. He'd done that last night with a curry, too, not having the benefit of the fictitious plans he'd told her of. Finally he'd ended up googling Two Houses; idly searching online for Hestle Hall and its mysteries, before throwing his phone across the bed. Those are Jay's manias, hers the obsession with the past. He is an architect, someone who builds; he wants to look to the future.

Now, though, the future feels more precarious. He's done his duty, he's seen Podge, and he has only to cross a few streets to where George thinks he lives so that he can pretend he's popped round the corner to meet her for dinner.

But his mind is as blank, suddenly, as that northern hillside he's been staring at for two months. He can't quite remember the configuration of the streets. He takes a wrong turn, ends up down a dead-end, and when he finally arrives she is waiting for him with a strange look on her face.

'Hello, George.' He is unnaturally jolly. 'Everything OK?'

'Sure.'

Simon's face falls along with his heart. 'Really?'

'I went to the house, Simon. Your house.'

'Oh.'

It is a dull, bitter kind of night. Even down here the rain is falling, dribbling meanly onto the pavements, the wind biting. Premature Christmas lights blink feebly behind fogged-up windows. The familiar sense of gloom that comes with everyone heading home, readying for work tomorrow, chins dug deeply into collars. Simon's loneliness is, in that moment, magnified a hundredfold.

'Why didn't you tell me?' she asks gently.

'What,' he scoffs, 'that we're between two half-empty homes and I'd rather stay in some grotty shoe-box hotel than come back to my own house?'

'Dear me,' she smiles sadly, 'is it as bad as all that?'

And it's not, actually, because she is there, and smiling at him. Emboldened, he takes her arm.

'No, of course not. Forgive me – I'm an old fool who's dragged you halfway across London for dinner when we could have just gone to bloody Islington.'

She laughs and pulls his arm. 'Come on, let's eat.'

He follows her, scarcely remembering that he'd suggested their favourite French restaurant. He orders Jay's favourite wine, the mussels they always share, the same duck dish as always for which she always teases him.

But this is not Jay, and Simon has almost forgotten what it is to have dinner with someone who doesn't really know you. To laugh and joke, and put on that better version of yourself for show. The wine arrives and is quickly replenished. Two bottles in, it allows him to brush the hair from her face, and to feel the frisson of her hand knocking oh-so-casually against his. It warms places inside him that have been cold a long time so that, lying alone in his stuffy hotel room, he is all ablaze, the frigid fellsides and their ruptured houses slipping entirely from his mind.

50

Rain, always the rain, even in these lonely pitch-dark nights it is there. Pelting against the cottage windows with the same beat as Heather's own quickened pulse. Like her pulse, it is rising. *Something's got to give*, she thinks, looking in the dark towards the rain-slammed glass, out in the direction of the pub, the bridge, the road to Two Houses. *Something's got to give.*

Her bedside lamp flickers, casting a feeble orange glow across the small room. Next to her, the radio gurgles through the usual overnight programmes. Heather tries to lie still, to trick her body into rest, but even beneath the weight of sheets, the press of all these blankets lying on top of her, still her hands flit and dance, answering to their own secret rhythms.

At five, the shipping forecast. The weather. Alone in her own dark, cold room, Heather imagines the weather forecaster in his. Going to work in these solitary, empty hours. How quiet the studios must be, and dark, and he alone in his little cubbyhole poring over the reports.

Severe weather warnings are in place across northern and western England. Winter storm Beatrice is set to bring heavy rain to parts of northern England . . .

And is that slight catch in his throat because they haven't said this soon enough? Because this storm is going to be bigger than they thought?

. . . up to three inches in the next twenty-four hours. Communities are on high alert . . .

Or maybe he just hasn't had his coffee yet.

The Prime Minister has promised all resources will be available . . . No community left unaided.

In spite of Joss's grumblings, Heather pulls back the covers, meets the shock of night air. She totters unsteadily towards the window, seeing nothing, just the lashings of water on glass. Tiny rivers course together down the icy panes, and is that, dimly, through the murk, a light? She cannot tell if the pale smudge is someone else, or just her solitary reflection staring back at her.

It is a light, a torchlight, and clamping it between his teeth, Tom is busy telling himself not to panic. *Don't panic, don't panic, don't panic.* He can't be losing his head, he can't be jumping to conclusions. The solicitor's words circle in his head, as fast and driving as the rain that pummels his face, slides helter-skelter down his collar, drenches his clothes. The worst thing to do would be to panic.

In the dark and the cold, Tom is heaving sandbags out of the coal shed. He, too, has heard the weather report, and he scoffed at the idea that there would be anyone coming to help them. Like Heather, he, too, was lying sleepless, because he could not reach Zoe on her phone last night, and yes, she's a teenager, yes, she might have been out, yes, the signal's rubbish up here at the best of times, but Tom cannot stop the queasy thundering of his heart that she has gone; that Lisa has taken her; that they are, at this moment, fleeing north; Lisa and Mike and his girl, his Zoe. Watch out for anything odd, anything different, Helen said. *Flight risk.* Tom closes his eyes and for a second the dark sky turns light in his mind, the sharp bright chill of October air, a blanket of pale-grey clouds above him and his knees bare in schoolboy's shorts as the elegant V of geese in sharp formation soars overhead, flying south for winter. His mam is gone, they tell him. Has left him. That childhood sadness compounded in his heart.

Heaving another sandbag up towards the pub, Tom slips on the wet stone.

'Shit!'

Winded, his breath clouds around him in sharp, painful bursts. Hauling himself up, slamming his fists into the sack-cloth, he repeats his new-found mantra.

Don't panic, don't panic.

And if anyone had been there to see him, they might almost have thought he was talking about the rain and the flood-waters inching their way towards him.

Alone at Two Houses, Jay is also keeping watch for the creeping dawn. Bella, fearful of the storm, has clambered up underneath the covers.

'There's no such thing as ghosts,' she whispers to them both, though she has believed in ghosts here. She has sought them out. But without Simon she feels her stomach laced with glacial fear. There was a woman found lying beneath this land. There are secrets hidden in these houses, and without him she cannot explain the objects that move by themselves in her absence. Even between leaving for the library and returning, the things in the living room have shifted, picked up and then replaced by someone else's hand, and would that he were here, with her, to deny doing it.

Abandoned.

Least preferred.

A mother who chose self-slaughter over me. She could not imagine life without my darling brother. A life with me was not worth living.

Below her in the house, something shifts. A movement, a noise. There is the rain, the wind, the ragged edges of her breath, but beyond all that she can hear something stirring. Bella stiffens at her side, and *there's no such thing as ghosts* does little for her now, not when she can see Maryanne in her mind's eye, pacing these floorboards as real and flesh and blood as Jay herself. Maryanne, who must have wanted children; and Jay can, unwillingly, remember what that feels like. Maryanne who fought so hard to keep the school open, who parcelled up those strange packages with strange care, who wrote down everything, both praise and punishment. Maryanne who was left behind by her mother, then left again, alone and forgotten beneath this sodden, wretched earth, because Jay is certain now, that it was her. Maryanne who deserves to have a name again. To be remembered.

I saw the pills, though they tried to shield me from them. Lying on her bed in her silk nightgown. Empty bottles strewn across the coverlet. Isobel Brathwane. The fine Lady Isobel Brathwane, so beautiful, so elegant, so adored by all the county.

Pale green she was, at her end. Pale green of her own making and I am glad. For she loved her looks; she did not deserve to die with them.

Clutching Bella to her chest, Jay thinks of them all – all the people who have thwarted her efforts. Who have denied this woman the identity she deserves. D.I. Mosby, with his toothache and his *historic cases*; Simon, who said the past was better left alone; Heather who told her to leave things be; Jacob wanting things left as they were; Angela shouting at her; Dev, even Dev, with his tentative advances, his unwillingness to commit. And Tom, at the end of it always Tom, with his moorgrass eyes and the electricity between them and the way she was so certain he would have told her, the mere millimetres he was away from her and she from him and he from finally spilling whatever this secret was.

Downstairs there is a crash, the sound of something falling. Leaving Bella in the tangle of bedsheets, Jay takes her life in her hands and darts across the frozen bedroom. Her bare feet trip lightly down the wooden staircase, through the living room with its ashes dead now in the grate, into the kitchen.

'Hello?' she says to nobody, no one, her breath rough and panicky. But turning on the light, her heart stops. The door is hanging open, the storm rattling it on its ancient hinges, rain spattering across the stone floor next to a trail of wet footprints.

51

All night the storm thrashes, hurling itself against the fellsides like a petulant child, arms and legs flailing, head thrown back in wild abandon. With the days grown so short, the light barely seems to arrive again before hastening its departure, and Jay does not wait for sunrise before she sets off. There is no sunrise anyway, just the thundering weight of cloud, the inundation of rain, the stinging assault of wind and water against her skin.

'Stay, Bella!' she cries uselessly, trying to inch her way out of the door without the dog slipping through. But the dog is persistent. She will not be left alone in the house, prefers instead to take her chances in the monsoon, its roaring torrents slicking her fur into silky ribbons. Relenting, Jay lets her into the car.

Pulling the heavy Volvo out of the driveway and on to the road, Jay banishes the thought that she shouldn't be driving in this at all. It is the rain that is driving; driving against the windscreen, against the creaking wipers, ineffectual against the deluge, driving the car itself as they slip and slide across the submerged roadway.

But she can't stop. Can't turn back. She sees in front of her, against the grey blur of rain and road, Maryanne's outline, monochrome like her photograph, black and white like this ravaged landscape. The steering wheel is cold as bone beneath her hands, and she cannot leave this, cannot let this woman lie forgotten. Untitled. A 'Jane Doe', they say on television. A number; neat pencil markings on a label looped around a toe. Nothing more.

'Here, Bella.' Jay leans perilously over to the passenger

seat, wrapping the dog in the blankets she has plopped herself down on. The same blanket, Jay thinks, as I was wrapped in when we came here.

She glances down at her phone, thrown casually into the space beneath the radio. She brought it out of habit, she tells herself, though there is no denying the faint hope that, as she nears the town, a few flickers of signal might appear and bring with them a word from Simon. Eventually the town appears out of the storm in front of her; the messages do not. It is an unusual silence, and deafening.

The market square is deserted. A few shops have piled sandbags in front of their doorways, but most seem simply to have jumped ship. There are no lights, no cars, nothing to suggest anyone at all. The police station alone shows signs of life, though Jay has to circle the empty streets a few times before she finds it, its door open, neon-jacketed officers running up and down its stone steps. The car skids through the last, gaping puddles, arriving in front of the station with a sudden, juddering stop.

Inside it is fluorescent lights and fluorescent jackets, radios crackling and phones ringing.

'I need to see D.I. Mosby.'

The man behind the desk looks up at her, and Jay realises that she is breathless, dishevelled, her coat dripping noisily onto the floor. *Drip, drip*. The man – sixty-odd and round, riding out these last years to retirement quietly – looks back down at the papers he's organising.

'He's a bit busy today, miss.'

'It's important.'

The man speaks to her slowly, as if explaining something to a small, difficult child.

'We've widespread flooding. Damaged homes. People needing evac—'

Frustration rushes in her like blood. 'I know, I know, but it's about a body.'

He cocks one eyebrow. 'A body?'

'Yes. I'm from Two Houses, there was a body found—'

'I know about Two Houses. I know who you are.'

Her fist lands against the counter with greater force than she'd intended. Years of working with her hands has given her a strength she occasionally forgets.

'Then can you *please* get D.I. Mosby?'

As if on cue, he appears, haggard as ever. He is clad today in waterproofs and wellingtons so that he rustles as he walks.

'What is it?' he asks abruptly. He hasn't slept either.

'I think I know who the body is.'

Mosby sighs, the release of breath and sinking of his shoulders so obvious to her eyes that it is as if she has deflated him with her words. Popped a pin into his skin to let the air out. As he opens the door to usher Jay towards the offices, a young officer appears.

'Sir—'

'I've already told him, Wood, he's got to get over to Lower Tarn. Get them out, or at least get them ready. If the river goes, it will be above there and they will be buggered, up shit creek and we've no assurances to give them about when we can get them a paddle.'

'Yes, sir.' Wood nods obediently, ready to rush back with his message.

'Wood?'

'Yes, sir?'

'Tell him not to give it to them in quite those terms.'

'No, sir.'

Mosby turns to Jay, his hand back in its habitual clutch around his jaw. 'Let's go somewhere else, shall we?'

Somewhere else turns out to be Mosby's office. A tiny cubbyhole of space cut from a sea of corporate cubicles, adrift with papers and files, piled so high and so wide that there are only three or four carpet tiles still free to walk on.

'You don't mind if I . . .?' Mosby shuts the door and pulls his flask from his jacket. 'Bloody tooth, bloody floods.'

'Is it already flooding?'

'It will.' He takes a second swig. 'Sit down if you can find . . .' He gestures towards the two chairs in front of his desk, but since these, too, are submerged beneath old case notes and ring binder folders, Jay stands, Bella close at her feet.

'So . . .' Mosby leans back against a filing cabinet. 'You've found our missing woman?'

'Yes. She—'

'Thing is, Mrs Wigmore—'

'My name is Jay.'

'OK. The thing is, Jay, everyone thinks they're a detective. Telly, films, they make it look glamorous when really . . .' He shrugs at the room around him and its detritus. 'What I mean is, not unkindly, like, but it's probably nothing.'

'It's not nothing.'

'Well—'

'It's not nothing if I've found her identity, found out who she is.'

'Was. No, but what I'm saying is you probably haven't.'

Jay cocks her head. 'You from Hestle, by any chance, D.I. Mosby?'

He snaps his head round to look at her, paying more attention now, the air between them humming like the wires between telephone poles before a storm. 'And what of it?'

'I'm just asking.'

'Yes, I was born in Hestle. Moved down here when I was a teenager, moved away, moved back, what of that?'

'Because you haven't even asked me what I've found. Almost as if you don't want to hear it.'

'Look.' His voice is hard, his fists clenched against the cabinets behind him, knuckles white against the metal. 'We've got a rush on. I've got more rain than Noah and no bleeding ark.'

Jay takes her heart in her hands.

'I think it's Maryanne.'

Eye to eye, each so intent on the other that there is barely room for breath, she watches Mosby hear that name. Watches for the flicker in his irises; the twitch at the corner of his lips; the slightest hesitation that might give him away. But he is just as careful, each word cautiously weighed up before being given breath.

'Maryanne who?'

'Maryanne Outhwaite. Tom's stepmother.'

Mosby breaks first, his eyes darting towards the main office, where an unanswered phone is ringing.

'I don't know what you're talking about.'

'What or who?' she tries to say, but he is pulling his office door open, yelling into the space: 'Can someone answer that bloody phone?'

He turns back towards her. 'Look—'

'You know, don't you?'

He sighs. 'Why?'

'Why what?'

'Why do you think it's Maryanne Outhwaite?'

'Because she left. Because I – we can't find a trace of her. Because her things are piled high in the attic at Two Houses, and she wasn't liked, and she was born in that house, at Two Houses, before it was made into two, and no one can tell me where she is.'

'Lots of people left.' Mosby is just inches from her now. 'You ever consider it strange to think you're the only people to actually *come* here?'

His words hang between them like a thread, a threat, broken only by his junior Wood appearing at the door.

'Sir—'

'What?'

'It's Tarn.'

'Lower or Upper?'

'Both, we can't get up there.'

'Jesus.' Mosby turns to Jay, but she is already gathering Bella's lead in her hands.

'Don't worry, I'm going.' She pauses right in front of him, so close that she can almost feel the shiver that runs along his skin. She storms past Wood back towards the entrance, towards the rain that takes neither respite nor prisoners.

'The past is past!' Mosby yells after her. 'Doesn't do any good digging it up for no reason.'

His words are met by silence and the door's slam.

52

You never see it coming, Dev thinks.

Is it in the nature of things or just the nature of him to worry about the small stuff? Paying the bills, keeping the roof from leaking, scraping together the pennies to be able to acquire at least a few new books each year. To sweat these minute details, these things that could all be swept away at a moment's notice. A flood. Water up to the windows of the village houses. Muck and mould, and those heartbroken people you see on the evening news shovelling mud and debris from what was once their living room. Days ago, they were worrying about dinner and what to watch on telly. You never see it coming.

Just before close of business the council sent an email round. More jittery than the usual corporate jargon, a lacing of panic to it, this one. *Latest advisories . . . weather warnings . . .* Rivers will break, that's the brunt of it. They will burst. And the damage depends on where it happens. Whether you're above or below or bobbing on the waterline, just trying to keep your head up. You never see it coming. Not for the first time, Dev thanked his stars that his library is up a hill.

'So I won't be seeing you then?' Gareth's voice low and plaintive on the phone, as if his words were fluttering his eyelashes.

'I can't be driving in this.' Dev held up the curtain to reveal the sound of rain hammering against the cottage windows. Just driving back from Two Houses had been hairy enough.

'You can't drive at the best of times,' came the response.

'Hey, don't be nasty. I have to be here in the morning anyway, if this damn water's going to rise.'

And it'll be a long stretch now, until they can meet again,

a desert eking out in front of them, hot and dry as bone. A long stretch until Gareth's parents are out of town again, until they, two grown men, get the secret, ungiven gift of an empty house for a few days. Flocked wallpaper, patterned carpet, and time, sweet, uninterrupted time.

'I'll be seeing you then,' Gareth sniffed.

'I'll be seeing you,' Dev replied, holding on just in case, hating to be the one who hangs up first. Because of course they won't be seeing each other, and you must be growing old, Dev told himself, not to jump in the car and drive through wind and rain to see the man. But he was kidding himself. He's never been that person. So it was back to the knitting, back to the lonely bed beneath the eaves with the wind buffeting the cottage as if it might take off, the rain falling as if in personal attack, uneasy sleep shattered at six o'clock with his mother phoning.

'Dev baby, I'm worried baby, they're saying floods, storms, rising waters.'

'Mum, I'm fine, I'm in bed.'

'But they're saying sandbags—'

And he was up, then, after the usual twenty-minute barrage of yes-Mum, no-Mum, whatever-you-want-me-to-do, Mum. And why is it, he growls to himself, phone clamped to his chin as he stirs his three sugars into his morning tea, that he never tells his mother to stop. To stop calling him Dev baby, to stop treating him as a child? She is still doing it as he struggles into his wellingtons and out into the miserable onslaught of weather.

They have sandbags, at the library. Doled out after the last floods as a precaution. Dev joked last time that a sandbag wasn't much good for a library up a set of steps on a hill, but as icy rain plummets down the back of his collar he's not laughing now. Breathless, staggering, cursing the weight of all those biscuits dragging around him, he lugs the sandbags out of the store.

Out of the rain, a voice, a figure, walking towards him.

'Let me give you a hand.'

You never see it coming. And how gullible must he have looked, straightening up, wiping his glasses; how stupidly grateful to those young arms, that kind offer. Later, he will imagine the narrow slits of eyes, the curl of an as yet hairless upper lip. But in the moment his glasses are flying through the air before he has a chance to properly look through them. The sandbag sails weightless towards him, until it clubs him to the ground. Schoolboy's shoes make a percussion of his ribs and arms, clattering against him, and Dev is back, a schoolboy too; back in the alley behind the house, back on the school bus, at the bus stop, on that street in town, the club in Huddersfield, all those places where people have pummelled his skin.

It doesn't hurt, in the moment of it. Not even as their voices fade, shoes rattling away from him down the pavement. He rests his head on the pavement and watches the raindrops splatter into the pool of blood in front of him. It strikes him, then, how very ordinary that blood looks. Red as any other.

Ordinary. An ordinary day.

'Nothing extraordinary to see here,' Heather announces to no one in particular, counting her pills out on to the kitchen counter. Seven, eight . . . She keeps them in a sandwich bag, now. Easier than a jar. She wants, most of all, for it to be easy. How many of these would you need? she wonders again. How do you make sure?

The rain with its drumbeat seems to announce her thoughts. *Not today, not today, not today,* even as her hands are dancing. Thirteen, fourteen . . . It's not bad enough today. Today is just an ordinary day.

Except it's not, for Jackie was on the phone at seven. *We can't get there, Mam. Are you ready? Are you prepared?* Then there was the radio, saying the same thing: *do you know what to do in the event of flooding?* She didn't, but she could see Tom heaving his sandbags about, him and a few others passing the extras up the abandoned bit of village road, so that the

259

few cottages still lived in now have great beige lumps outside their front doors.

She gets to twenty-six and decides to go to the library.

'Give Dev a hand, eh, Jossy? What good these hands are.'

The dog looks up with mournful eyes. Heather cannot but read reproach in that face, as if Joss knows only too well what it is she is counting.

'You stay here, Joss. It's raining cats and whatsits out there.'

And it is. Cats and dogs and any other creature the good Lord has to pelt at them. Wind buffeting like she has never known it, too much, almost, to keep upright. Heather inches along, clinging to the houses. They did this as children, when the weather was bad, but it didn't maul her then as it does now, it was not this fierce. She can hardly see through the roar, the whole world cast silver-blue in the weight of water.

'That daft man,' she says, squinting at the blur of a sandbag at the bottom of the library steps. 'What's he gone and left that there for?'

She is almost on top of the sandbag before she realises that it is on top of Dev. That he is lying, drenched and beaten, on the ground.

'Dev!' Her heart pounding in her chest like it hasn't for years. 'Dev, are you alright?'

'Heather.'

His lips hardly move, but somehow over the rage of the storm she hears her name, sees him try to smile at the sight of her. Not that he can see, for his specs are lying shattered behind him. With all her might she hauls at the sandbag, tries to get him upright.

'What happened? Who did this?'

'I'm fine, I'm fine.'

'You're not.'

And that fierce rush of blood in her heart. That maternal instinct that makes her think of lions and cubs. That feeling she had when Jackie fell and broke her wrist and the thing she wailed most over was her little gold bracelet, lost or stolen somewhere. When Jacob came running to her, blood trickling down his jumper, his little legs black and blue with bruises, screaming about his dog. When, at last, she found out what was happening and all she wanted to do was protect those children. And here she is, soaked to the bone, with a great big grown man, clutching him to her as if he were hers. As if he needed her protection.

'Come on, come back to the house.'

She heaves him up, lugs at his bulk with strength she didn't know she had. His lovely face battered and blue, one eye puffed up like a black egg, his chin dripping blood on to the both of them. It is an agonising stagger back to her cottage, along the one village street, the same street she has walked along every day of her life. And where is Tom, now? Where is anybody? All shut up against the storm so she and Dev must lurch together.

Finally, she settles him into a kitchen chair. Hot towel for this, bag of frozen peas for that. Tea, always tea; a cup of tea with three sugars – maybe four or five for Dev, on this occasion – a cup of tea solves everything.

'Don't tell me who, you don't have to. That bloody woman, those bloody hooligans. Put this on your eye. There'll be hell to pay when I see her, hell to pay.' She pauses. 'Here. Tea.'

And it is only then as he looks at her through blurred, bloodshot eyes, eyes that take in the sweep of her, the bag of pills still out on the table, that he says quietly, 'Heather, what's wrong with your hands?'

53

Jay's hands grip the steering wheel, clenched so tightly that she can feel her pulse beating against the wheel's cold leather. It is insistent, like the thud in her chest, the voice in her brain that says *keep going, keep going.*

The clouds are dark as slate, making an evening out of day, the rain flashing white as it slams against the windscreen. They keep going up the Nelder road. Past the turning for Two Houses, where Bella cocks her head in surprise. Her furry eyebrows jiggle, as if to say, *can't we go home yet?*

'Not yet, Bell. Not yet.'

The sky hangs overhead like wet clay, thick and drab and so heavy it feels as if it might come crashing down on top of them. *Splat*, clay hitting the wheel. *Splash*, water from the road whirring up beside them, smacking into the glass. Water trickling down the back of her neck, making the fine hairs of her skin stand tantalisingly up on end. Hair dripping, nose dripping, the seat beneath her growing soggy from the weight of water held in her coat. *Keep going, keep going*, her brain says, waiting for the village to come into view.

Tom looks at his phone again. Pointless; the signal has gone now. Happens when big storms come in. There's nothing, not a tremor, not even that little dance between symbols. Phones cut off, roads cut off. Nothing to do but wait it out, and fight the fear in his chest that with every minute's passing Zoe travels further away from him.

Rainwater is running along the village street. Still falling, it is one long crescendo of water on stone, pouring down into a river that, since first light, has been fit to bursting.

'River's going, Tom!'

John shouts up to him from down by the bridge. A few of them have gathered in raincoats and wellies to watch the torrent of brown, peaty water rushing past. Tom joins them, water coursing down his cheeks, dropping cold into his boots, and sure enough, the water has broken its banks now, is creeping up over the roadway, seeping through the stone on to the bridge itself.

'Think the bridge'll hold?' he shouts at John. They stand shoulder to shoulder, watching. John sucks at his teeth and Tom remembers the weight of the dead sheep that washed up here last time, the way the rotten flesh gave under his hands.

But before he has time to reply, there is a new hum above the water's roar. A car appears around the bend in the road. Before he sets eyes on it, Tom knows that it is Jay. He steps towards the water.

'Go back!' Arms waving. 'It's flooding, go back!'

But she can't hear him, won't hear him, and the Volvo creeps down to the bridge, to what is now the river's edge. Water is trickling over the roadway, a steady stream of it, tearing through the cement that holds the stones as it goes. It must be about to go.

'The bridge is going!' he shouts. 'Please!'

They lock eyes, but even as they stare at each other he hears the engine rev and roar, is almost bowled over by it as the car swings suddenly, lurchingly, across the bridge. Gasping for breath, he slams his hands down on the bonnet.

'What the hell are you playing at?'

She steps out of the car, long hair whipping around her face in the wind.

'Don't shout at me.'

'That was a bloody stupid thing to do. Can't you see the water, see that the bridge is going to go?'

She is just centimetres from him. He can read constellations in her freckles, can count the minute flecks of amber in her turquoise eyes, the raindrops landing on her cheeks.

'I know who she is.'

Tom says nothing. Does nothing. He is locked in her stare, in the way the rain falls like teardrops across her pale face.

'And I know,' she continues, her words almost whisper now, secret to the others, standing further up, out the way, watching this strange encounter, 'that you know too.'

'Jay . . .' He cannot think of what to say besides her name, her strange and beautiful name. 'Jay.'

'You knew, and you didn't tell me.'

'Don't—'

'Don't tell me what to do. I am sick of being told what to do.' She walks back to the car door. 'I'm going to the farmhouse.'

The burst river is lapping at Tom's boots, and even if it weren't he would feel its tug, the force of its riptide, everything she says ripping at him, tearing what's left of his world from him.

'You can't,' his hands try to grasp the closing door. 'The road, it'll be dangerous in this, washed away.'

But with a creak and a roar, the Volvo springs to life and she is gone. Tom wheels around, slams his palms against the nearest wall.

'Shit!'

John and the others inch further away, transfixed. Pushing past them, Tom makes to follow her.

What a hovel that farmhouse is. What a coming down in the world, as if taking a profession wasn't ignominy enough.

I was married for convenience, there's no need to dress it up, to sugar the facts. That is the truth of it. A widower with children needing taking care of, and who was I? Where had I to go? No children of my own to have, that became clear quickly enough. Other children inherited, passed on to me, fobbed off.

A whole life spent in someone else's shadow. Trying to step into someone else's shoes.

They were little boys, to boot. I never had time for little boys. Everyone's so damn fond of little boys.

Outside the wind flies over the exposed fellside like a banshee, howling and shrieking, but inside the farmhouse it is silent as the grave. Damp and cold, the same stinking assault that Jay remembered. Her eyes strain against the murk of unlit rooms and dirt-clad windows. The air is soupy, thick and still, her clothes heavy, wet and dripping around her.

Taking a few steps into the kitchen, she is almost feeling sure of herself until something moves silently past her leg.

'Jesus Christ!'

It is a cat, the sharp movement of her foot hurrying its journey across the room with a hiss and a yelp.

'She won't hurt,' comes the low, gravelled voice from the doorway to the next room.

'Mr Outhwaite.' Her heart sits bulbous and slippery in her mouth.

'Thought I'd be seeing you again.' He shuffles towards his fireside chair, not seeing her at all, the milky orbs of his wizened face fixed instead a few inches above her head. He drops heavily into the chair.

'You took my photograph,' he says, without accusation.

'Yes.'

He takes out his pipe. His fingers are swollen with age, thick and purple, so that the act of filling it up takes long, painstaking seconds.

The pipe is wedged between his dentures. 'Some people don't like a thief.'

'Mr Outhwaite, I live at Two Houses—'

'I know where you live.'

'Your wife . . . I found your wife.'

For the first time, his eyes meet hers. Cataract-clouded, they fill slowly, until they are wet with more than just age, glistening across the dark room.

'My wife?'

He looks at her with such innocence. A child, childishly delighted by a new word or toy. His question – inflected with the echoes of hope and happiness – hangs between them in the mottled air.

'Your wife.'

'My wife,' he echoes, a smile spreading like sun over the landscape of his wrinkled face. 'Oh she were lovely my wife, my Peggie.'

'Mr Outhwaite . . .' Jay doesn't know why tears are rising in her eyes, but they are, trembling over her lower lids and down on to her cheeks. 'Not Peggie, Mr Outhwaite. Maryanne.'

This is it. She can almost taste it. She is almost at the moment of knowing, of finally understanding why that bone was beneath that earth. Why it was her who touched it, why she alone reached out. Why, in those long seconds of contact, it became so important for her to know who that woman was, and why she, too, has been buried, submerged, waiting to come up for air.

Through the low, grime-streaked window, Jay sees Tom's car pull up in front of the farm. Almost before it stops he is charging towards the door.

'Mr Outhwaite—'

She hears the cat moving behind her again.

'I have to know why—'

The front door opens. Wheeling around to face the blast of air and light, she realises too late that it was not the cat moving behind her, but Jacob, a rock held high in his hand. Tom is through the door, lunging towards her, and as the world slows on its axis, its seconds drawn out far longer than a heartbeat, she looks at him and wonders if his cry is for her or Jacob. The rock lands before she can hear the second syllable, and everything is black.

54

The ground beneath her is cold, familiar.

She is in her studio, all her works staring down at her from dusty shelves.

London, this is her London workplace, yet there is no sound at all. Not builders, not cars, not aeroplanes overhead. Just a silence so total it is shrill in her ears. Ringing, reverberating.

She is lying on the floor. She does not know why, but she recognises this scuffed and battered earth. She looks again at her works – pots, vases, dishes, the great moon vessel, not broken any more, staring down at her like so many pale, placid faces – and they, like the silence, are reverberating. Humming.

At first it is almost imperceptible, just a faint jostling together, but the delicate clink of porcelain grows louder, the polite rattle rising to a roar until they are falling – everything – all these things she has poured her life into – falling down to earth. But she is not scared. Because even as they crack and break, even as she watches their earthbound tumble, she knows that they will fall softly, touch down lightly, transforming into just so many dusty fragments of bone.

'Jay?'

It is dark, and quiet, but this is not her studio floor.

This is not London.

That's not Simon calling her name.

She scrabbles to move her legs, to jump to her feet, but she is made of jelly, her limbs of lead, and the back of her head is aflame, pain roaring across her skull.

'Jay.'

'Tom.' His name escapes her lips before his face swims into focus.

'You're OK, you're OK.'

He has his arms on hers, trying to tug her down, to keep her grounded, for she is halfway to the galaxy now, stars and constellations flickering across her vision. Dimly, there are figures standing on the other side of the room. Something hard behind her – a chest, a sideboard? – catching her slump. She tries to look but her head, her head . . .

'Jay.'

Tom again. His moorgrass eyes.

'What happened?' Her voice is a croak, her mouth a desert, and yet she remembers rain, so much rain. And is that Bella, barking in the distance? 'Where's Bella?'

Tom looks over his shoulder. 'Get her, will you?'

And a pair of boots trudge out of her vision.

Tom lifts her into a chair, places Bella – a rush of wet barks, rain-soaked fluff and hot breath – in her lap. Jay buries her face in the soft, familiar fur.

'What happened?'

Silence.

'Tom, what happened?'

His voice is little more than air, the faintest breeze tickling the long grasses. 'He didn't mean it.'

'Who didn't?'

Tom leans one hand against the table behind him. She hasn't noticed the table before. Next to his hand there is a rock, one side dark and glistening. And it floods back to her. The farmhouse. The drive. Mosby lying, Tom pleading with her, rushing in at the door, and Jacob, his hand held high.

'Oh my god.' Fear beats in her head, her heart. She watches Tom curl his hands around the back of a chair. She watches as he leans over it, defeated, his head hung low. For a moment, no one moves. Not the shadowy figures by the window. Not Tom. Not even Bella, who seems to sense the question on the air.

'Why?'

Her word echoes around the room, huge and reverberating. Why then, why now. 'What did she ever do to you?' Jay whispers.

With a jolt, Tom looks up at her.

'What did she ever do to us?' he asks, his voice light, quiet. 'What did she ever do to us?' His eyes glint as he moves towards her, yanking up the sleeve of his shirt. 'This, this is what she did to us' – thrusting out an arm of silvery scars. 'Jacob, get over here.' But Jacob doesn't move, and Tom is dragging him now, pulling his brother towards her seat, pulling at his jumper, revealing a pale side of scrawny ribs, a sunken belly laced with the same ghost marks, the pale trace of cuts, tears, burns. 'This is what she did to us!'

'But . . . but she was a teacher.' Jay can't make her battered brain think fast enough. The Mothers' Group, the school, those packages wrapped up with such care. The way she'd written out all those names, the little stinging punishments, yes, but the floral paper, the record cards, the photographs she kept. *Twelve strikes for trouser-wetting. Made to wash her mouth out. The standing stone.*

'No, lass.' Ned Outhwaite shuffles forward now. With a touch of his hand he loosens Tom's grip on Jacob, who, whimpering, flees his brother's grasp. Yanking down his jumper, he cowers in the corner, rocking back and forth. 'She didn't love children. She wanted them, would have loved her own, mebbe, but she didn't love other folk's.'

He drops into the chair beside her, his milky eyes meeting hers.

'Took me a long time to see that. Too long. The mind makes excuses for what the heart doesn't want to hear.'

A voice, a woman's voice, from over by the doorway. 'Shouldn't be so hard on yourself, Ned. None of us wanted to see it.'

It is Heather, entering slowly into their strange half-circle in the kitchen.

'Heather.' Tom does not look at her, but she puts a wavering hand on his shoulder as she passes.

'What's happening here then?' She gives Bella an affectionate pat on the head, her coat falling open to reveal a jumper smeared with blood. 'Oh, it's not mine,' she says in response to Tom's half-started question. 'Dev had a little run-in. He's fine now, sleeping it off on my sofa. No,' she says, removing her coat and rolling up her sleeves, 'it's not blood that's wrong with me.'

Heather's cold hands are sweet relief on Jay's raging forehead. The older woman looks over her head, tenderly finding the bloodied bump at the back.

'Now then lovey, let's get some ice on this.'

The rest of them are silent as Heather potters authoritatively towards the freezer.

'Hello Jacob, love,' she says in passing. 'I finally made it up here.'

Although Jay receives the frozen peas gratefully, her mouth struggles to form the questions racing through her brain.

'But what . . . how . . .?'

'We'll tell you, missy.' Heather strokes Jay's hair. 'Lord knows you're not giving up on this one.' Heather pulls up a chair next to Ned. 'Get the fire on, Tom. We'll catch our deaths without.'

And so, with the wind howling, the fire slowly licking its way to warmth, they tell her. Ned, first, in slow, stuttering words, words that he has held secret for thirty years.

'It weren't easy, after Peggie died. I don't say that as an excuse. There are no excuses. They were my boys, my blood. I have no excuse for not acting. Not seeing the bruises, not putting two and two together.' His old voice cracks and wavers. 'But like you, I thought, *she's a teacher*. She said, *boys will be boys*. I couldn't manage on my own and she was there . . . and—'

'And it was easy to believe her.' Heather takes over. 'Said she liked kids, did Maryanne. Always wanting to be involved, Mothering Sunday, school outings. And it wasn't her fault that Ned and I . . . that we had our history. I didn't want to be jealous, didn't want to dislike her just because she was married to the man I loved.'

The word *loved* seems to fill the room, all these years of silence finally coming up for air.

'She was left, you see. At Two Houses. Well, it wasn't Two Houses then but you know that. Her brother was born weak, a sickly little thing. And when he died, her mother didn't want to go on living. Took her life, like the story said. And left Maryanne behind. You can see, then, that she wouldn't like children. 'Specially once she learned she couldn't have her own. It was a coming down in the world to her, to be a teacher. To marry a farmer and live like this. All that anger . . .' Heather shudders. 'All the anger began to work its way out.

'I'm sorry, Jacob.' Heather turns to him, cowed and broken in the corner. 'You came to me. And I did nothing. I will always be sorry for that.'

Heather looks back to Jay.

'Two Houses were empty, later on. You know that, of course. Maryanne treated them as if they were hers, though she didn't inherit. She didn't like the children playing down there. Paid some of them the odd penny to keep an eye on things for her. So Angela knew, of course, about me and Ned. Nasty piece of work, Angela, even as a kiddie. She saw us one day, one day down at Two Houses. Said she'd tell Maryanne, tell my Harry.' Heather sighs, a sigh so heavy it seems to hold the whole world in its wings. 'So, for all the usual, stupid reasons, I did nothing. Said nothing, even when the kids complained, when they came back from school with bumps and bruises. And then, suddenly, it was too late.'

'Too late?' Jay whispers.

'He didn't mean to do it,' Tom says quietly.

'Who didn't?'

'Jacob. He didn't mean it. But she was a monster . . . And there . . .' his voice breaks, '. . . there is only so much one person can bear.'

Jay looks back at the bloodied rock on the table. Jacob, at home with stone. Jacob, desperate that she didn't uncover the history at Two Houses, that she didn't dig into its secrets and sorrows. Suddenly, with a crack in her heart, she understands.

From the corner, Jacob's voice is low and plaintive. He is in darkness, but she can hear the tears in his voice, knows that they are streaming down his face, a waterfall without the roar. She can see him. A boy. Motherless, scabbed and bruised. Raising up one of his precious rocks. The *thud* of its landing. The release.

'You all said no one could know. You all said no one could ever know.'

Heather goes over and kneels in front of him, not touching him, even now; this man, this boy, so hurt by human hands, so bent and broken by them.

'I know we did, Jacob. And I'm sorry for that. I am so very sorry.'

55

The afternoon dips into milky halflight, the wind dropping to mere breath above them, the rain to drizzle. Jay stirs, and when she makes to leave it is Tom who helps her to her feet, who puts an arm around her shoulders to guide her out of this dark, dank kitchen, thick with sorrow. She does not see Jacob's face as she passes: he remains in his corner, hunched over; his long, ungainly limbs scrunched into a ball.

Outside the world is cloud-coloured, full of hush, the hazy rain silent as it falls. Jay and Tom stand for a moment, looking out on it: on the tops, the steep-sided valley, Nelderdale opening up beneath them, indistinct beneath the mist.

'Don't drive,' he says. 'Let me take you.'

'Will he be alright?' she asks, as Tom opens the passenger door for her.

'Aye,' Tom replies softly, looking out at the empty fellside rising above them. 'He'll be alright.'

Clutching Bella to her chest, Jay closes her eyes. Night is falling quickly now, sudden, like a blanket aired above a bed that gathers speed in its descent. She does not want to see the farmhouse disappearing behind them, or the village gradually coming into view. She does not want to see or think anything at all.

'I'll get your car tomorrow,' Tom says into the darkness.

Down in the village, he doesn't stop at the pub, turning the corner to survey the bridge.

'Looks like it's holding,' he mutters, squinting beyond the windscreen.

'Yes,' Jay murmurs. 'It's holding.'

Nevertheless, Tom pulls the car around and back to the pub. 'Stay here tonight,' he says, somewhere between demand and question, statement and plea.

She says nothing, but gets out of the car.

Inside it is cold. He rattles the radiators until they begin to hiss their way to warmth. Tom turns on the oven, makes to fill the kettle.

'I'll make you some tea.'

'I don't want tea,' she says quietly.

He pauses, his back to her, and in the dim light cast by the table-top lamp, its pink velvet trim as incongruous as ever, she can see the muscles in his shoulders tense.

'What do you want?'

'I don't know. Gin.'

He turns. 'Have some tea. And then?'

'And then what?'

'That's what I asked you.'

A minute passes, the silence broken only by the whir of the oven coming up to temperature and the rumbling boil of the unwanted kettle. *And then?* Tom's question echoes in the air around them. Jay closes her eyes again, leans back into the throbbing of her head. She wanted so much to find that woman. To put a name to the bone, a face to the name. It is hard, now, to think that this is not what she came here for. That, in setting out from London and its barren wastes, the summer and everything that was so empty in it, she did not know she was coming here to search for this. And now what? She was wrong. She followed the breadcrumbs but they did not lead her where she thought they would. These last weeks have been a rescue attempt; she was trying to rescue Maryanne, but Maryanne, it turns out, was beyond rescuing. Maybe, after all this – all the money, all the miles, all the months of trying to get away from it – it is still her, Jay, who needs to be rescued.

Tom places a heavily sugared tea down in front of her, the clunk on the table startling her reverie.

'Well?'

'I don't know.' It is all she can think to say.

Tom rubs his face roughly with his hands, as if he can hardly bear to say the words. 'Will you tell?'

The kettle is still whistling, its hot-steam shriek insistent and ghostly, somewhere between the howl of the wind and the human cries that ring out in Jay's mind. The hurt, the pain, those little boys missing their mother, and she knows what that, at least, feels like.

Abruptly, she pushes back her chair, pushes past him to pull the kettle off the heat. The metal handle sears her palm, an angry red welt flashing up across the map of her hand. For a moment she pauses, looks at the panting flesh with strange fascination, before Tom pulls her wrist beneath the cold tap.

'It's fine.'

'It's burned.'

'My hands are bashed up anyway.'

And it is true, the left hand that she turns over and back for him bears the scars, faded now, of all the years on the wheel, the years with the kiln. Just so many faint marks, snowflakes imprinted in the skin. He has not let go of her wrist, and she knows they are both thinking of the marks on his arms, the old welts on Jacob.

He is close enough now that she can feel his heart beating. She feels his breath on her neck as she gently pushes up his shirtsleeve, runs her finger across the traces of those ancient wounds. Turning to face him, she can smell the hillsides, damp earth and sharp air as if it is caught in his very being. His eyes are so close to hers now, his long nose, his lips. She stares at it all, drinks him in. The tap is still running behind them, and she is surprised that it is he who speaks first, who brings low, whispered words into this not-quite-embrace.

'In another life,' he murmurs, 'I'd kiss you.'

'In another life,' she echoes, and it is like striking a flint against her own heart, the brief flicker and glow receding into darkness.

'Come on,' Tom says eventually, making his way towards the kitchen door. They lean against the floral-patterned wall, kicking off their muddied boots, thick with earth. Slowly, they climb the steep, narrow stairs, Tom's hand on Jay's back to steady her still-woozy step.

Outside the bedroom door, he hovers on the threshold.

'You can come in,' she murmurs, slipping fully-dressed beneath the blankets.

He lies down next to her.

'You shouldn't sleep just yet,' he says. 'Your head. Try not to sleep just yet.'

In the light cast by a half-moon, each can see the other's eyes. He cups a hand around her cheek. She places the tips of her fingers against his stubble. They do not speak. No sweet nothings here, no sugared words to pretend that the world is not what it is, that they are not who they are, each with their own burden. The weight of land and family, heavy as clay.

56

In another life, Heather would have stayed on with Ned at the farmhouse. She would have reached out a hand to that old, sunken face. Laid her head against the shoulder that was once so familiar to her, now just ragged bone beneath his shirt. In another life.

But in this one it is too hard. Too long ago. Too tied up with all these secrets, all this hurt. There is Jacob, still crouched and murmuring to himself in the corner. There is Dev to be getting back to. There are some gulfs, she thinks, looking out into the dark at the ravine that falls away in front of them, that are simply too big to bridge.

'You're shaking,' Ned says gruffly.

'Parkinson's.' The word comes out without her thinking about it, and this once, to this one person, it is a relief to simply speak the truth. 'Bad, they say. No help for it.'

Ned nods matter of factly, as if he already knew. And perhaps it is better to keep things in the realm of fact. To keep the heart tightly bound, as it has been for so many of these long, hard years.

'How long?' he asks. This is a man used to the cycles of life and death, wrenching creatures into the world and sending them back out of it.

'They don't know. Could be one year, could be five,' she replies, parroting out the same words the doctor used. She leaves off *ten at a push*. 'They don't know,' she says again, her voice wavering slightly in her throat. 'But I don't think I'll be waiting around that long.'

Ned looks at her, his eyes milky.

'I've done enough waiting, Ned,' she whispers. And it is easier to speak to him while tidying the tea things, folding the tea towels over the chairs. 'But I've been wanting to come up. To see you.' In spite of everything, she laughs a little. 'Been walking almost all the way up here most nights trying to pluck up the courage.'

'To say goodbye.'

It is not a question.

'Yes.'

Tears well in Heather's eyes, so that her sight, too, is clouded over. Tears for what so briefly was. For what might have been.

'I never told.'

'I know, Ned.'

They speak in whispers now, though Jacob is beyond the point of hearing them.

'Your girl.'

'Jacqueline.'

'She doesn't know?'

Heather shakes her head.

'Better that way,' he replies. She wonders if it is only age that makes his lower lip tremble.

'Yes.' She wipes her cheeks with the back of her hands. 'Well. I'll be going, then, Ned.'

'Aye.' He nods, but will not bring himself to watch her go, and as she stumbles out of the dark house on to the dark of the hillside, she thinks, maybe, that it is better. They are not what they once were. It is all so much harder and more painful than what it might once have been. She starts her little car and pulls off down the unlit, roughshod track. She is glad, for once, not to have Joss with her. No one – not even the dog – needs to see these tears.

The village is dark, quiet. Much like any other night, save that today has been so unusual she almost expected the streets to be abuzz with it. For the pub to have its lights on. For folk to be talking about the river, the floods, even if they do not talk about Two Houses and the farmhouse and their quiet revelations.

Like Tom, Heather gets out of the car and walks down to survey the bridge as best she can on this moon-dappled night. It is much colder suddenly, her breath making clouds in the black air. Winter on its way after autumn's final storm. Tom's car is outside the pub, but there is no sign of life, and Heather cannot help but wonder where they are; what was said between them once they left the hilltops.

Fumbling with the torch she keeps in her pocket, Heather squints into the dark night and she thinks, too, that the bridge has held, though the rush of water is loud above the silence. Turning back towards the cottage, a voice comes to her out of the darkness, a form illuminated only by the glow of a cigarette end.

'Heather.'

It's Angela, on her way to the pub, presumably. For a moment, Heather is tempted to fib, to embellish, to tell her that Jay is in there now, with him, just for the spite of making Angela wince at it.

'They're good kids, your boys are.'

'What?'

In the dark, the other woman is thrown by the compliment, her surly voice momentarily unsure of itself.

'I said they're good kids. But you – and not Tony, *you*, Angela – are going to ruin them if you keep this up.'

'Keep what up? I don't know what you're—'

'Save it,' Heather interrupts. 'I don't want to hear it. You know exactly what they've done, what you've done to them. He's lying on my sofa, Dev is, bruised and bloodied. But it's your boys you're hurting, Angela. His bruises will fade, but you keep this up and those boys will end up no better than their father.' Heather is shaking with rage, the tremors in her hands subsumed by the animal anger rising in her, loosed by the night and the day and all it has raked up. 'Now, we won't say anything this time, but I swear to God, if it happens again, I will come down on you so hard Angela Metcalfe. The police, the social, so help me I will do it.'

For once Angela is silent; no retort comes across the night air. Even her cigarette has extinguished itself.

'Now,' Heather regains her composure, pats down her hair and jacket as if smoothing herself out after a gust of wind. 'Not everyone gets what they want in life, Angela. But they do get the chance to make it right. Go home, look after those boys. He's not here.'

'But his car—' Angela gestures to the pub then stops herself, realising she's given the game away.

'He's not here. Get home with you.'

Inside Heather's cottage, the air is laced with disinfectant. From the doorway she can make out Dev's bulbous form beneath the blankets on the sofa. She has almost forgotten what it is to come home to somebody; to hold your breath when easing off your shoes, the effort in trying to stop a coat from rustling. Joss, who has been keeping watch, waddles over to greet her.

'Hello old girl,' she whispers, and on the sofa, Dev stirs.

Heather comes forward, placing an icy hand on his forehead.

'How are you feeling?'

'Better.'

'Don't get up, let me make you some tea.'

Heather totters into the kitchen. The bag of pills are still on the table. They jump out at her and set her heart to thumping, but she knows that Dev is watching her, and that it would be more obvious to move them than to pretend they are not there. There's the bottle of TCP, too, the detritus of bandages, plasters, Savlon. Nothing special to look at here.

'Heather . . .'

Dev has dragged himself upright now. Even in the lamp-light, he looks awful, swollen and discoloured.

'Yes?'

'The pills . . .'

Heather sets the mugs she's been filling down on the counter. She is, suddenly, exhausted; drained by this day and all it has thrown at her. She presses her hands up to her eyes and, of course, now that she's no longer shouting at Angela, the tremors are back.

'I have to have a way out, Dev.'

She brings his sugared tea over and perches beside him on the sofa.

'I have to have an out.'

Dev swallows, looking down into his still-swirling drink.

'I know, but . . . I'd miss you.'

Beneath her ribcage, her heart swells. 'Dev—'

'And you know . . .' He struggles, now, to find the words. 'You know you have friends who'd help you. If it got really bad, I mean.'

'I know.'

'No, I mean, friends who'd really help.' He looks at her with those round, chipmunk eyes, under a thick glitter of tears. 'Who'd help at the end.'

Heather puts an arm around him, pulls him into a half hug that threatens to send both mugfuls of tea onto the carpet.

'You need to rest,' she says after a little while. 'Let me get you another blanket.'

Like a good little boy, Dev finishes his tea and lies back down on the sagging sofa. Heather drapes the blanket on top of him and, fumbling only a little, turns out the light. At the foot of the stairs she turns back to him.

'Dev?'

He raises his head from the thick mass of wool and pillows.

'Thank you.'

57

Daylight sneaks quietly in between the open curtains. They are lying where they first placed their heads, the centimetres between them preserved in sleep; she with her mane of auburn curls, he with his moorgrass eyes closed against the world. Almost simultaneously their phones start beeping. The storm has passed, the signal returns, and with a start they awake into the day.

Dad, I was at Megan's. What's up?

Jay, how are you?

For a moment they each peer, bleary-eyed, at their glowing screens. Tom lets out a sigh of relief.

'Good news?' Jay asks quietly, as if there is someone who might overhear them.

'My daughter, she . . . I thought her mother might have . . .' He shakes his head, pulling back from the strange intimacy this shared bed and her turquoise eyes invite. 'It's nothing. You?'

'Simon.'

'Simon,' he repeats with a solemn nod. Of course, there is always Simon. Simon whose spectre has been hanging over them all evening. 'When will he be back?'

'I don't know, it's . . . complicated.'

'Does he know?'

Jay shakes her head, wincing as yesterday's wound presses against the pillow.

'Are you—' Tom leans forward.

'I'm fine.'

'Do you want a shower?' Though even as he asks it, he

realises that the thought of her bare skin in the next-door room would be too much for his battered heart to bear.

'No, thank you. I should be getting back.'

He nods, an inexplicable lump rising in his throat. 'You should be getting back. I'll drive you.'

Back at Two Houses, Jay looks down at her abandoned pots, the sludge on the wheel, her half-sculpted pieces of bone. *Porcelain has memory*, she'd told Tom in the car, though she doesn't know why. She picks up one of the bones and bends it, just for the sake of almost breaking it. She'd hardly known she was making them. And now, and now.

'It was Heather he ran to,' Tom had said, outside, in the still air. There was no more rain. It was as if the sky had shed all the tears it had left. 'Heather and my da who . . . Covered in blood he was, I remember that. Covered in blood and howling for his dog, his precious Mac. She'd shot the beast right in front of him. And for what? Because Jacob was playing down Two Houses again, and she felt they were hers by rights.'

'I thought it was Isobel,' Jay had whispered, and without the wind to which she's now grown accustomed, not even the long grasses whisper back. Just the two of them, alone, beneath the vast sky.

'I know. But Isobel killed herself, they say, after the death of her boy.'

'Jacob recited it to me, the story.'

'She used to make us learn it by rote.'

'It doesn't mention a daughter.'

'I think that's the point. Left. Forgotten. Turns you hard, something like that. God, was she bitter, putting her pain on to those little bodies . . .'

He turned from her then, looking out at the grey world spread below them. She reached out a hand.

'You don't have to—'

He shook his head. 'No, I'll only say this once in life. I don't know why, but it's you. You're the one I have to say it to.' He turned back then, his face so close to hers that she might almost feel his breath upon her cheek.

'Da and Heather, they took care of it. Cleaned it up. I was told later. They sat us down in the kitchen, told us no one could ever know. We had to keep it a secret. And we did, for the most part. Angela knew somehow, she's always known everything. I suppose other folk must have wondered. But we never said. Never. It's eaten Jacob alive, I think.'

Jay thought then of the attic, of all the things she found in it.

'His jumper . . . It was with her things. I thought it was mud, on his jumper . . .'

'I can't . . .' Tom pressed his lips together, screwed shut his eyes. 'Heather did all that. Found all the things she'd been breaking or stealing. Wrapped them all up, hid them away. In case anyone ever went looking. But no one did. Until you.'

And how thin and inadequate the words felt in her mouth when she tried to call his name, to say 'Tom, I'm sorry.'

He just shook his head again, wiped his eyes. 'No use being sorry.' And for a moment, on the battered hillside, he clasped her hands. But almost before her fingers had found his, they were gone again, and he was leaving her. 'No use for sorry up here.'

Inside the house is quiet as death. Nothing stirs, not even Bella. Jay drifts through the half-empty rooms, her fingers tracing half-remembered patterns over her books and papers. It seemed so important, when they came, to find the truth. To put name to bone, to dig up these secrets, to finally give them air. Yet this morning, Jay sees things in a different light. Secrets carried for so many years, held so tight and so close and time has done nothing to blunt their pain. To take off that raw edge.

It must have been Jacob, she realises now, who was coming to the house. Moving things around. Looking for whatever it was that she was finding, desperate to keep his secret as he had been told to do. Jacob, with his sloping shoulders, his calloused hands. Jacob with his miscoloured eyes – one green for earth, one blue for heaven – and she remembers thinking when she first saw him that he was not of this world.

With a pang as sharp and real as a pinprick to her heart muscle, she thinks of Simon. Realises that she misses Simon. Simon, whose absence has thrown the world off kilter. Simon, who, if he were here, would give her a shoulder on which to rest her battered head. Simon who waited, patiently, through all of her worst, most silent, desperate days. And what would he do, Simon, with this knowledge? Will he say *I told you so*? Will it be another *when will you ever learn, Jay-bird*? Or will it hurt him more than her, this truth that he did not think worth pursuing?

In spite of the rain, the storm, the open door, a faint smell of woodsmoke still clings to the air. Jay looks down at her carefully written notes, and with a rush of clarity sharp as the morning air, she knows what she must do.

58

Morning in Nelderdale, this northerly world awake, but two hundred miles south Simon is only just rising to the surface. His skin is caught between sticky sheets, his parched and blubbery tongue stuck to the roof of his mouth. He can smell beer, and bodies, and his eyes feel like they're revolving in his sockets as he looks around him at the bright, flower-scented bedroom. This is not his windowless hotel room. Not with the light pouring in and the vase of flowers and the pretty feminine objects cast about the place. Head and heart pounding, he realises with quickening nausea exactly where he is.

Beyond the bedroom he can hear tinkly music playing. The gentle clatter of pots and pans, a coffee pot hissing as it boils. Casting about for his clothes, he realises with a dull, metallic horror that he is naked. Like in those paralysing school dreams, but this is true and worse.

Collapsing back for a moment into the pale-pink sheets, Simon is hit with guilt like a punch to the stomach. He knew. He knew exactly what he was getting himself into. That dinner at *Chez Jacques*, the wine, the flirtation. They inched closer with every sip, and by evening's end, when she murmured, 'Why don't you let me cook tomorrow?' they both knew exactly what that meant. He knew all through a sleepless Sunday night, through all of Monday, all through those excruciating meetings, all those minutes that were dragged out beyond all hope and yet seemed to dash terrifyingly by, until he was standing on her doorstep with a bunch of supermarket flowers, and there was no way that either of them didn't know what they were doing.

Overwhelmed with self-loathing, he is just into his T-shirt and boxers, hands trembling, when George appears in the doorway.

'Good morning,' she smiles, seemingly untroubled to find him here.

'Morning,' he croaks in weak reply.

What to say, what to say? What is there to say that is not hackneyed, clichéd? Everything that springs into his aching brain is so trite, so well-trodden, so easily tripped off the tongue in films and on television that it has no meaning in this horribly real world in which he finds himself.

'I was just making breakfast,' she smiles again, more hesitantly this time. She moves to sit next to him on the bed and Simon cannot for the life of him prevent the jolt that moves him away from her.

'George . . .' It is all he can utter. Feeble guilt, worthless apology. Her face crumbles. 'I'm sorry . . .'

She waves him quiet with a hand and, like a coward, he is silenced.

'It's fine,' she murmurs without looking at him, her voice strangely contracted in her throat. 'I knew anyway.' She turns to face him, her eyes pinched and sad. 'You're in love with your wife.'

Simon nods. 'I'm so sorry to have dragged you into all this.'

She is up and across the room, arms folded across her chest.

'Don't. It's fine. Just go, please?'

And Simon is only too happy to oblige.

Stumbling out into the street is like coming up for air, quenching the thirst of oxygen-starved, sea-drenched lungs. Simon starts down the road at a run, before a violent collapse into a hedge – stars swimming before his eyes, bile rising in his throat – forces him to a walk. It is a quiet weekday morning, and the pounding of his feet on the pavements seems to spell out her name. *Jay. Jay. Jay.* He is sweating, glancing around himself like a criminal in fear of being caught. He fishes in his jacket for his mobile. Still some charge. He rings. *Jay. Jay.*

There is no answer, and in this haze of guilt and hangover he is convinced that she knows. That she is up there, at Two Houses, watching his name flash on her mobile, letting his newly installed landline ring into infinity, punishing his infidelity.

Infidelity. The very word sets a new trembling to Simon's hands. He never once thought that it would be him. That he would be the one to be unfaithful. His mind, always a goody-two-shoes, wants to make excuses. To say that it's been a hard year, diminish the magnitude of what he's done. But he will not let it. Again, he phones. *Jay.*

At King's Cross, he pleads with the man behind the counter to get him north on the fastest route possible.

'Can't guarantee the service, sir. The flooding and all.'

And clasping his clutch of tickets in his hand, Simon looks for the first time at the newspapers. The flooded fields. The houses with water rising to their windows. The bridges washed away and roads deluged.

Her voicemail again, and this time he leaves a message.

'Jay, it's me, Simon. I'm coming back. I'm worried. Are you alright, is everything alright? The flooding, it . . . I hope you're OK, that Bella's OK. I'm coming home today.'

Slowly, heavily, the first of his trains pulls out of the station. As Simon lays his head on the plastic table, a few pathetic tears leak out of his eyes. He watches them judder their way across the scratched plastic, and prays, to everyone and no one in particular, that it is not too late.

59

Dusk falls over the valley, turning the still air purple. The temperature has dropped and winter is surely on its way now, with this tang of frost on the air, the new bite of earth underfoot. There is not a breath of wind, as if all that could be said has already been spoken and not even nature has the energy for more.

Life is, at the end of this day, all that it has always been: Ned in his kitchen, Angela at her till, Heather gazing out of the kitchen window as the suds in the washing-up bowl turn slowly back to water. And yet everything is not quite what it was. There has been a shift, a rebalancing, as subtle as wind through leaves, rain through earth. Just as the water recedes, leaving a ghostly trace to mark its height, so everything continues with the world turned ever so slightly on its axis, this minute readjustment of breath and dirt. Things are the same and they are different, and when Dev next goes to the Co-op, Angela will not meet his eye but she will bite her tongue; when Jackie next rings, Heather will say, 'Yes, love, I'm fine', but she will know that Dev, sitting across the living room or on the other side of the library desk, knows differently.

There are no customers in the pub tonight. Perhaps it will be one of the nights where no one comes at all. Tom doesn't mind, for it is the beginning of a new week with Zoe. She is in her bedroom again, mute and moody, but he stands behind his bar with relief in his heart. She is safe, she is here, and, for whatever brief moment of childhood remains, she is still his. And he does not let himself dwell on what else his heart would have liked to hold, its other reaches and yearnings. In his mind, he puts Jay up on the felltops, with the dream of a farm that is still a farm, on the land that he knows by heart and whose paths he has traversed as surely as his veins course through him. He will not dwell, and one day, perhaps, he will even smile to think of her up on that wild moor, in the wild air.

And up in his corner of the wide world, among the deserted mine workings, Jacob sets a fire in the abandoned grate, makes all his usual spells and mutterings. The cold does not bother him, nor the clouds that approach, pink-tinged, across the vast horizon. He thinks of Mac, of the secret, of the woman with the red hair who makes things like he does. 'Goodnight Mac,' he says to the nettles and the crumbled stones, to the buzzard circling and the rabbits out for the last of the light.

Simon arrives at Two Houses breathless and dread-laden. How he has raced to get here, running between trains, promising the bemused taxi driver the most exorbitant fare, and yet now he shrinks from it, the very object of his hurried desire. How he wishes that he could tarry, delay, dawdle. That the muddied walk up to the house were four, five times as long. That he had untold hours more in which to compose himself.

But suddenly, she is here, opening the door to greet him. Or not to greet him, in fact, for she is startled, her eyes wide like a bird's before flight. She is wearing one of his big woollen jumpers, so vast on her thin frame that it hangs from her, a sail billowing in the wind, and beneath its folds he is vaguely aware that she is carrying something. But it is her eyes, her turquoise eyes, that transfix Simon, that pin him down just as they did when first they met.

'Oh, it's you.'

'It's me,' he echoes, trying to read her voice, her face, to see if she has – in her strange, otherworldly way – already found him out.

Jay, for her part, is knocked off course by her heart's pang,

290

for she had thought for a moment that it was Tom, and yet she is glad to see Simon, her Simon. And how strange for the heart to ache in two directions at once, to pull itself two different ways, as if it, too, at the end, is nothing more than clay.

'How have you been?' he asks, and there is something strange in the way that he asks it.

'Fine, good,' she replies, looking at him looking at her, but she cannot read what his eyes are saying. Brushing her hair back with one hand, she decides she has had enough of reading anyway. 'I'm having a bonfire.'

'Oh!'

With what surprise he says that. *Can you not smell it?* she thinks.

Hasn't it been raining? he wonders, his business shoes sinking into the mulchy ground.

It's taken all day to get it to light, she counters in her head.

But neither of them say these things. She says, 'You can come. If you like,' and he follows her, her Simon in his London suit, to the back of the house where she dumps the papers from her hands and a small bundle of what looks to him like muddied wool on to a gently smouldering pile. A thin smoke rises, the colour of cloud. Already, books and paper have turned to ash, flakes of white powder swirling in the air, not far off snow. They are white, bone white, clay white, and perhaps, Jay thinks, this will finally be the end of it.

They stand, shivering, as the ends of flames lick and crack at photographs and paper, words and images curling then disappearing in the heat. Heavy clouds arrive over the hillside, turning the world to grey, and under the murk of a sinking twilight the drystone walls look like just so many old scars. Time passes, the light wanes, and it is mere glimmer above the hilltops when the first sleet starts.

Jay had imagined it to be quiet, snow. Not in the city, of course, those faint, quickly muddied dustings that fall amid the glare and roar. But up here she had thought it would be quiet, peaceful. It is anything but, this sleet, clattering like icy pins to the cold ground.

Eventually Simon turns to her, still in his city coat, still clutching his city bag.

'I'll be going in, then.'

She nods. 'I'll be right with you.'

But she stays a while longer, looking off to the distance towards the village. From the kitchen, he watches as she drinks in the cold, the last light, the dying embers fading in front of her, before making her way slowly back to the echoing house.

Salvage

60

The Two Houses sit grey and brooding beneath a pale sky. They cling to the hillside, cowering from the wind, because always, before everything up here, there is the wind, even at this height of summer, on this seemingly unending day that marks the apex of the world's turn.

Below, the valley rolls away as it has always done. Thousands of buttercups have sprung up in the low pastures. There is no hay-time now, and left to their own devices the hillsides quiver like liquid gold. The air is sweet with grass, and meadow flowers, and the lavender that Jay has planted either side of the doorway, in whose stone a long-forgotten hand once carved *1712*.

Slumped low in an ancient deckchair, a jaunty panama shading his brow, Simon is working on the crossword. He pouts, puffs, hums to himself, his pencil busily scribbling at his clues. Thick with bees, the lavender hums too, and with the rippling of the wind, the creak of the deckchair, they form a peaceful symphony.

Hands newly calloused, fingernails freshly clad in clay, Jay walks out from the space between, from the houses that, in 1712, were built as one, and which have now been made into one again. For Simon has earned his restive deckchair: his renovation is complete, a joining wrought in glass and stone that has brought the two houses together again. For where she has clay, he has concrete, and the one has been formed to fit the other's work.

A studio for her, an office for him. A house that is no longer half-empty. They have rented out their London home, just for the time being, of course; just to see if they really like it here. Already, their minds are playing tricks on them, and each day it grows harder to remember the division, to remember the houses as they were when first they came. Placing down her pots and porcelain and glazes in their new home, Jay did wonder, briefly, whether Bella would baulk at this studio space between; whether some unearthly trace would persist in this wide, windowed room, the glass of its ceiling so high above her as she works that she feels open to the elements. But the dog trotted happily in, slumped at her mistress's feet as she always had.

Things have stopped moving around the houses since that day at the farm, and Jay is forced to admit that the ghosts we make for ourselves are sometimes the most potent. She does not think of Isobel too often, nor Maryanne, nor Jacob and his scars. She does not often think of Tom. Walking season, and he is busy now, the pub peopled with muddy boots just passing through, though he and Jay smile politely at each other in the village whenever fate decides their paths should cross. His daughter has expressed an interest in ceramics, he tells her. Jay says that she should visit the studio, one day, perhaps.

Perhaps.

But for now it is enough to lay a cool hand on Simon's sunburned neck, to have him reach up and clasp that hand in his. To hold on to flesh, not bone, and stand in front of the two houses made one as the fields turn to amber in the violet dusk.

Acknowledgements

It has been a great privilege to work with the wonderful Hodder team again, and I owe special thanks to Abby Parsons, Natalie Chen, Alice Morley and Veronique Norton for their help and support. I am enormously grateful to my marvellous agent, Lucy Morris, for always reading so closely, making exactly the right suggestions, and saving my bacon with deadlines. The greatest thanks are owed to Emma Herdman, the most incisive, thoughtful and encouraging of editors.

The staff at Clay Time on Blackstock Road – especially Sonja and Sinead – not only taught me to make some very wonky ceramics, but also answered a hundred questions about clay and porcelain. At the other end of the country, Margaret Reynolds's knowledge of mole-lore was invaluable!

Finally, a big thank you to my parents, sister and in-laws, who are saint-like in their support of the ups and downs of a writing life. I could not write at all without my beloved Alex and Chip at my side.

Do you wish this wasn't the end?

Join us at www.hodder.co.uk, or follow us on
Twitter @hodderbooks to be a part of our community
of people who love the very best in books and reading.

Whether you want to discover more about a book
or an author, watch trailers and interviews, have the
chance to win early limited editions, or simply browse
our expert readers' selection of the very best books,
we think you'll find what you're looking for.

And if you don't,
that's the place to tell us what's missing.

We love what we do, and we'd love you to be part of it.

www.hodder.co.uk

@hodderbooks

HodderBooks

HodderBooks